T0144359

The Bishop and Other Stories

The Bishop and Other Stories

Anton Chekhov

MINT EDITIONS

The Bishop and Other Stories was first published in 1902.

This edition published by Mint Editions 2021.

ISBN 9781513269153 | E-ISBN 9781513274157

Published by Mint Editions®

 **MINT EDITIONS**

minteditionbooks.com

Publishing Director: Jennifer Newens
Design & Production: Rachel Lopez Metzger
Translated by: Constance Garnett
Typesetting: Westchester Publishing Services

Contents

The Bishop

I

The evening service was being celebrated on the eve of Palm Sunday in the Old Petrovsky Convent. When they began distributing the palm it was close upon ten o'clock, the candles were burning dimly, the wicks wanted snuffing; it was all in a sort of mist. In the twilight of the church the crowd seemed heaving like the sea, and to Bishop Pyotr, who had been unwell for the last three days, it seemed that all the faces—old and young, men's and women's—were alike, that everyone who came up for the palm had the same expression in his eyes. In the mist he could not see the doors; the crowd kept moving and looked as though there were no end to it. The female choir was singing, a nun was reading the prayers for the day.

How stifling, how hot it was! How long the service went on! Bishop Pyotr was tired. His breathing was laboured and rapid, his throat was parched, his shoulders ached with weariness, his legs were trembling. And it disturbed him unpleasantly when a religious maniac uttered occasional shrieks in the gallery. And then all of a sudden, as though in a dream or delirium, it seemed to the bishop as though his own mother Marya Timofyevna, whom he had not seen for nine years, or some old woman just like his mother, came up to him out of the crowd, and, after taking a palm branch from him, walked away looking at him all the while good-humouredly with a kind, joyful smile until she was lost in the crowd. And for some reason tears flowed down his face. There was peace in his heart, everything was well, yet he kept gazing fixedly towards the left choir, where the prayers were being read, where in the dusk of evening you could not recognize anyone, and—wept. Tears glistened on his face and on his beard. Here someone close at hand was weeping, then someone else farther away, then others and still others, and little by little the church was filled with soft weeping. And a little later, within five minutes, the nuns' choir was singing; no one was weeping and everything was as before.

Soon the service was over. When the bishop got into his carriage to drive home, the gay, melodious chime of the heavy, costly bells was filling the whole garden in the moonlight. The white walls, the white crosses on the tombs, the white birch-trees and black shadows, and the far-away moon in the sky exactly over the convent, seemed now living their own life, apart and incomprehensible, yet very near to man. It was the beginning of April, and after the warm spring day it turned cool; there was a faint touch of frost, and the breath of spring could be felt in the soft, chilly air. The road from the convent to the town was sandy, the horses had to go at a walking pace, and on both sides of the carriage in the brilliant, peaceful moonlight there were people trudging along home from church through the sand. And all was silent, sunk in thought; everything around seemed kindly, youthful, akin, everything— trees and sky and even the moon, and one longed to think that so it would be always.

At last the carriage drove into the town and rumbled along the principal street. The shops were already shut, but at Erakin's, the millionaire shopkeeper's, they were trying the new electric lights, which flickered brightly, and a crowd of people were gathered round. Then came wide, dark, deserted streets, one after another; then the highroad, the open country, the fragrance of pines. And suddenly there rose up before the bishop's eyes a white turreted wall, and behind it a tall belfry in the full moonlight, and beside it five shining, golden cupolas: this was the Pankratievsky Monastery, in which Bishop Pyotr lived. And here, too, high above the monastery, was the silent, dreamy moon. The carriage drove in at the gate, crunching over the sand; here and there in the moonlight there were glimpses of dark monastic figures, and there was the sound of footsteps on the flag-stones. . .

"You know, your holiness, your mamma arrived while you were away," the lay brother informed the bishop as he went into his cell.

"My mother? When did she come?"

"Before the evening service. She asked first where you were and then she went to the convent."

"Then it was her I saw in the church, just now! Oh, Lord!"

And the bishop laughed with joy.

"She bade me tell your holiness," the lay brother went on, "that she would come to-morrow. She had a little girl with her—her grandchild, I suppose. They are staying at Ovsyannikov's inn."

"What time is it now?"

"A little after eleven."

"Oh, how vexing!"

The bishop sat for a little while in the parlour, hesitating, and as it were refusing to believe it was so late. His arms and legs were stiff,

ANTON CHEKHOV

his head ached. He was hot and uncomfortable. After resting a little he went into his bedroom, and there, too, he sat a little, still thinking of his mother; he could hear the lay brother going away, and Father Sisoy coughing the other side of the wall. The monastery clock struck a quarter.

The bishop changed his clothes and began reading the prayers before sleep. He read attentively those old, long familiar prayers, and at the same time thought about his mother. She had nine children and about forty grandchildren. At one time, she had lived with her husband, the deacon, in a poor village; she had lived there a very long time from the age of seventeen to sixty. The bishop remembered her from early childhood, almost from the age of three, and—how he had loved her! Sweet, precious childhood, always fondly remembered! Why did it, that long-past time that could never return, why did it seem brighter, fuller, and more festive than it had really been? When in his childhood or youth he had been ill, how tender and sympathetic his mother had been! And now his prayers mingled with the memories, which gleamed more and more brightly like a flame, and the prayers did not hinder his thinking of his mother.

When he had finished his prayers he undressed and lay down, and at once, as soon as it was dark, there rose before his mind his dead father, his mother, his native village Lesopolye. . . the creak of wheels, the bleat of sheep, the church bells on bright summer mornings, the gypsies under the window—oh, how sweet to think of it! He remembered the priest of Lesopolye, Father Simeon—mild, gentle, kindly; he was a lean little man, while his son, a divinity student, was a huge fellow and talked in a roaring bass voice. The priest's son had flown into a rage with the cook and abused her: "Ah, you Jehud's ass!" and Father Simeon overhearing it, said not a word, and was only ashamed because he could not remember where such an ass was mentioned in the Bible. After him the priest at Lesopolye had been Father Demyan, who used to drink heavily, and at times drank till he saw green snakes, and was even nicknamed Demyan Snakeseer. The schoolmaster at Lesopolye was Matvey Nikolaitch, who had been a divinity student, a kind and intelligent man, but he, too, was a drunkard; he never beat the schoolchildren, but for some reason he always had hanging on his wall a bunch of birch-twigs, and below it an utterly meaningless inscription in Latin: "Betula kinderbalsamica secuta." He had a shaggy black dog whom he called Syntax.

And his holiness laughed. Six miles from Lesopolye was the village Obnino with a wonder-working ikon. In the summer they used to carry the ikon in procession about the neighbouring villages and ring the bells the whole day long; first in one village and then in another, and it used to seem to the bishop then that joy was quivering in the air, and he (in those days his name was Pavlusha) used to follow the ikon, bareheaded and barefoot, with naïve faith, with a naïve smile, infinitely happy. In Obnino, he remembered now, there were always a lot of people, and the priest there, Father Alexey, to save time during mass, used to make his deaf nephew Ilarion read the names of those for whose health or whose souls' peace prayers were asked. Ilarion used to read them, now and then getting a five or ten kopeck piece for the service, and only when he was grey and bald, when life was nearly over, he suddenly saw written on one of the pieces of paper: "What a fool you are, Ilarion." Up to fifteen at least Pavlusha was undeveloped and idle at his lessons, so much so that they thought of taking him away from the clerical school and putting him into a shop; one day, going to the post at Obnino for letters, he had stared a long time at the post-office clerks and asked: "Allow me to ask, how do you get your salary, every month or every day?"

His holiness crossed himself and turned over on the other side, trying to stop thinking and go to sleep.

"My mother has come," he remembered and laughed.

The moon peeped in at the window, the floor was lighted up, and there were shadows on it. A cricket was chirping. Through the wall Father Sisoy was snoring in the next room, and his aged snore had a sound that suggested loneliness, forlornness, even vagrancy. Sisoy had once been housekeeper to the bishop of the diocese, and was called now "the former Father Housekeeper"; he was seventy years old, he lived in a monastery twelve miles from the town and stayed sometimes in the town, too. He had come to the Pankratievsky Monastery three days before, and the bishop had kept him that he might talk to him at his leisure about matters of business, about the arrangements here. . .

At half-past one they began ringing for matins. Father Sisoy could be heard coughing, muttering something in a discontented voice, then he got up and walked barefoot about the rooms.

"Father Sisoy," the bishop called.

Sisoy went back to his room and a little later made his appearance in his boots, with a candle; he had on his cassock over his underclothes and on his head was an old faded skull-cap.

"I can't sleep," said the bishop, sitting up. "I must be unwell. And what it is I don't know. Fever!"

"You must have caught cold, your holiness. You must be rubbed with tallow." Sisoy stood a little and yawned. "O Lord, forgive me, a sinner."

"They had the electric lights on at Erakin's today," he said; "I don't like it!"

Father Sisoy was old, lean, bent, always dissatisfied with something, and his eyes were angry-looking and prominent as a crab's.

"I don't like it," he said, going away. "I don't like it. Bother it!"

II

Next day, Palm Sunday, the bishop took the service in the cathedral in the town, then he visited the bishop of the diocese, then visited a very sick old lady, the widow of a general, and at last drove home. Between one and two o'clock he had welcome visitors dining with him—his mother and his niece Katya, a child of eight years old. All dinner-time the spring sunshine was streaming in at the windows, throwing bright light on the white tablecloth and on Katya's red hair. Through the double windows they could hear the noise of the rooks and the notes of the starlings in the garden.

"It is nine years since we have met," said the old lady. "And when I looked at you in the monastery yesterday, good Lord! you've not changed a bit, except maybe you are thinner and your beard is a little longer. Holy Mother, Queen of Heaven! Yesterday at the evening service no one could help crying. I, too, as I looked at you, suddenly began crying, though I couldn't say why. His Holy Will!"

And in spite of the affectionate tone in which she said this, he could see she was constrained as though she were uncertain whether to address him formally or familiarly, to laugh or not, and that she felt herself more a deacon's widow than his mother. And Katya gazed without blinking at her uncle, his holiness, as though trying to discover what sort of a person he was. Her hair sprang up from under the comb and the velvet ribbon and stood out like a halo; she had a turned-up nose and sly eyes. The child had broken a glass before sitting down to dinner, and now her grandmother, as she talked, moved away from Katya first a wineglass and then a tumbler. The bishop listened to his mother and remembered how many, many years ago she used to take him and his brothers and sisters to relations whom she considered rich;

in those days she was taken up with the care of her children, now with her grandchildren, and she had brought Katya. . .

"Your sister, Varenka, has four children," she told him; "Katya, here, is the eldest. And your brother-in-law Father Ivan fell sick, God knows of what, and died three days before the Assumption; and my poor Varenka is left a beggar."

"And how is Nikanor getting on?" the bishop asked about his eldest brother.

"He is all right, thank God. Though he has nothing much, yet he can live. Only there is one thing: his son, my grandson Nikolasha, did not want to go into the Church; he has gone to the university to be a doctor. He thinks it is better; but who knows! His Holy Will!"

"Nikolasha cuts up dead people," said Katya, spilling water over her knees.

"Sit still, child," her grandmother observed calmly, and took the glass out of her hand. "Say a prayer, and go on eating."

"How long it is since we have seen each other!" said the bishop, and he tenderly stroked his mother's hand and shoulder; "and I missed you abroad, mother, I missed you dreadfully."

"Thank you."

"I used to sit in the evenings at the open window, lonely and alone; often there was music playing, and all at once I used to be overcome with homesickness and felt as though I would give everything only to be at home and see you."

His mother smiled, beamed, but at once she made a grave face and said:

"Thank you."

His mood suddenly changed. He looked at his mother and could not understand how she had come by that respectfulness, that timid expression of face: what was it for? And he did not recognize her. He felt sad and vexed. And then his head ached just as it had the day before; his legs felt fearfully tired, and the fish seemed to him stale and tasteless; he felt thirsty all the time. . .

After dinner two rich ladies, landowners, arrived and sat for an hour and a half in silence with rigid countenances; the archimandrite, a silent, rather deaf man, came to see him about business. Then they began ringing for vespers; the sun was setting behind the wood and the day was over. When he returned from church, he hurriedly said his prayers, got into bed, and wrapped himself up as warm as possible.

ANTON CHEKHOV

It was disagreeable to remember the fish he had eaten at dinner. The moonlight worried him, and then he heard talking. In an adjoining room, probably in the parlour, Father Sisoy was talking politics:

"There's war among the Japanese now. They are fighting. The Japanese, my good soul, are the same as the Montenegrins; they are the same race. They were under the Turkish yoke together."

And then he heard the voice of Marya Timofyevna:

"So, having said our prayers and drunk tea, we went, you know, to Father Yegor at Novokatnoye, so. . ."

And she kept on saying, "having had tea" or "having drunk tea," and it seemed as though the only thing she had done in her life was to drink tea.

The bishop slowly, languidly, recalled the seminary, the academy. For three years he had been Greek teacher in the seminary: by that time he could not read without spectacles. Then he had become a monk; he had been made a school inspector. Then he had defended his thesis for his degree. When he was thirty-two he had been made rector of the seminary, and consecrated archimandrite: and then his life had been so easy, so pleasant; it seemed so long, so long, no end was in sight. Then he had begun to be ill, had grown very thin and almost blind, and by the advice of the doctors had to give up everything and go abroad.

"And what then?" asked Sisoy in the next room.

"Then we drank tea. . ." answered Marya Timofyevna.

"Good gracious, you've got a green beard," said Katya suddenly in surprise, and she laughed.

The bishop remembered that the grey-headed Father Sisoy's beard really had a shade of green in it, and he laughed.

"God have mercy upon us, what we have to put up with with this girl!" said Sisoy, aloud, getting angry. "Spoilt child! Sit quiet!"

The bishop remembered the perfectly new white church in which he had conducted the services while living abroad, he remembered the sound of the warm sea. In his flat he had five lofty light rooms; in his study he had a new writing-table, lots of books. He had read a great deal and often written. And he remembered how he had pined for his native land, how a blind beggar woman had played the guitar under his window every day and sung of love, and how, as he listened, he had always for some reason thought of the past. But eight years had passed and he had been called back to Russia, and now he was a suffragan bishop, and all the past had retreated far away into the mist as though it were a dream. . .

Father Sisoy came into the bedroom with a candle.

"I say!" he said, wondering, "are you asleep already, your holiness?"

"What is it?"

"Why, it's still early, ten o'clock or less. I bought a candle to-day; I wanted to rub you with tallow."

"I am in a fever. . ." said the bishop, and he sat up. "I really ought to have something. My head is bad. . ."

Sisoy took off the bishop's shirt and began rubbing his chest and back with tallow.

"That's the way. . . that's the way. . ." he said. "Lord Jesus Christ. . . that's the way. I walked to the town to-day; I was at what's-his-name's—the chief priest Sidonsky's. . . I had tea with him. I don't like him. Lord Jesus Christ. . . That's the way. I don't like him."

III

THE BISHOP OF THE DIOCESE, a very fat old man, was ill with rheumatism or gout, and had been in bed for over a month. Bishop Pyotr went to see him almost every day, and saw all who came to ask his help. And now that he was unwell he was struck by the emptiness, the triviality of everything which they asked and for which they wept; he was vexed at their ignorance, their timidity; and all this useless, petty business oppressed him by the mass of it, and it seemed to him that now he understood the diocesan bishop, who had once in his young days written on "The Doctrines of the Freedom of the Will," and now seemed to be all lost in trivialities, to have forgotten everything, and to have no thoughts of religion. The bishop must have lost touch with Russian life while he was abroad; he did not find it easy; the peasants seemed to him coarse, the women who sought his help dull and stupid, the seminarists and their teachers uncultivated and at times savage. And the documents coming in and going out were reckoned by tens of thousands; and what documents they were! The higher clergy in the whole diocese gave the priests, young and old, and even their wives and children, marks for their behaviour—a five, a four, and sometimes even a three; and about this he had to talk and to read and write serious reports. And there was positively not one minute to spare; his soul was troubled all day long, and the bishop was only at peace when he was in church.

He could not get used, either, to the awe which, through no wish of his own, he inspired in people in spite of his quiet, modest disposition.

All the people in the province seemed to him little, scared, and guilty when he looked at them. Everyone was timid in his presence, even the old chief priests; everyone "flopped" at his feet, and not long previously an old lady, a village priest's wife who had come to consult him, was so overcome by awe that she could not utter a single word, and went empty away. And he, who could never in his sermons bring himself to speak ill of people, never reproached anyone because he was so sorry for them, was moved to fury with the people who came to consult him, lost his temper and flung their petitions on the floor. The whole time he had been here, not one person had spoken to him genuinely, simply, as to a human being; even his old mother seemed now not the same! And why, he wondered, did she chatter away to Sisoy and laugh so much; while with him, her son, she was grave and usually silent and constrained, which did not suit her at all. The only person who behaved freely with him and said what he meant was old Sisoy, who had spent his whole life in the presence of bishops and had outlived eleven of them. And so the bishop was at ease with him, although, of course, he was a tedious and nonsensical man.

After the service on Tuesday, his holiness Pyotr was in the diocesan bishop's house receiving petitions there; he got excited and angry, and then drove home. He was as unwell as before; he longed to be in bed, but he had hardly reached home when he was informed that a young merchant called Erakin, who subscribed liberally to charities, had come to see him about a very important matter. The bishop had to see him. Erakin stayed about an hour, talked very loud, almost shouted, and it was difficult to understand what he said.

"God grant it may," he said as he went away. "Most essential! According to circumstances, your holiness! I trust it may!"

After him came the Mother Superior from a distant convent. And when she had gone they began ringing for vespers. He had to go to church.

In the evening the monks sang harmoniously, with inspiration. A young priest with a black beard conducted the service; and the bishop, hearing of the Bridegroom who comes at midnight and of the Heavenly Mansion adorned for the festival, felt no repentance for his sins, no tribulation, but peace at heart and tranquillity. And he was carried back in thought to the distant past, to his childhood and youth, when, too, they used to sing of the Bridegroom and of the Heavenly Mansion; and now that past rose up before him—living, fair, and joyful as in all likelihood it never had been. And perhaps in the other world, in the life to come, we shall think of the distant past, of our life here, with the same feeling. Who knows? The bishop was sitting near the altar. It was dark; tears flowed down his face. He thought that here he had attained everything a man in his position could attain; he had faith and yet everything was not clear, something was lacking still. He did not want to die; and he still felt that he had missed what was most important, something of which he had dimly dreamed in the past; and he was troubled by the same hopes for the future as he had felt in childhood, at the academy and abroad.

"How well they sing to-day!" he thought, listening to the singing. "How nice it is!"

IV

On Thursday he celebrated mass in the cathedral; it was the Washing of Feet. When the service was over and the people were going home, it was sunny, warm; the water gurgled in the gutters, and the unceasing trilling of the larks, tender, telling of peace, rose from the fields outside the town. The trees were already awakening and smiling a welcome, while above them the infinite, fathomless blue sky stretched into the distance, God knows whither.

On reaching home his holiness drank some tea, then changed his clothes, lay down on his bed, and told the lay brother to close the shutters on the windows. The bedroom was darkened. But what weariness, what pain in his legs and his back, a chill heavy pain, what a noise in his ears! He had not slept for a long time—for a very long time, as it seemed to him now, and some trifling detail which haunted his brain as soon as his eyes were closed prevented him from sleeping. As on the day before, sounds reached him from the adjoining rooms through the walls, voices, the jingle of glasses and teaspoons. . . Marya Timofyevna was gaily telling Father Sisoy some story with quaint turns of speech, while the latter answered in a grumpy, ill-humoured voice: "Bother them! Not likely! What next!" And the bishop again felt vexed and then hurt that with other people his old mother behaved in a simple, ordinary way, while with him, her son, she was shy, spoke little, and did not say what she meant, and even, as he fancied, had during all those three days kept trying in his presence to find an excuse for standing up, because she was embarrassed at sitting before him. And his father? He, too, probably, if he had been living, would not have been able to utter a word in the bishop's presence. . .

Something fell down on the floor in the adjoining room and was broken; Katya must have dropped a cup or a saucer, for Father Sisoy suddenly spat and said angrily:

"What a regular nuisance the child is! Lord forgive my transgressions! One can't provide enough for her."

Then all was quiet, the only sounds came from outside. And when the bishop opened his eyes he saw Katya in his room, standing motionless, staring at him. Her red hair, as usual, stood up from under the comb like a halo.

"Is that you, Katya?" he asked. "Who is it downstairs who keeps opening and shutting a door?"

"I don't hear it," answered Katya; and she listened.

"There, someone has just passed by."

"But that was a noise in your stomach, uncle."

He laughed and stroked her on the head.

"So you say Cousin Nikolasha cuts up dead people?" he asked after a pause.

"Yes, he is studying."

"And is he kind?"

"Oh, yes, he's kind. But he drinks vodka awfully."

"And what was it your father died of?"

"Papa was weak and very, very thin, and all at once his throat was bad. I was ill then, too, and brother Fedya; we all had bad throats. Papa died, uncle, and we got well."

Her chin began quivering, and tears gleamed in her eyes and trickled down her cheeks.

"Your holiness," she said in a shrill voice, by now weeping bitterly, "uncle, mother and all of us are left very wretched. . . Give us a little money. . . do be kind. . . uncle darling. . ."

He, too, was moved to tears, and for a long time was too much touched to speak. Then he stroked her on the head, patted her on the shoulder and said:

"Very good, very good, my child. When the holy Easter comes, we will talk it over. . . I will help you. . . I will help you. . ."

His mother came in quietly, timidly, and prayed before the ikon. Noticing that he was not sleeping, she said:

"Won't you have a drop of soup?"

"No, thank you," he answered, "I am not hungry."

"You seem to be unwell, now I look at you. I should think so; you may well be ill! The whole day on your legs, the whole day. . . And, my goodness, it makes one's heart ache even to look at you! Well, Easter is not far off; you will rest then, please God. Then we will have a talk, too, but now I'm not going to disturb you with my chatter. Come along, Katya; let his holiness sleep a little."

And he remembered how once very long ago, when he was a boy, she had spoken exactly like that, in the same jestingly respectful tone, with a Church dignitary. . . Only from her extraordinarily kind eyes and the timid, anxious glance she stole at him as she went out of the room could one have guessed that this was his mother. He shut his eyes and seemed to sleep, but twice heard the clock strike and Father Sisoy coughing the other side of the wall. And once more his mother came in and looked timidly at him for a minute. Someone drove up to the steps, as he could hear, in a coach or in a chaise. Suddenly a knock, the door slammed, the lay brother came into the bedroom.

"Your holiness," he called.

"Well?"

"The horses are here; it's time for the evening service."

"What o'clock is it?"

"A quarter past seven."

He dressed and drove to the cathedral. During all the "Twelve Gospels" he had to stand in the middle of the church without moving, and the first gospel, the longest and the most beautiful, he read himself. A mood of confidence and courage came over him. That first gospel, "Now is the Son of Man glorified," he knew by heart; and as he read he raised his eyes from time to time, and saw on both sides a perfect sea of lights and heard the splutter of candles, but, as in past years, he could not see the people, and it seemed as though these were all the same people as had been round him in those days, in his childhood and his youth; that they would always be the same every year and till such time as God only knew.

His father had been a deacon, his grandfather a priest, his great-grandfather a deacon, and his whole family, perhaps from the days when Christianity had been accepted in Russia, had belonged to the priesthood; and his love for the Church services, for the priesthood, for the peal of the bells, was deep in him, ineradicable, innate. In church, particularly when he took part in the service, he felt vigorous, of good cheer, happy. So it was now. Only when the eighth gospel had been read, he felt that his voice had grown weak, even his cough was inaudible. His head had begun to ache intensely, and he was troubled by a fear that he might fall down. And his legs were indeed quite numb, so that by degrees he ceased to feel them and could not understand how or on what he was standing, and why he did not fall. . .

It was a quarter to twelve when the service was over. When he reached home, the bishop undressed and went to bed at once without even saying his prayers. He could not speak and felt that he could not have stood up. When he had covered his head with the quilt he felt a sudden longing to be abroad, an insufferable longing! He felt that he would give his life not to see those pitiful cheap shutters, those low ceilings, not to smell that heavy monastery smell. If only there were one person to whom he could have talked, have opened his heart!

For a long while he heard footsteps in the next room and could not tell whose they were. At last the door opened, and Sisoy came in with a candle and a tea-cup in his hand.

"You are in bed already, your holiness?" he asked. "Here I have come to rub you with spirit and vinegar. A thorough rubbing does a great deal of good. Lord Jesus Christ!. . . That's the way. . . that's the way. . . I've just been in our monastery. . . I don't like it. I'm going away from here to-morrow, your holiness; I don't want to stay longer. Lord Jesus Christ. . . That's the way. . ."

Sisoy could never stay long in the same place, and he felt as though he had been a whole year in the Pankratievsky Monastery. Above all, listening to him it was difficult to understand where his home was, whether he cared for anyone or anything, whether he believed in God. . . He did not know himself why he was a monk, and, indeed, he did not think about it, and the time when he had become a monk had long passed out of his memory; it seemed as though he had been born a monk.

"I'm going away to-morrow; God be with them all."

"I should like to talk to you. . . I can't find the time," said the bishop softly with an effort. "I don't know anything or anybody here. . ."

"I'll stay till Sunday if you like; so be it, but I don't want to stay longer. I am sick of them!"

"I ought not to be a bishop," said the bishop softly. "I ought to have been a village priest, a deacon. . . or simply a monk. . . All this oppresses me. . . oppresses me."

"What? Lord Jesus Christ. . . That's the way. Come, sleep well, your holiness!. . . What's the good of talking? It's no use. Good-night!"

The bishop did not sleep all night. And at eight o'clock in the morning he began to have hemorrhage from the bowels. The lay brother was alarmed, and ran first to the archimandrite, then for the monastery doctor, Ivan Andreyitch, who lived in the town. The doctor, a stout old man with a long grey beard, made a prolonged examination of the bishop, and kept shaking his head and frowning, then said:

"Do you know, your holiness, you have got typhoid?"

After an hour or so of hemorrhage the bishop looked much thinner, paler, and wasted; his face looked wrinkled, his eyes looked bigger, and he seemed older, shorter, and it seemed to him that he was thinner, weaker, more insignificant than any one, that everything that had been had retreated far, far away and would never go on again or be repeated.

"How good," he thought, "how good!"

His old mother came. Seeing his wrinkled face and his big eyes, she was frightened, she fell on her knees by the bed and began kissing his face, his shoulders, his hands. And to her, too, it seemed that he was thinner, weaker, and more insignificant than anyone, and now she forgot that he was a bishop, and kissed him as though he were a child very near and very dear to her.

"Pavlusha, darling," she said; "my own, my darling son!. . . Why are you like this? Pavlusha, answer me!"

Katya, pale and severe, stood beside her, unable to understand what was the matter with her uncle, why there was such a look of suffering on her grandmother's face, why she was saying such sad and touching things. By now he could not utter a word, he could understand nothing, and he imagined he was a simple ordinary man, that he was walking quickly, cheerfully through the fields, tapping with his stick, while above him was the open sky bathed in sunshine, and that he was free now as a bird and could go where he liked!

"Pavlusha, my darling son, answer me," the old woman was saying. "What is it? My own!"

"Don't disturb his holiness," Sisoy said angrily, walking about the room. "Let him sleep. . . what's the use. . . it's no good. . ."

Three doctors arrived, consulted together, and went away again. The day was long, incredibly long, then the night came on and passed slowly, slowly, and towards morning on Saturday the lay brother went in to the old mother who was lying on the sofa in the parlour, and asked her to go into the bedroom: the bishop had just breathed his last.

Next day was Easter Sunday. There were forty-two churches and six monasteries in the town; the sonorous, joyful clang of the bells hung over the town from morning till night unceasingly, setting the spring air aquiver; the birds were singing, the sun was shining brightly. The big market square was noisy, swings were going, barrel organs were playing, accordions were squeaking, drunken voices were shouting. After midday people began driving up and down the principal street.

In short, all was merriment, everything was satisfactory, just as it had been the year before, and as it will be in all likelihood next year.

A month later a new suffragan bishop was appointed, and no one thought anything more of Bishop Pyotr, and afterwards he was completely forgotten. And only the dead man's old mother, who is living to-day with her son-in-law the deacon in a remote little district town, when she goes out at night to bring her cow in and meets other women at the pasture, begins talking of her children and her grandchildren, and says that she had a son a bishop, and this she says timidly, afraid that she may not be believed. . .

And, indeed, there are some who do not believe her.

The Letter

The clerical superintendent of the district, his Reverence Father Fyodor Orlov, a handsome, well-nourished man of fifty, grave and important as he always was, with an habitual expression of dignity that never left his face, was walking to and fro in his little drawing-room, extremely exhausted, and thinking intensely about the same thing: "When would his visitor go?" The thought worried him and did not leave him for a minute. The visitor, Father Anastasy, the priest of one of the villages near the town, had come to him three hours before on some very unpleasant and dreary business of his own, had stayed on and on, was now sitting in the corner at a little round table with his elbow on a thick account book, and apparently had no thought of going, though it was getting on for nine o'clock in the evening.

Not everyone knows when to be silent and when to go. It not infrequently happens that even diplomatic persons of good worldly breeding fail to observe that their presence is arousing a feeling akin to hatred in their exhausted or busy host, and that this feeling is being concealed with an effort and disguised with a lie. But Father Anastasy perceived it clearly, and realized that his presence was burdensome and inappropriate, that his Reverence, who had taken an early morning service in the night and a long mass at midday, was exhausted and longing for repose; every minute he was meaning to get up and go, but he did not get up, he sat on as though he were waiting for something. He was an old man of sixty-five, prematurely aged, with a bent and bony figure, with a sunken face and the dark skin of old age, with red eyelids and a long narrow back like a fish's; he was dressed in a smart cassock of a light lilac colour, but too big for him (presented to him by the widow of a young priest lately deceased), a full cloth coat with a broad leather belt, and clumsy high boots the size and hue of which showed clearly that Father Anastasy dispensed with goloshes. In spite of his position and his venerable age, there was something pitiful, crushed and humiliated in his lustreless red eyes, in the strands of grey hair with a shade of green in it on the nape of his neck, and in the big shoulder-blades on his lean back. . . He sat without speaking or moving, and coughed with circumspection, as though afraid that the sound of his coughing might make his presence more noticeable.

The old man had come to see his Reverence on business. Two months before he had been prohibited from officiating till further notice, and his case was being inquired into. His shortcomings were numerous. He was intemperate in his habits, fell out with the other clergy and the commune, kept the church records and accounts carelessly—these were the formal charges against him; but besides all that, there had been rumours for a long time past that he celebrated unlawful marriages for money and sold certificates of having fasted and taken the sacrament to officials and officers who came to him from the town. These rumours were maintained the more persistently that he was poor and had nine children to keep, who were as incompetent and unsuccessful as himself. The sons were spoilt and uneducated, and stayed at home doing nothing, while the daughters were ugly and did not get married.

Not having the moral force to be open, his Reverence walked up and down the room and said nothing or spoke in hints.

"So you are not going home to-night?" he asked, stopping near the dark window and poking with his little finger into the cage where a canary was asleep with its feathers puffed out.

Father Anastasy started, coughed cautiously and said rapidly:

"Home? I don't care to, Fyodor Ilyitch. I cannot officiate, as you know, so what am I to do there? I came away on purpose that I might not have to look the people in the face. One is ashamed not to officiate, as you know. Besides, I have business here, Fyodor Ilyitch. To-morrow after breaking the fast I want to talk things over thoroughly with the Father charged with the inquiry."

"Ah!. . ." yawned his Reverence, "and where are you staying?"

"At Zyavkin's."

Father Anastasy suddenly remembered that within two hours his Reverence had to take the Easter-night service, and he felt so ashamed of his unwelcome burdensome presence that he made up his mind to go away at once and let the exhausted man rest. And the old man got up to go. But before he began saying good-bye he stood clearing his throat for a minute and looking searchingly at his Reverence's back, still with the same expression of vague expectation in his whole figure; his face was working with shame, timidity, and a pitiful forced laugh such as one sees in people who do not respect themselves. Waving his hand as it were resolutely, he said with a husky quavering laugh:

"Father Fyodor, do me one more kindness: bid them give me at leave-taking. . . one little glass of vodka."

"It's not the time to drink vodka now," said his Reverence sternly. "One must have some regard for decency."

Father Anastasy was still more overwhelmed by confusion; he laughed, and, forgetting his resolution to go away, he dropped back on his chair. His Reverence looked at his helpless, embarrassed face and his bent figure and he felt sorry for the old man.

"Please God, we will have a drink to-morrow," he said, wishing to soften his stem refusal. "Everything is good in due season."

His Reverence believed in people's reforming, but now when a feeling of pity had been kindled in him it seemed to him that this disgraced, worn-out old man, entangled in a network of sins and weaknesses, was hopelessly wrecked, that there was no power on earth that could straighten out his spine, give brightness to his eyes and restrain the unpleasant timid laugh which he laughed on purpose to smoothe over to some slight extent the repulsive impression he made on people.

The old man seemed now to Father Fyodor not guilty and not vicious, but humiliated, insulted, unfortunate; his Reverence thought of his wife, his nine children, the dirty beggarly shelter at Zyavkin's; he thought for some reason of the people who are glad to see priests drunk and persons in authority detected in crimes; and thought that the very best thing Father Anastasy could do now would be to die as soon as possible and to depart from this world for ever.

There were a sound of footsteps.

"Father Fyodor, you are not resting?" a bass voice asked from the passage.

"No, deacon; come in."

Orlov's colleague, the deacon Liubimov, an elderly man with a big bald patch on the top of his head, though his hair was still black and he was still vigorous-looking, with thick black eyebrows like a Georgian's, walked in. He bowed to Father Anastasy and sat down.

"What good news have you?" asked his Reverence.

"What good news?" answered the deacon, and after a pause he went on with a smile: "When your children are little, your trouble is small; when your children are big, your trouble is great. Such goings on, Father Fyodor, that I don't know what to think of it. It's a regular farce, that's what it is."

He paused again for a little, smiled still more broadly and said:

"Nikolay Matveyitch came back from Harkov to-day. He has been telling me about my Pyotr. He has been to see him twice, he tells me."

"What has he been telling you, then?"

"He has upset me, God bless him. He meant to please me but when I came to think it over, it seems there is not much to be pleased at. I ought to grieve rather than be pleased. . . 'Your Petrushka,' said he, 'lives in fine style. He is far above us now,' said he. 'Well thank God for that,' said I. 'I dined with him,' said he, 'and saw his whole manner of life. He lives like a gentleman,' he said; 'you couldn't wish to live better.' I was naturally interested and I asked, 'And what did you have for dinner?' 'First,' he said, 'a fish course something like fish soup, then tongue and peas,' and then he said, 'roast turkey.' 'Turkey in Lent? that is something to please me,' said I. 'Turkey in Lent? Eh?'"

"Nothing marvellous in that," said his Reverence, screwing up his eyes ironically. And sticking both thumbs in his belt, he drew himself up and said in the tone in which he usually delivered discourses or gave his Scripture lessons to the pupils in the district school: "People who do not keep the fasts are divided into two different categories: some do not keep them through laxity, others through infidelity. Your Pyotr does not keep them through infidelity. Yes."

The deacon looked timidly at Father Fyodor's stern face and said:

"There is worse to follow. . . We talked and discussed one thing and another, and it turned out that my infidel of a son is living with some madame, another man's wife. She takes the place of wife and hostess in his flat, pours out the tea, receives visitors and all the rest of it, as though she were his lawful wife. For over two years he has been keeping up this dance with this viper. It's a regular farce. They have been living together for three years and no children."

"I suppose they have been living in chastity!" chuckled Father Anastasy, coughing huskily. "There are children, Father Deacon— there are, but they don't keep them at home! They send them to the Foundling! He-he-he!. . ." Anastasy went on coughing till he choked.

"Don't interfere, Father Anastasy," said his Reverence sternly.

"Nikolay Matveyitch asked him, 'What madame is this helping the soup at your table?'" the deacon went on, gloomily scanning Anastasy's bent figure. "'That is my wife,' said he. 'When was your wedding?' Nikolay Matveyitch asked him, and Pyotr answered, 'We were married at Kulikov's restaurant.'"

His Reverence's eyes flashed wrathfully and the colour came into his temples. Apart from his sinfulness, Pyotr was not a person he liked. Father Fyodor had, as they say, a grudge against him. He remembered him a boy at school—he remembered him distinctly, because even then the boy had seemed to him not normal. As a schoolboy, Petrushka had been ashamed to serve at the altar, had been offended at being addressed without ceremony, had not crossed himself on entering the room, and what was still more noteworthy, was fond of talking a great deal and with heat—and, in Father Fyodor's opinion, much talking was unseemly in children and pernicious to them; moreover Petrushka had taken up a contemptuous and critical attitude to fishing, a pursuit to which both his Reverence and the deacon were greatly addicted. As a student Pyotr had not gone to church at all, had slept till midday, had looked down on people, and had been given to raising delicate and insoluble questions with a peculiarly provoking zest.

"What would you have?" his Reverence asked, going up to the deacon and looking at him angrily. "What would you have? This was to be expected! I always knew and was convinced that nothing good would come of your Pyotr! I told you so, and I tell you so now. What you have sown, that now you must reap! Reap it!"

"But what have I sown, Father Fyodor?" the deacon asked softly, looking up at his Reverence.

"Why, who is to blame if not you? You're his father, he is your offspring! You ought to have admonished him, have instilled the fear of God into him. A child must be taught! You have brought him into the world, but you haven't trained him up in the right way. It's a sin! It's wrong! It's a shame!"

His Reverence forgot his exhaustion, paced to and fro and went on talking. Drops of perspiration came out on the deacon's bald head and forehead. He raised his eyes to his Reverence with a look of guilt, and said:

"But didn't I train him, Father Fyodor? Lord have mercy on us, haven't I been a father to my children? You know yourself I spared nothing for his good; I have prayed and done my best all my life to give him a thorough education. He went to the high school and I got him tutors, and he took his degree at the University. And as to my not being able to influence his mind, Father Fyodor, why, you can judge for yourself that I am not qualified to do so! Sometimes when he used to come here as a student, I would begin admonishing him in my way, and he wouldn't heed me. I'd say to him, 'Go to church,' and he would answer, 'What for?' I would begin explaining, and he would say, 'Why? what for?' Or he would slap me on the shoulder and say, 'Everything in this world is relative, approximate and conditional. I don't know anything, and you don't know anything either, dad.'"

Father Anastasy laughed huskily, cleared his throat and waved his fingers in the air as though preparing to say something. His Reverence glanced at him and said sternly:

"Don't interfere, Father Anastasy."

The old man laughed, beamed, and evidently listened with pleasure to the deacon as though he were glad there were other sinful persons in this world besides himself. The deacon spoke sincerely, with an aching heart, and tears actually came into his eyes. Father Fyodor felt sorry for him.

"You are to blame, deacon, you are to blame," he said, but not so sternly and heatedly as before. "If you could beget him, you ought to know how to instruct him. You ought to have trained him in his childhood; it's no good trying to correct a student."

A silence followed; the deacon clasped his hands and said with a sigh:

"But you know I shall have to answer for him!"

"To be sure you will!"

After a brief silence his Reverence yawned and sighed at the same moment and asked:

"Who is reading the 'Acts'?"

"Yevstrat. Yevstrat always reads them."

The deacon got up and, looking imploringly at his Reverence, asked:

"Father Fyodor, what am I to do now?"

"Do as you please; you are his father, not I. You ought to know best."

"I don't know anything, Father Fyodor! Tell me what to do, for goodness' sake! Would you believe it, I am sick at heart! I can't sleep now, nor keep quiet, and the holiday will be no holiday to me. Tell me what to do, Father Fyodor!"

"Write him a letter."

"What am I to write to him?"

"Write that he mustn't go on like that. Write shortly, but sternly and circumstantially, without softening or smoothing away his guilt. It is your parental duty; if you write, you will have done your duty and will be at peace."

"That's true. But what am I to write to him, to what effect? If I write to him, he will answer, 'Why? what for? Why is it a sin?'"

Father Anastasy laughed hoarsely again, and brandished his fingers.

"Why? what for? why is it a sin?" he began shrilly. "I was once confessing a gentleman, and I told him that excessive confidence in the Divine Mercy is a sin; and he asked, 'Why?' I tried to answer him, but——" Anastasy slapped himself on the forehead. "I had nothing here. He-he-he-he!. . ."

Anastasy's words, his hoarse jangling laugh at what was not laughable, had an unpleasant effect on his Reverence and on the deacon. The former was on the point of saying, "Don't interfere" again, but he did not say it, he only frowned.

"I can't write to him," sighed the deacon.

"If you can't, who can?"

"Father Fyodor!" said the deacon, putting his head on one side and pressing his hand to his heart. "I am an uneducated slow-witted man, while the Lord has vouchsafed you judgment and wisdom. You know everything and understand everything. You can master anything, while I don't know how to put my words together sensibly. Be generous. Instruct me how to write the letter. Teach me what to say and how to say it. . ."

"What is there to teach? There is nothing to teach. Sit down and write."

"Oh, do me the favour, Father Fyodor! I beseech you! I know he will be frightened and will attend to your letter, because, you see, you are a cultivated man too. Do be so good! I'll sit down, and you'll dictate to me. It will be a sin to write to-morrow, but now would be the very time; my mind would be set at rest."

His Reverence looked at the deacon's imploring face, thought of the disagreeable Pyotr, and consented to dictate. He made the deacon sit down to his table and began.

"Well, write. . . 'Christ is risen, dear son. . .' exclamation mark. 'Rumours have reached me, your father,' then in parenthesis, 'from what source is no concern of yours. . .' close the parenthesis. . . Have you written it? 'That you are leading a life inconsistent with the laws both of God and of man. Neither the luxurious comfort, nor the worldly splendour, nor the culture with which you seek outwardly to disguise it, can hide your heathen manner of life. In name you are a Christian, but in your real nature a heathen as pitiful and wretched as all other heathens—more wretched, indeed, seeing that those heathens who know not Christ are lost from ignorance, while you are lost in that, possessing a treasure, you neglect it. I will not enumerate here your vices, which you know well enough; I will say that I see the cause of your ruin in your infidelity. You imagine yourself to be wise, boast of your knowledge of science, but refuse to see that science without faith, far from elevating a man, actually degrades him to the level of a lower animal, inasmuch as. . .'" The whole letter was in this strain.

When he had finished writing it the deacon read it aloud, beamed all over and jumped up.

"It's a gift, it's really a gift!" he said, clasping his hands and looking enthusiastically at his Reverence. "To think of the Lord's bestowing a gift like that! Eh? Holy Mother! I do believe I couldn't write a letter like that in a hundred years. Lord save you!"

Father Anastasy was enthusiastic too.

"One couldn't write like that without a gift," he said, getting up and wagging his fingers—"that one couldn't! His rhetoric would trip any philosopher and shut him up. Intellect. Brilliant intellect! If you weren't married, Father Fyodor, you would have been a bishop long ago, you would really!"

Having vented his wrath in a letter, his Reverence felt relieved; his fatigue and exhaustion came back to him. The deacon was an old friend, and his Reverence did not hesitate to say to him:

"Well deacon, go, and God bless you. I'll have half an hour's nap on the sofa; I must rest."

The deacon went away and took Anastasy with him. As is always the case on Easter Eve, it was dark in the street, but the whole sky was sparkling with bright luminous stars. There was a scent of spring and holiday in the soft still air.

"How long was he dictating?" the deacon said admiringly. "Ten minutes, not more! It would have taken someone else a month to compose such a letter. Eh! What a mind! Such a mind that I don't know what to call it! It's a marvel! It's really a marvel!"

"Education!" sighed Anastasy as he crossed the muddy street, holding up his cassock to his waist. "It's not for us to compare ourselves with him. We come of the sacristan class, while he has had a learned education. Yes, he's a real man, there is no denying that."

"And you listen how he'll read the Gospel in Latin at mass to-day! He knows Latin and he knows Greek. . . Ah Petrushka, Petrushka!" the deacon said, suddenly remembering. "Now that will make him scratch his head! That will shut his mouth, that will bring it home to him! Now he won't ask 'Why.' It is a case of one wit to outwit another! Haha-ha!"

The deacon laughed gaily and loudly. Since the letter had been written to Pyotr he had become serene and more cheerful. The consciousness of having performed his duty as a father and his faith in the power of the letter had brought back his mirthfulness and good-humour.

"Pyotr means a stone," said he, as he went into his house. "My Pyotr is not a stone, but a rag. A viper has fastened upon him and he pampers her, and hasn't the pluck to kick her out. Tfoo! To think there should be women like that, God forgive me! Eh? Has she no shame? She has fastened upon the lad, sticking to him, and keeps him tied to her apron strings. . . Fie upon her!"

"Perhaps it's not she keeps hold of him, but he of her?"

"She is a shameless one anyway! Not that I am defending Pyotr. . . He'll catch it. He'll read the letter and scratch his head! He'll burn with shame!"

"It's a splendid letter, only you know I wouldn't send it, Father Deacon. Let him alone."

"What?" said the deacon, disconcerted.

"Why. . . Don't send it, deacon! What's the sense of it? Suppose you send it; he reads it, and. . . and what then? You'll only upset him. Forgive him. Let him alone!"

The deacon looked in surprise at Anastasy's dark face, at his unbuttoned cassock, which looked in the dusk like wings, and shrugged his shoulders.

"How can I forgive him like that?" he asked. "Why I shall have to answer for him to God!"

"Even so, forgive him all the same. Really! And God will forgive you for your kindness to him."

"But he is my son, isn't he? Ought I not to teach him?"

"Teach him? Of course—why not? You can teach him, but why call him a heathen? It will hurt his feelings, you know, deacon. . ."

The deacon was a widower, and lived in a little house with three windows. His elder sister, an old maid, looked after his house for him, though she had three years before lost the use of her legs and was confined to her bed; he was afraid of her, obeyed her, and did nothing without her advice. Father Anastasy went in with him. Seeing his table already laid with Easter cakes and red eggs, he began weeping for some reason, probably thinking of his own home, and to turn these tears into a jest, he at once laughed huskily.

"Yes, we shall soon be breaking the fast," he said. "Yes. . . it wouldn't come amiss, deacon, to have a little glass now. Can we? I'll drink it so that the old lady does not hear," he whispered, glancing sideways towards the door.

Without a word the deacon moved a decanter and wineglass towards him. He unfolded the letter and began reading it aloud. And now the letter pleased him just as much as when his Reverence had dictated it to him. He beamed with pleasure and wagged his head, as though he had been tasting something very sweet.

"A-ah, what a letter!" he said. "Petrushka has never dreamt of such a letter. It's just what he wants, something to throw him into a fever. . ."

"Do you know, deacon, don't send it!" said Anastasy, pouring himself out a second glass of vodka as though unconsciously. "Forgive him, let him alone! I am telling you. . . what I really think. If his own father can't forgive him, who will forgive him? And so he'll live without forgiveness. Think, deacon: there will be plenty to chastise him without you, but you should look out for some who will show mercy to your son! I'll. . . I'll. . . have just one more. The last, old man. . . Just sit down and write straight off to him, 'I forgive you Pyotr!' He will under-sta-and! He will fe-el it! I understand it from myself, you see old man. . . deacon, I mean. When I lived like other people, I hadn't much to trouble about, but now since I lost the image and semblance, there is only one thing I care about, that good people should forgive me. And remember, too, it's not the righteous but sinners we must forgive. Why should you forgive your old woman if she is not sinful? No, you must forgive a man when he is a sad sight to look at. . . yes!"

Anastasy leaned his head on his fist and sank into thought.

"It's a terrible thing, deacon," he sighed, evidently struggling with the desire to take another glass—"a terrible thing! In sin my mother bore me, in sin I have lived, in sin I shall die. . . God forgive me, a sinner! I have gone astray, deacon! There is no salvation for me! And it's not as though I had gone astray in my life, but in old age—at death's door. . . I. . ."

The old man, with a hopeless gesture, drank off another glass, then got up and moved to another seat. The deacon, still keeping the letter in his hand, was walking up and down the room. He was thinking of his son. Displeasure, distress and anxiety no longer troubled him; all that had gone into the letter. Now he was simply picturing Pyotr; he imagined his face, he thought of the past years when his son used to come to stay with him for the holidays. His thoughts were only of what was good, warm, touching, of which one might think for a whole lifetime without wearying. Longing for his son, he read the letter through once more and looked questioningly at Anastasy.

"Don't send it," said the latter, with a wave of his hand.

"No, I must send it anyway; I must. . . bring him to his senses a little, all the same. It's just as well. . ."

The deacon took an envelope from the table, but before putting the letter into it he sat down to the table, smiled and added on his own account at the bottom of the letter:

"They have sent us a new inspector. He's much friskier than the old one. He's a great one for dancing and talking, and there's nothing he can't do, so that all the Govorovsky girls are crazy over him. Our military chief, Kostyrev, will soon get the sack too, they say. High time he did!" And very well pleased, without the faintest idea that with this postscript he had completely spoiled the stern letter, the deacon addressed the envelope and laid it in the most conspicuous place on the table.

Easter Eve

I was standing on the bank of the River Goltva, waiting for the ferry-boat from the other side. At ordinary times the Goltva is a humble stream of moderate size, silent and pensive, gently glimmering from behind thick reeds; but now a regular lake lay stretched out before me. The waters of spring, running riot, had overflowed both banks and flooded both sides of the river for a long distance, submerging vegetable gardens, hayfields and marshes, so that it was no unusual thing to meet poplars and bushes sticking out above the surface of the water and looking in the darkness like grim solitary crags.

The weather seemed to me magnificent. It was dark, yet I could see the trees, the water and the people. . . The world was lighted by the stars, which were scattered thickly all over the sky. I don't remember ever seeing so many stars. Literally one could not have put a finger in between them. There were some as big as a goose's egg, others tiny as hempseed. . . They had come out for the festival procession, every one of them, little and big, washed, renewed and joyful, and everyone of them was softly twinkling its beams. The sky was reflected in the water; the stars were bathing in its dark depths and trembling with the quivering eddies. The air was warm and still. . . Here and there, far away on the further bank in the impenetrable darkness, several bright red lights were gleaming. . .

A couple of paces from me I saw the dark silhouette of a peasant in a high hat, with a thick knotted stick in his hand.

"How long the ferry-boat is in coming!" I said.

"It is time it was here," the silhouette answered.

"You are waiting for the ferry-boat, too?"

"No I am not," yawned the peasant—"I am waiting for the illumination. I should have gone, but to tell you the truth, I haven't the five kopecks for the ferry."

"I'll give you the five kopecks."

"No; I humbly thank you. . . With that five kopecks put up a candle for me over there in the monastery. . . That will be more interesting, and I will stand here. What can it mean, no ferry-boat, as though it had sunk in the water!"

The peasant went up to the water's edge, took the rope in his hands, and shouted; "Ieronim! Ieron—im!"

As though in answer to his shout, the slow peal of a great bell floated across from the further bank. The note was deep and low, as from the thickest string of a double bass; it seemed as though the darkness itself had hoarsely uttered it. At once there was the sound of a cannon shot. It rolled away in the darkness and ended somewhere in the far distance behind me. The peasant took off his hat and crossed himself.

"'Christ is risen,'" he said.

Before the vibrations of the first peal of the bell had time to die away in the air a second sounded, after it at once a third, and the darkness was filled with an unbroken quivering clamour. Near the red lights fresh lights flashed, and all began moving together and twinkling restlessly.

"Ieron—im!" we heard a hollow prolonged shout.

"They are shouting from the other bank," said the peasant, "so there is no ferry there either. Our Ieronim has gone to sleep."

The lights and the velvety chimes of the bell drew one towards them. . . I was already beginning to lose patience and grow anxious, but behold at last, staring into the dark distance, I saw the outline of something very much like a gibbet. It was the long-expected ferry. It moved towards us with such deliberation that if it had not been that its lines grew gradually more definite, one might have supposed that it was standing still or moving to the other bank.

"Make haste! Ieronim!" shouted my peasant. "The gentleman's tired of waiting!"

The ferry crawled to the bank, gave a lurch and stopped with a creak. A tall man in a monk's cassock and a conical cap stood on it, holding the rope.

"Why have you been so long?" I asked jumping upon the ferry.

"Forgive me, for Christ's sake," Ieronim answered gently. "Is there no one else?"

"No one. . ."

Ieronim took hold of the rope in both hands, bent himself to the figure of a mark of interrogation, and gasped. The ferry-boat creaked and gave a lurch. The outline of the peasant in the high hat began slowly retreating from me—so the ferry was moving off. Ieronim soon drew himself up and began working with one hand only. We were silent, gazing towards the bank to which we were floating. There the illumination for which the peasant was waiting had begun. At the water's edge barrels of tar were flaring like huge camp fires. Their reflections, crimson as the rising moon, crept to meet us in long broad streaks. The burning barrels

ANTON CHEKHOV

lighted up their own smoke and the long shadows of men flitting about the fire; but further to one side and behind them from where the velvety chime floated there was still the same unbroken black gloom. All at once, cleaving the darkness, a rocket zigzagged in a golden ribbon up the sky; it described an arc and, as though broken to pieces against the sky, was scattered crackling into sparks. There was a roar from the bank like a far-away hurrah.

"How beautiful!" I said.

"Beautiful beyond words!" sighed Ieronim. "Such a night, sir! Another time one would pay no attention to the fireworks, but to-day one rejoices in every vanity. Where do you come from?"

I told him where I came from.

"To be sure. . . a joyful day to-day. . ." Ieronim went on in a weak sighing tenor like the voice of a convalescent. "The sky is rejoicing and the earth and what is under the earth. All the creatures are keeping holiday. Only tell me kind sir, why, even in the time of great rejoicing, a man cannot forget his sorrows?"

I fancied that this unexpected question was to draw me into one of those endless religious conversations which bored and idle monks are so fond of. I was not disposed to talk much, and so I only asked:

"What sorrows have you, father?"

"As a rule only the same as all men, kind sir, but to-day a special sorrow has happened in the monastery: at mass, during the reading of the Bible, the monk and deacon Nikolay died."

"Well, it's God's will!" I said, falling into the monastic tone. "We must all die. To my mind, you ought to rejoice indeed. . . They say if anyone dies at Easter he goes straight to the kingdom of heaven."

"That's true."

We sank into silence. The figure of the peasant in the high hat melted into the lines of the bank. The tar barrels were flaring up more and more.

"The Holy Scripture points clearly to the vanity of sorrow and so does reflection," said Ieronim, breaking the silence, "but why does the heart grieve and refuse to listen to reason? Why does one want to weep bitterly?"

Ieronim shrugged his shoulders, turned to me and said quickly:

"If I died, or anyone else, it would not be worth notice perhaps; but, you see, Nikolay is dead! No one else but Nikolay! Indeed, it's hard to believe that he is no more! I stand here on my ferry-boat and every minute I keep fancying that he will lift up his voice from the bank. He always used to come to the bank and call to me that I might not be afraid on the ferry. He used to get up from his bed at night on purpose for that. He was a kind soul. My God! how kindly and gracious! Many a mother is not so good to her child as Nikolay was to me! Lord, save his soul!"

Ieronim took hold of the rope, but turned to me again at once.

"And such a lofty intelligence, your honour," he said in a vibrating voice. "Such a sweet and harmonious tongue! Just as they will sing immediately at early matins: 'Oh lovely! oh sweet is Thy Voice!' Besides all other human qualities, he had, too, an extraordinary gift!"

"What gift?" I asked.

The monk scrutinized me, and as though he had convinced himself that he could trust me with a secret, he laughed good-humouredly.

"He had a gift for writing hymns of praise," he said. "It was a marvel, sir; you couldn't call it anything else! You would be amazed if I tell you about it. Our Father Archimandrite comes from Moscow, the Father Sub-Prior studied at the Kazan academy, we have wise monks and elders, but, would you believe it, no one could write them; while Nikolay, a simple monk, a deacon, had not studied anywhere, and had not even any outer appearance of it, but he wrote them! A marvel! A real marvel!" Ieronim clasped his hands and, completely forgetting the rope, went on eagerly:

"The Father Sub-Prior has great difficulty in composing sermons; when he wrote the history of the monastery he worried all the brotherhood and drove a dozen times to town, while Nikolay wrote canticles! Hymns of praise! That's a very different thing from a sermon or a history!"

"Is it difficult to write them?" I asked.

"There's great difficulty!" Ieronim wagged his head. "You can do nothing by wisdom and holiness if God has not given you the gift. The monks who don't understand argue that you only need to know the life of the saint for whom you are writing the hymn, and to make it harmonize with the other hymns of praise. But that's a mistake, sir. Of course, anyone who writes canticles must know the life of the saint to perfection, to the least trivial detail. To be sure, one must make them harmonize with the other canticles and know where to begin and what to write about. To give you an instance, the first response begins everywhere with 'the chosen' or 'the elect.'. . . The first line must always begin with the 'angel.' In the canticle of praise to Jesus the Most

Sweet, if you are interested in the subject, it begins like this: 'Of angels Creator and Lord of all powers!' In the canticle to the Holy Mother of God: 'Of angels the foremost sent down from on high,' to Nikolay, the Wonder-worker—'An angel in semblance, though in substance a man,' and so on. Everywhere you begin with the angel. Of course, it would be impossible without making them harmonize, but the lives of the saints and conformity with the others is not what matters; what matters is the beauty and sweetness of it. Everything must be harmonious, brief and complete. There must be in every line softness, graciousness and tenderness; not one word should be harsh or rough or unsuitable. It must be written so that the worshipper may rejoice at heart and weep, while his mind is stirred and he is thrown into a tremor. In the canticle to the Holy Mother are the words: 'Rejoice, O Thou too high for human thought to reach! Rejoice, O Thou too deep for angels' eyes to fathom!' In another place in the same canticle: 'Rejoice, O tree that bearest the fair fruit of light that is the food of the faithful! Rejoice, O tree of gracious spreading shade, under which there is shelter for multitudes!'"

Ieronim hid his face in his hands, as though frightened at something or overcome with shame, and shook his head.

"Tree that bearest the fair fruit of light. . . tree of gracious spreading shade. . ." he muttered. "To think that a man should find words like those! Such a power is a gift from God! For brevity he packs many thoughts into one phrase, and how smooth and complete it all is! 'Light-radiating torch to all that be. . .' comes in the canticle to Jesus the Most Sweet. 'Light-radiating!' There is no such word in conversation or in books, but you see he invented it, he found it in his mind! Apart from the smoothness and grandeur of language, sir, every line must be beautified in every way, there must be flowers and lightning and wind and sun and all the objects of the visible world. And every exclamation ought to be put so as to be smooth and easy for the ear. 'Rejoice, thou flower of heavenly growth!' comes in the hymn to Nikolay the Wonder-worker. It's not simply 'heavenly flower,' but 'flower of heavenly growth.' It's smoother so and sweet to the ear. That was just as Nikolay wrote it! Exactly like that! I can't tell you how he used to write!"

"Well, in that case it is a pity he is dead," I said; "but let us get on, father, or we shall be late."

Ieronim started and ran to the rope; they were beginning to peal all the bells. Probably the procession was already going on near the monastery, for all the dark space behind the tar barrels was now dotted with moving lights.

"Did Nikolay print his hymns?" I asked Ieronim.

"How could he print them?" he sighed. "And indeed, it would be strange to print them. What would be the object? No one in the monastery takes any interest in them. They don't like them. They knew Nikolay wrote them, but they let it pass unnoticed. No one esteems new writings nowadays, sir!"

"Were they prejudiced against him?"

"Yes, indeed. If Nikolay had been an elder perhaps the brethren would have been interested, but he wasn't forty, you know. There were some who laughed and even thought his writing a sin."

"What did he write them for?"

"Chiefly for his own comfort. Of all the brotherhood, I was the only one who read his hymns. I used to go to him in secret, that no one else might know of it, and he was glad that I took an interest in them. He would embrace me, stroke my head, speak to me in caressing words as to a little child. He would shut his cell, make me sit down beside him, and begin to read. . ."

Ieronim left the rope and came up to me.

"We were dear friends in a way," he whispered, looking at me with shining eyes. "Where he went I would go. If I were not there he would miss me. And he cared more for me than for anyone, and all because I used to weep over his hymns. It makes me sad to remember. Now I feel just like an orphan or a widow. You know, in our monastery they are all good people, kind and pious, but. . . there is no one with softness and refinement, they are just like peasants. They all speak loudly, and tramp heavily when they walk; they are noisy, they clear their throats, but Nikolay always talked softly, caressingly, and if he noticed that anyone was asleep or praying he would slip by like a fly or a gnat. His face was tender, compassionate. . ."

Ieronim heaved a deep sigh and took hold of the rope again. We were by now approaching the bank. We floated straight out of the darkness and stillness of the river into an enchanted realm, full of stifling smoke, crackling lights and uproar. By now one could distinctly see people moving near the tar barrels. The flickering of the lights gave a strange, almost fantastic, expression to their figures and red faces. From time to time one caught among the heads and faces a glimpse of a horse's head motionless as though cast in copper.

"They'll begin singing the Easter hymn directly,. . ." said Ieronim, "and Nikolay is gone; there is no one to appreciate it. . . There was nothing written dearer to him than that hymn. He used to take in every word! You'll be there, sir, so notice what is sung; it takes your breath away!"

"Won't you be in church, then?"

"I can't;. . . I have to work the ferry. . ."

"But won't they relieve you?"

"I don't know. . . I ought to have been relieved at eight; but, as you see, they don't come!. . . And I must own I should have liked to be in the church. . ."

"Are you a monk?"

"Yes. . . that is, I am a lay-brother."

The ferry ran into the bank and stopped. I thrust a five-kopeck piece into Ieronim's hand for taking me across and jumped on land. Immediately a cart with a boy and a sleeping woman in it drove creaking onto the ferry. Ieronim, with a faint glow from the lights on his figure, pressed on the rope, bent down to it, and started the ferry back. . .

I took a few steps through mud, but a little farther walked on a soft freshly trodden path. This path led to the dark monastery gates, that looked like a cavern through a cloud of smoke, through a disorderly crowd of people, unharnessed horses, carts and chaises. All this crowd was rattling, snorting, laughing, and the crimson light and wavering shadows from the smoke flickered over it all. . . A perfect chaos! And in this hubbub the people yet found room to load a little cannon and to sell cakes. There was no less commotion on the other side of the wall in the monastery precincts, but there was more regard for decorum and order. Here there was a smell of juniper and incense. They talked loudly, but there was no sound of laughter or snorting. Near the tombstones and crosses people pressed close to one another with Easter cakes and bundles in their arms. Apparently many had come from a long distance for their cakes to be blessed and now were exhausted. Young lay brothers, making a metallic sound with their boots, ran busily along the iron slabs that paved the way from the monastery gates to the church door. They were busy and shouting on the belfry, too.

"What a restless night!" I thought. "How nice!"

One was tempted to see the same unrest and sleeplessness in all nature, from the night darkness to the iron slabs, the crosses on the tombs and the trees under which the people were moving to and fro.

But nowhere was the excitement and restlessness so marked as in the church. An unceasing struggle was going on in the entrance between the inflowing stream and the outflowing stream. Some were going in, others going out and soon coming back again to stand still for a little and begin moving again. People were scurrying from place to place, lounging about as though they were looking for something. The stream flowed from the entrance all round the church, disturbing even the front rows, where persons of weight and dignity were standing. There could be no thought of concentrated prayer. There were no prayers at all, but a sort of continuous, childishly irresponsible joy, seeking a pretext to break out and vent itself in some movement, even in senseless jostling and shoving.

The same unaccustomed movement is striking in the Easter service itself. The altar gates are flung wide open, thick clouds of incense float in the air near the candelabra; wherever one looks there are lights, the gleam and splutter of candles. . . There is no reading; restless and lighthearted singing goes on to the end without ceasing. After each hymn the clergy change their vestments and come out to burn the incense, which is repeated every ten minutes.

I had no sooner taken a place, when a wave rushed from in front and forced me back. A tall thick-set deacon walked before me with a long red candle; the grey-headed archimandrite in his golden mitre hurried after him with the censer. When they had vanished from sight the crowd squeezed me back to my former position. But ten minutes had not passed before a new wave burst on me, and again the deacon appeared. This time he was followed by the Father Sub-Prior, the man who, as Ieronim had told me, was writing the history of the monastery.

As I mingled with the crowd and caught the infection of the universal joyful excitement, I felt unbearably sore on Ieronim's account. Why did they not send someone to relieve him? Why could not someone of less feeling and less susceptibility go on the ferry? 'Lift up thine eyes, O Sion, and look around,' they sang in the choir, 'for thy children have come to thee as to a beacon of divine light from north and south, and from east and from the sea. . .'

I looked at the faces; they all had a lively expression of triumph, but not one was listening to what was being sung and taking it in, and not one was 'holding his breath.' Why was not Ieronim released? I could fancy Ieronim standing meekly somewhere by the wall, bending forward and hungrily drinking in the beauty of the holy phrase. All

ANTON CHEKHOV

this that glided by the ears of the people standing by me he would have eagerly drunk in with his delicately sensitive soul, and would have been spell-bound to ecstasy, to holding his breath, and there would not have been a man happier than he in all the church. Now he was plying to and fro over the dark river and grieving for his dead friend and brother.

The wave surged back. A stout smiling monk, playing with his rosary and looking round behind him, squeezed sideways by me, making way for a lady in a hat and velvet cloak. A monastery servant hurried after the lady, holding a chair over our heads.

I came out of the church. I wanted to have a look at the dead Nikolay, the unknown canticle writer. I walked about the monastery wall, where there was a row of cells, peeped into several windows, and, seeing nothing, came back again. I do not regret now that I did not see Nikolay; God knows, perhaps if I had seen him I should have lost the picture my imagination paints for me now. I imagine the lovable poetical figure solitary and not understood, who went out at nights to call to Ieronim over the water, and filled his hymns with flowers, stars and sunbeams, as a pale timid man with soft mild melancholy features. His eyes must have shone, not only with intelligence, but with kindly tenderness and that hardly restrained childlike enthusiasm which I could hear in Ieronim's voice when he quoted to me passages from the hymns.

When we came out of church after mass it was no longer night. The morning was beginning. The stars had gone out and the sky was a morose greyish blue. The iron slabs, the tombstones and the buds on the trees were covered with dew There was a sharp freshness in the air. Outside the precincts I did not find the same animated scene as I had beheld in the night. Horses and men looked exhausted, drowsy, scarcely moved, while nothing was left of the tar barrels but heaps of black ash. When anyone is exhausted and sleepy he fancies that nature, too, is in the same condition. It seemed to me that the trees and the young grass were asleep. It seemed as though even the bells were not pealing so loudly and gaily as at night. The restlessness was over, and of the excitement nothing was left but a pleasant weariness, a longing for sleep and warmth.

Now I could see both banks of the river; a faint mist hovered over it in shifting masses. There was a harsh cold breath from the water. When I jumped on to the ferry, a chaise and some two dozen men and women were standing on it already. The rope, wet and as I fancied drowsy, stretched far away across the broad river and in places disappeared in the white mist.

"Christ is risen! Is there no one else?" asked a soft voice.

I recognized the voice of Ieronim. There was no darkness now to hinder me from seeing the monk. He was a tall narrow-shouldered man of five-and-thirty, with large rounded features, with half-closed listless-looking eyes and an unkempt wedge-shaped beard. He had an extraordinarily sad and exhausted look.

"They have not relieved you yet?" I asked in surprise.

"Me?" he answered, turning to me his chilled and dewy face with a smile. "There is no one to take my place now till morning. They'll all be going to the Father Archimandrite's to break the fast directly."

With the help of a little peasant in a hat of reddish fur that looked like the little wooden tubs in which honey is sold, he threw his weight on the rope; they gasped simultaneously, and the ferry started.

We floated across, disturbing on the way the lazily rising mist. Everyone was silent. Ieronim worked mechanically with one hand. He slowly passed his mild lustreless eyes over us; then his glance rested on the rosy face of a young merchant's wife with black eyebrows, who was standing on the ferry beside me silently shrinking from the mist that wrapped her about. He did not take his eyes off her face all the way.

There was little that was masculine in that prolonged gaze. It seemed to me that Ieronim was looking in the woman's face for the soft and tender features of his dead friend.

A Nightmare

Kunin, a young man of thirty, who was a permanent member of the Rural Board, on returning from Petersburg to his district, Borisovo, immediately sent a mounted messenger to Sinkino, for the priest there, Father Yakov Smirnov.

Five hours later Father Yakov appeared.

"Very glad to make your acquaintance," said Kunin, meeting him in the entry. "I've been living and serving here for a year; it seems as though we ought to have been acquainted before. You are very welcome! But. . . how young you are!" Kunin added in surprise. "What is your age?"

"Twenty-eight,. . ." said Father Yakov, faintly pressing Kunin's outstretched hand, and for some reason turning crimson.

Kunin led his visitor into his study and began looking at him more attentively.

"What an uncouth womanish face!" he thought.

There certainly was a good deal that was womanish in Father Yakov's face: the turned-up nose, the bright red cheeks, and the large grey-blue eyes with scanty, scarcely perceptible eyebrows. His long reddish hair, smooth and dry, hung down in straight tails on to his shoulders. The hair on his upper lip was only just beginning to form into a real masculine moustache, while his little beard belonged to that class of good-for-nothing beards which among divinity students are for some reason called "ticklers." It was scanty and extremely transparent; it could not have been stroked or combed, it could only have been pinched. . . All these scanty decorations were put on unevenly in tufts, as though Father Yakov, thinking to dress up as a priest and beginning to gum on the beard, had been interrupted halfway through. He had on a cassock, the colour of weak coffee with chicory in it, with big patches on both elbows.

"A queer type," thought Kunin, looking at his muddy skirts. "Comes to the house for the first time and can't dress decently.

"Sit down, Father," he began more carelessly than cordially, as he moved an easy-chair to the table. "Sit down, I beg you."

Father Yakov coughed into his fist, sank awkwardly on to the edge of the chair, and laid his open hands on his knees. With his short figure, his narrow chest, his red and perspiring face, he made from the first moment a most unpleasant impression on Kunin. The latter could never have imagined that there were such undignified and pitiful-looking priests in Russia; and in Father Yakov's attitude, in the way he held his hands on his knees and sat on the very edge of his chair, he saw a lack of dignity and even a shade of servility.

"I have invited you on business, Father. . ." Kunin began, sinking back in his low chair. "It has fallen to my lot to perform the agreeable duty of helping you in one of your useful undertakings. . . On coming back from Petersburg, I found on my table a letter from the Marshal of Nobility. Yegor Dmitrevitch suggests that I should take under my supervision the church parish school which is being opened in Sinkino. I shall be very glad to, Father, with all my heart. . . More than that, I accept the proposition with enthusiasm."

Kunin got up and walked about the study.

"Of course, both Yegor Dmitrevitch and probably you, too, are aware that I have not great funds at my disposal. My estate is mortgaged, and I live exclusively on my salary as the permanent member. So that you cannot reckon on very much assistance, but I will do all that is in my power. . . And when are you thinking of opening the school Father?"

"When we have the money,. . ." answered Father Yakov.

"You have some funds at your disposal already?"

"Scarcely any. . . The peasants settled at their meeting that they would pay, every man of them, thirty kopecks a year; but that's only a promise, you know! And for the first beginning we should need at least two hundred roubles. . ."

"M'yes. . . Unhappily, I have not that sum now," said Kunin with a sigh. "I spent all I had on my tour and got into debt, too. Let us try and think of some plan together."

Kunin began planning aloud. He explained his views and watched Father Yakov's face, seeking signs of agreement or approval in it. But the face was apathetic and immobile, and expressed nothing but constrained shyness and uneasiness. Looking at it, one might have supposed that Kunin was talking of matters so abstruse that Father Yakov did not understand and only listened from good manners, and was at the same time afraid of being detected in his failure to understand.

"The fellow is not one of the brightest, that's evident. . ." thought Kunin. "He's rather shy and much too stupid."

Father Yakov revived somewhat and even smiled only when the footman came into the study bringing in two glasses of tea on a tray and a cake-basket full of biscuits. He took his glass and began drinking at once.

"Shouldn't we write at once to the bishop?" Kunin went on, meditating aloud. "To be precise, you know, it is not we, not the Zemstvo, but the higher ecclesiastical authorities, who have raised the question of the church parish schools. They ought really to apportion the funds. I remember I read that a sum of money had been set aside for the purpose. Do you know nothing about it?"

Father Yakov was so absorbed in drinking tea that he did not answer this question at once. He lifted his grey-blue eyes to Kunin, thought a moment, and as though recalling his question, he shook his head in the negative. An expression of pleasure and of the most ordinary prosaic appetite overspread his face from ear to ear. He drank and smacked his lips over every gulp. When he had drunk it to the very last drop, he put his glass on the table, then took his glass back again, looked at the bottom of it, then put it back again. The expression of pleasure faded from his face. . . Then Kunin saw his visitor take a biscuit from the cake-basket, nibble a little bit off it, then turn it over in his hand and hurriedly stick it in his pocket.

"Well, that's not at all clerical!" thought Kunin, shrugging his shoulders contemptuously. "What is it, priestly greed or childishness?"

After giving his visitor another glass of tea and seeing him to the entry, Kunin lay down on the sofa and abandoned himself to the unpleasant feeling induced in him by the visit of Father Yakov.

"What a strange wild creature!" he thought. "Dirty, untidy, coarse, stupid, and probably he drinks. . . My God, and that's a priest, a spiritual father! That's a teacher of the people! I can fancy the irony there must be in the deacon's face when before every mass he booms out: 'Thy blessing, Reverend Father!' A fine reverend Father! A reverend Father without a grain of dignity or breeding, hiding biscuits in his pocket like a schoolboy. . . Fie! Good Lord, where were the bishop's eyes when he ordained a man like that? What can he think of the people if he gives them a teacher like that? One wants people here who. . ."

And Kunin thought what Russian priests ought to be like.

"If I were a priest, for instance. . . An educated priest fond of his work might do a great deal. . . I should have had the school opened long ago. And the sermons? If the priest is sincere and is inspired by love for his work, what wonderful rousing sermons he might give!"

Kunin shut his eyes and began mentally composing a sermon. A little later he sat down to the table and rapidly began writing.

"I'll give it to that red-haired fellow, let him read it in church,. . ." he thought.

The following Sunday Kunin drove over to Sinkino in the morning to settle the question of the school, and while he was there to make acquaintance with the church of which he was a parishioner. In spite of the awful state of the roads, it was a glorious morning. The sun was shining brightly and cleaving with its rays the layers of white snow still lingering here and there. The snow as it took leave of the earth glittered with such diamonds that it hurt the eyes to look, while the young winter corn was hastily thrusting up its green beside it. The rooks floated with dignity over the fields. A rook would fly, drop to earth, and give several hops before standing firmly on its feet. . .

The wooden church up to which Kunin drove was old and grey; the columns of the porch had once been painted white, but the colour had now completely peeled off, and they looked like two ungainly shafts. The ikon over the door looked like a dark smudged blur. But its poverty touched and softened Kunin. Modestly dropping his eyes, he went into the church and stood by the door. The service had only just begun. An old sacristan, bent into a bow, was reading the "Hours" in a hollow indistinct tenor. Father Yakov, who conducted the service without a deacon, was walking about the church, burning incense. Had it not been for the softened mood in which Kunin found himself on entering the poverty-stricken church, he certainly would have smiled at the sight of Father Yakov. The short priest was wearing a crumpled and extremely long robe of some shabby yellow material; the hem of the robe trailed on the ground.

The church was not full. Looking at the parishioners, Kunin was struck at the first glance by one strange circumstance: he saw nothing but old people and children. . . Where were the men of working age? Where was the youth and manhood? But after he had stood there a little and looked more attentively at the aged-looking faces, Kunin saw that he had mistaken young people for old. He did not, however, attach any significance to this little optical illusion.

The church was as cold and grey inside as outside. There was not one spot on the ikons nor on the dark brown walls which was not begrimed and defaced by time. There were many windows, but the general effect of colour was grey, and so it was twilight in the church.

"Anyone pure in soul can pray here very well," thought Kunin. "Just as in St. Peter's in Rome one is impressed by grandeur, here one is touched by the lowliness and simplicity."

But his devout mood vanished like smoke as soon as Father Yakov went up to the altar and began mass. Being still young and having come straight from the seminary bench to the priesthood, Father Yakov had not yet formed a set manner of celebrating the service. As he read he seemed to be vacillating between a high tenor and a thin bass; he bowed clumsily, walked quickly, and opened and shut the gates abruptly. . . The old sacristan, evidently deaf and ailing, did not hear the prayers very distinctly, and this very often led to slight misunderstandings. Before Father Yakov had time to finish what he had to say, the sacristan began chanting his response, or else long after Father Yakov had finished the old man would be straining his ears, listening in the direction of the altar and saying nothing till his skirt was pulled. The old man had a sickly hollow voice and an asthmatic quavering lisp. . . The complete lack of dignity and decorum was emphasized by a very small boy who seconded the sacristan and whose head was hardly visible over the railing of the choir. The boy sang in a shrill falsetto and seemed to be trying to avoid singing in tune. Kunin stayed a little while, listened and went out for a smoke. He was disappointed, and looked at the grey church almost with dislike.

"They complain of the decline of religious feeling among the people. . ." he sighed. "I should rather think so! They'd better foist a few more priests like this one on them!"

Kunin went back into the church three times, and each time he felt a great temptation to get out into the open air again. Waiting till the end of the mass, he went to Father Yakov's. The priest's house did not differ outwardly from the peasants' huts, but the thatch lay more smoothly on the roof and there were little white curtains in the windows. Father Yakov led Kunin into a light little room with a clay floor and walls covered with cheap paper; in spite of some painful efforts towards luxury in the way of photographs in frames and a clock with a pair of scissors hanging on the weight the furnishing of the room impressed him by its scantiness. Looking at the furniture, one might have supposed that Father Yakov had gone from house to house and collected it in bits; in one place they had given him a round three-legged table, in another a stool, in a third a chair with a back bent violently backwards; in a fourth a chair with an upright back, but the seat smashed in; while in a fifth they had been liberal and given him a semblance of a sofa with a flat back and a lattice-work seat.

This semblance had been painted dark red and smelt strongly of paint. Kunin meant at first to sit down on one of the chairs, but on second thoughts he sat down on the stool.

"This is the first time you have been to our church?" asked Father Yakov, hanging his hat on a huge misshapen nail.

"Yes it is. I tell you what, Father, before we begin on business, will you give me some tea? My soul is parched."

Father Yakov blinked, gasped, and went behind the partition wall. There was a sound of whispering.

"With his wife, I suppose," thought Kunin; "it would be interesting to see what the red-headed fellow's wife is like."

A little later Father Yakov came back, red and perspiring and with an effort to smile, sat down on the edge of the sofa.

"They will heat the samovar directly," he said, without looking at his visitor.

"My goodness, they have not heated the samovar yet!" Kunin thought with horror. "A nice time we shall have to wait."

"I have brought you," he said, "the rough draft of the letter I have written to the bishop. I'll read it after tea; perhaps you may find something to add. . ."

"Very well."

A silence followed. Father Yakov threw furtive glances at the partition wall, smoothed his hair, and blew his nose.

"It's wonderful weather,. . ." he said.

"Yes. I read an interesting thing yesterday. . . the Volsky Zemstvo have decided to give their schools to the clergy, that's typical."

Kunin got up, and pacing up and down the clay floor, began to give expression to his reflections.

"That would be all right," he said, "if only the clergy were equal to their high calling and recognized their tasks. I am so unfortunate as to know priests whose standard of culture and whose moral qualities make them hardly fit to be army secretaries, much less priests. You will agree that a bad teacher does far less harm than a bad priest."

Kunin glanced at Father Yakov; he was sitting bent up, thinking intently about something and apparently not listening to his visitor.

"Yasha, come here!" a woman's voice called from behind the partition. Father Yakov started and went out. Again a whispering began.

Kunin felt a pang of longing for tea.

"No; it's no use my waiting for tea here," he thought, looking at his watch. "Besides I fancy I am not altogether a welcome visitor. My host has not deigned to say one word to me; he simply sits and blinks."

Kunin took up his hat, waited for Father Yakov to return, and said good-bye to him.

"I have simply wasted the morning," he thought wrathfully on the way home. "The blockhead! The dummy! He cares no more about the school than I about last year's snow. . . No, I shall never get anything done with him! We are bound to fail! If the Marshal knew what the priest here was like, he wouldn't be in such a hurry to talk about a school. We ought first to try and get a decent priest, and then think about the school."

By now Kunin almost hated Father Yakov. The man, his pitiful, grotesque figure in the long crumpled robe, his womanish face, his manner of officiating, his way of life and his formal restrained respectfulness, wounded the tiny relic of religious feeling which was stored away in a warm corner of Kunin's heart together with his nurse's other fairy tales. The coldness and lack of attention with which Father Yakov had met Kunin's warm and sincere interest in what was the priest's own work was hard for the former's vanity to endure. . .

On the evening of the same day Kunin spent a long time walking about his rooms and thinking. Then he sat down to the table resolutely and wrote a letter to the bishop. After asking for money and a blessing for the school, he set forth genuinely, like a son, his opinion of the priest at Sinkino.

"He is young," he wrote, "insufficiently educated, leads, I fancy, an intemperate life, and altogether fails to satisfy the ideals which the Russian people have in the course of centuries formed of what a pastor should be."

After writing this letter Kunin heaved a deep sigh, and went to bed with the consciousness that he had done a good deed.

On Monday morning, while he was still in bed, he was informed that Father Yakov had arrived. He did not want to get up, and instructed the servant to say he was not at home. On Tuesday he went away to a sitting of the Board, and when he returned on Saturday he was told by the servants that Father Yakov had called every day in his absence.

"He liked my biscuits, it seems," he thought.

Towards evening on Sunday Father Yakov arrived. This time not only his skirts, but even his hat, was bespattered with mud. Just as on his first visit, he was hot and perspiring, and sat down on the edge of his chair as he had done then. Kunin determined not to talk about the school—not to cast pearls.

"I have brought you a list of books for the school, Pavel Mihailovitch,. . ." Father Yakov began.

"Thank you."

But everything showed that Father Yakov had come for something else besides the list. Has whole figure was expressive of extreme embarrassment, and at the same time there was a look of determination upon his face, as on the face of a man suddenly inspired by an idea. He struggled to say something important, absolutely necessary, and strove to overcome his timidity.

"Why is he dumb?" Kunin thought wrathfully. "He's settled himself comfortably! I haven't time to be bothered with him."

To smoothe over the awkwardness of his silence and to conceal the struggle going on within him, the priest began to smile constrainedly, and this slow smile, wrung out on his red perspiring face, and out of keeping with the fixed look in his grey-blue eyes, made Kunin turn away. He felt moved to repulsion.

"Excuse me, Father, I have to go out," he said.

Father Yakov started like a man asleep who has been struck a blow, and, still smiling, began in his confusion wrapping round him the skirts of his cassock. In spite of his repulsion for the man, Kunin felt suddenly sorry for him, and he wanted to soften his cruelty.

"Please come another time, Father," he said, "and before we part I want to ask you a favour. I was somehow inspired to write two sermons the other day. . . I will give them to you to look at. If they are suitable, use them."

"Very good," said Father Yakov, laying his open hand on Kunin's sermons which were lying on the table. "I will take them."

After standing a little, hesitating and still wrapping his cassock round him, he suddenly gave up the effort to smile and lifted his head resolutely.

"Pavel Mihailovitch," he said, evidently trying to speak loudly and distinctly.

"What can I do for you?"

"I have heard that you. . . er. . . have dismissed your secretary, and. . . and are looking for a new one. . ."

"Yes, I am. . . Why, have you someone to recommend?"

"I. . . er. . . you see. . . I. . . Could you not give the post to me?"

"Why, are you giving up the Church?" said Kunin in amazement.

"No, no," Father Yakov brought out quickly, for some reason turning pale and trembling all over. "God forbid! If you feel doubtful, then never mind, never mind. You see, I could do the work between whiles,. . so as to increase my income. . . Never mind, don't disturb yourself!"

"H'm!. . . your income. . . But you know, I only pay my secretary twenty roubles a month."

"Good heavens! I would take ten," whispered Father Yakov, looking about him. "Ten would be enough! You. . . you are astonished, and everyone is astonished. The greedy priest, the grasping priest, what does he do with his money? I feel myself I am greedy,. . . and I blame myself, I condemn myself. . . I am ashamed to look people in the face. . . I tell you on my conscience, Pavel Mihailovitch. . . I call the God of truth to witness. . ."

Father Yakov took breath and went on:

"On the way here I prepared a regular confession to make you, but. . . I've forgotten it all; I cannot find a word now. I get a hundred and fifty roubles a year from my parish, and everyone wonders what I do with the money. . . But I'll explain it all truly. . . I pay forty roubles a year to the clerical school for my brother Pyotr. He has everything found there, except that I have to provide pens and paper."

"Oh, I believe you; I believe you! But what's the object of all this?" said Kunin, with a wave of the hand, feeling terribly oppressed by this outburst of confidence on the part of his visitor, and not knowing how to get away from the tearful gleam in his eyes.

"Then I have not yet paid up all that I owe to the consistory for my place here. They charged me two hundred roubles for the living, and I was to pay ten roubles a month. . . You can judge what is left! And, besides, I must allow Father Avraamy at least three roubles a month."

"What Father Avraamy?"

"Father Avraamy who was priest at Sinkino before I came. He was deprived of the living on account of. . . his failing, but you know, he is still living at Sinkino! He has nowhere to go. There is no one to keep him. Though he is old, he must have a corner, and food and clothing—I can't let him go begging on the roads in his position! It would be on my conscience if anything happened! It would be my fault! He is. . . in debt all round; but, you see, I am to blame for not paying for him."

Father Yakov started up from his seat and, looking frantically at the floor, strode up and down the room.

"My God, my God!" he muttered, raising his hands and dropping them again. "Lord, save us and have mercy upon us! Why did you take such a calling on yourself if you have so little faith and no strength? There is no end to my despair! Save me, Queen of Heaven!"

"Calm yourself, Father," said Kunin.

"I am worn out with hunger, Pavel Mihailovitch," Father Yakov went on. "Generously forgive me, but I am at the end of my strength. . . I know if I were to beg and to bow down, everyone would help, but. . . I cannot! I am ashamed. How can I beg of the peasants? You are on the Board here, so you know. . . How can one beg of a beggar? And to beg of richer people, of landowners, I cannot! I have pride! I am ashamed!"

Father Yakov waved his hand, and nervously scratched his head with both hands.

"I am ashamed! My God, I am ashamed! I am proud and can't bear people to see my poverty! When you visited me, Pavel Mihailovitch, I had no tea in the house! There wasn't a pinch of it, and you know it was pride prevented me from telling you! I am ashamed of my clothes, of these patches here. . . I am ashamed of my vestments, of being hungry. . . And is it seemly for a priest to be proud?"

Father Yakov stood still in the middle of the study, and, as though he did not notice Kunin's presence, began reasoning with himself.

"Well, supposing I endure hunger and disgrace—but, my God, I have a wife! I took her from a good home! She is not used to hard work; she is soft; she is used to tea and white bread and sheets on her bed. . . At home she used to play the piano. . . She is young, not twenty yet. . . She would like, to be sure, to be smart, to have fun, go out to see people. . . And she is worse off with me than any cook; she is ashamed to show herself in the street. My God, my God! Her only treat is when I bring an apple or some biscuit from a visit. . ."

Father Yakov scratched his head again with both hands.

"And it makes us feel not love but pity for each other. . . I cannot look at her without compassion! And the things that happen in this life, O Lord! Such things that people would not believe them if they saw them in the newspaper. . . And when will there be an end to it all!"

"Hush, Father!" Kunin almost shouted, frightened at his tone. "Why take such a gloomy view of life?"

"Generously forgive me, Pavel Mihailovitch. . ." muttered Father Yakov as though he were drunk, "Forgive me, all this. . . doesn't matter,

ANTON CHEKHOV

and don't take any notice of it. . . Only I do blame myself, and always shall blame myself. . . always."

Father Yakov looked about him and began whispering:

"One morning early I was going from Sinkino to Lutchkovo; I saw a woman standing on the river bank, doing something. . . I went up close and could not believe my eyes. . . It was horrible! The wife of the doctor, Ivan Sergeitch, was sitting there washing her linen. . . A doctor's wife, brought up at a select boarding-school! She had got up you see, early and gone half a mile from the village that people should not see her. . . She couldn't get over her pride! When she saw that I was near her and noticed her poverty, she turned red all over. . . I was flustered—I was frightened, and ran up to help her, but she hid her linen from me; she was afraid I should see her ragged chemises. . ."

"All this is positively incredible," said Kunin, sitting down and looking almost with horror at Father Yakov's pale face.

"Incredible it is! It's a thing that has never been! Pavel Mihailovitch, that a doctor's wife should be rinsing the linen in the river! Such a thing does not happen in any country! As her pastor and spiritual father, I ought not to allow it, but what can I do? What? Why, I am always trying to get treated by her husband for nothing myself! It is true that, as you say, it is all incredible! One can hardly believe one's eyes. During Mass, you know, when I look out from the altar and see my congregation, Avraamy starving, and my wife, and think of the doctor's wife—how blue her hands were from the cold water—would you believe it, I forget myself and stand senseless like a fool, until the sacristan calls to me. . . It's awful!"

Father Yakov began walking about again.

"Lord Jesus!" he said, waving his hands, "holy Saints! I can't officiate properly. . . Here you talk to me about the school, and I sit like a dummy and don't understand a word, and think of nothing but food. . . Even before the altar. . . But. . . what am I doing?" Father Yakov pulled himself up suddenly. "You want to go out. Forgive me, I meant nothing. . . Excuse. . ."

Kunin shook hands with Father Yakov without speaking, saw him into the hall, and going back into his study, stood at the window. He saw Father Yakov go out of the house, pull his wide-brimmed rusty-looking hat over his eyes, and slowly, bowing his head, as though ashamed of his outburst, walk along the road.

"I don't see his horse," thought Kunin.

Kunin did not dare to think that the priest had come on foot every day to see him; it was five or six miles to Sinkino, and the mud on the road was impassable. Further on he saw the coachman Andrey and the boy Paramon, jumping over the puddles and splashing Father Yakov with mud, run up to him for his blessing. Father Yakov took off his hat and slowly blessed Andrey, then blessed the boy and stroked his head.

Kunin passed his hand over his eyes, and it seemed to him that his hand was moist. He walked away from the window and with dim eyes looked round the room in which he still seemed to hear the timid droning voice. He glanced at the table. Luckily, Father Yakov, in his haste, had forgotten to take the sermons. Kunin rushed up to them, tore them into pieces, and with loathing thrust them under the table.

"And I did not know!" he moaned, sinking on to the sofa. "After being here over a year as member of the Rural Board, Honorary Justice of the Peace, member of the School Committee! Blind puppet, egregious idiot! I must make haste and help them, I must make haste!"

He turned from side to side uneasily, pressed his temples and racked his brains.

"On the twentieth I shall get my salary, two hundred roubles. . . On some good pretext I will give him some, and some to the doctor's wife. . . I will ask them to perform a special service here, and will get up an illness for the doctor. . . In that way I shan't wound their pride. And I'll help Father Avraamy too. . ."

He reckoned his money on his fingers, and was afraid to own to himself that those two hundred roubles would hardly be enough for him to pay his steward, his servants, the peasant who brought the meat. . . He could not help remembering the recent past when he was senselessly squandering his father's fortune, when as a puppy of twenty he had given expensive fans to prostitutes, had paid ten roubles a day to Kuzma, his cab-driver, and in his vanity had made presents to actresses. Oh, how useful those wasted rouble, three-rouble, ten-rouble notes would have been now!

"Father Avraamy lives on three roubles a month!" thought Kunin. "For a rouble the priest's wife could get herself a chemise, and the doctor's wife could hire a washerwoman. But I'll help them, anyway! I must help them."

Here Kunin suddenly recalled the private information he had sent to the bishop, and he writhed as from a sudden draught of cold air. This remembrance filled him with overwhelming shame before his inner self and before the unseen truth.

So had begun and had ended a sincere effort to be of public service on the part of a well-intentioned but unreflecting and over-comfortable person.

The Murder

I

The evening service was being celebrated at Progonnaya Station. Before the great ikon, painted in glaring colours on a background of gold, stood the crowd of railway servants with their wives and children, and also of the timbermen and sawyers who worked close to the railway line. All stood in silence, fascinated by the glare of the lights and the howling of the snow-storm which was aimlessly disporting itself outside, regardless of the fact that it was the Eve of the Annunciation. The old priest from Vedenyapino conducted the service; the sacristan and Matvey Terehov were singing.

Matvey's face was beaming with delight; he sang stretching out his neck as though he wanted to soar upwards. He sang tenor and chanted the "Praises" too in a tenor voice with honied sweetness and persuasiveness. When he sang "Archangel Voices" he waved his arms like a conductor, and trying to second the sacristan's hollow bass with his tenor, achieved something extremely complex, and from his face it could be seen that he was experiencing great pleasure.

At last the service was over, and they all quietly dispersed, and it was dark and empty again, and there followed that hush which is only known in stations that stand solitary in the open country or in the forest when the wind howls and nothing else is heard and when all the emptiness around, all the dreariness of life slowly ebbing away is felt.

Matvey lived not far from the station at his cousin's tavern. But he did not want to go home. He sat down at the refreshment bar and began talking to the waiter in a low voice.

"We had our own choir in the tile factory. And I must tell you that though we were only workmen, our singing was first-rate, splendid. We were often invited to the town, and when the Deputy Bishop, Father Ivan, took the service at Trinity Church, the bishop's singers sang in the right choir and we in the left. Only they complained in the town that we kept the singing on too long: 'the factory choir drag it out,' they used to say. It is true we began St. Andrey's prayers and the Praises between six and seven, and it was past eleven when we finished, so that it was sometimes after midnight when we got home to the factory. It was good," sighed Matvey. "Very good it was, indeed, Sergey

ANTON CHEKHOV

Nikanoritch! But here in my father's house it is anything but joyful. The nearest church is four miles away; with my weak health I can't get so far; there are no singers there. And there is no peace or quiet in our family; day in day out, there is an uproar, scolding, uncleanliness; we all eat out of one bowl like peasants; and there are beetles in the cabbage soup. . . God has not given me health, else I would have gone away long ago, Sergey Nikanoritch."

Matvey Terehov was a middle-aged man about forty-five, but he had a look of ill-health; his face was wrinkled and his lank, scanty beard was quite grey, and that made him seem many years older. He spoke in a weak voice, circumspectly, and held his chest when he coughed, while his eyes assumed the uneasy and anxious look one sees in very apprehensive people. He never said definitely what was wrong with him, but he was fond of describing at length how once at the factory he had lifted a heavy box and had ruptured himself, and how this had led to "the gripes," and had forced him to give up his work in the tile factory and come back to his native place; but he could not explain what he meant by "the gripes."

"I must own I am not fond of my cousin," he went on, pouring himself out some tea. "He is my elder; it is a sin to censure him, and I fear the Lord, but I cannot bear it in patience. He is a haughty, surly, abusive man; he is the torment of his relations and workmen, and constantly out of humour. Last Sunday I asked him in an amiable way, 'Brother, let us go to Pahomovo for the Mass!' but he said 'I am not going; the priest there is a gambler;' and he would not come here to-day because, he said, the priest from Vedenyapino smokes and drinks vodka. He doesn't like the clergy! He reads Mass himself and the Hours and the Vespers, while his sister acts as sacristan; he says, 'Let us pray unto the Lord'! and she, in a thin little voice like a turkey-hen, 'Lord, have mercy upon us!. . .' It's a sin, that's what it is. Every day I say to him, 'Think what you are doing, brother! Repent, brother!' and he takes no notice."

Sergey Nikanoritch, the waiter, poured out five glasses of tea and carried them on a tray to the waiting-room. He had scarcely gone in when there was a shout:

"Is that the way to serve it, pig's face? You don't know how to wait!"

It was the voice of the station-master. There was a timid mutter, then again a harsh and angry shout:

"Get along!"

The waiter came back greatly crestfallen.

"There was a time when I gave satisfaction to counts and princes," he said in a low voice; "but now I don't know how to serve tea. . . He called me names before the priest and the ladies!"

The waiter, Sergey Nikanoritch, had once had money of his own, and had kept a buffet at a first-class station, which was a junction, in the principal town of a province. There he had worn a swallow-tail coat and a gold chain. But things had gone ill with him; he had squandered all his own money over expensive fittings and service; he had been robbed by his staff, and getting gradually into difficulties, had moved to another station less bustling. Here his wife had left him, taking with her all the silver, and he moved to a third station of a still lower class, where no hot dishes were served. Then to a fourth. Frequently changing his situation and sinking lower and lower, he had at last come to Progonnaya, and here he used to sell nothing but tea and cheap vodka, and for lunch hard-boiled eggs and dry sausages, which smelt of tar, and which he himself sarcastically said were only fit for the orchestra. He was bald all over the top of his head, and had prominent blue eyes and thick bushy whiskers, which he often combed out, looking into the little looking-glass. Memories of the past haunted him continually; he could never get used to sausage "only fit for the orchestra," to the rudeness of the station-master, and to the peasants who used to haggle over the prices, and in his opinion it was as unseemly to haggle over prices in a refreshment room as in a chemist's shop. He was ashamed of his poverty and degradation, and that shame was now the leading interest of his life.

"Spring is late this year," said Matvey, listening. "It's a good job; I don't like spring. In spring it is very muddy, Sergey Nikanoritch. In books they write: Spring, the birds sing, the sun is setting, but what is there pleasant in that? A bird is a bird, and nothing more. I am fond of good company, of listening to folks, of talking of religion or singing something agreeable in chorus; but as for nightingales and flowers—bless them, I say!"

He began again about the tile factory, about the choir, but Sergey Nikanoritch could not get over his mortification, and kept shrugging his shoulders and muttering. Matvey said good-bye and went home.

There was no frost, and the snow was already melting on the roofs, though it was still falling in big flakes; they were whirling rapidly round and round in the air and chasing one another in white clouds along the

ANTON CHEKHOV

railway line. And the oak forest on both sides of the line, in the dim light of the moon which was hidden somewhere high up in the clouds, resounded with a prolonged sullen murmur. When a violent storm shakes the trees, how terrible they are! Matvey walked along the causeway beside the line, covering his face and his hands, while the wind beat on his back. All at once a little nag, plastered all over with snow, came into sight; a sledge scraped along the bare stones of the causeway, and a peasant, white all over, too, with his head muffled up, cracked his whip. Matvey looked round after him, but at once, as though it had been a vision, there was neither sledge nor peasant to be seen, and he hastened his steps, suddenly scared, though he did not know why.

Here was the crossing and the dark little house where the signalman lived. The barrier was raised, and by it perfect mountains had drifted and clouds of snow were whirling round like witches on broomsticks. At that point the line was crossed by an old highroad, which was still called "the track." On the right, not far from the crossing, by the roadside stood Terehov's tavern, which had been a posting inn. Here there was always a light twinkling at night.

When Matvey reached home there was a strong smell of incense in all the rooms and even in the entry. His cousin Yakov Ivanitch was still reading the evening service. In the prayer-room where this was going on, in the corner opposite the door, there stood a shrine of old-fashioned ancestral ikons in gilt settings, and both walls to right and to left were decorated with ikons of ancient and modern fashion, in shrines and without them. On the table, which was draped to the floor, stood an ikon of the Annunciation, and close by a cyprus-wood cross and the censer; wax candles were burning. Beside the table was a reading desk. As he passed by the prayer-room, Matvey stopped and glanced in at the door. Yakov Ivanitch was reading at the desk at that moment, his sister Aglaia, a tall lean old woman in a dark-blue dress and white kerchief, was praying with him. Yakov Ivanitch's daughter Dashutka, an ugly freckled girl of eighteen, was there, too, barefoot as usual, and wearing the dress in which she had at nightfall taken water to the cattle.

"Glory to Thee Who hast shown us the light!" Yakov Ivanitch boomed out in a chant, bowing low.

Aglaia propped her chin on her hand and chanted in a thin, shrill, drawling voice. And upstairs, above the ceiling, there was the sound of vague voices which seemed menacing or ominous of evil. No one had lived on the storey above since a fire there a long time ago. The windows were boarded up, and empty bottles lay about on the floor between the beams. Now the wind was banging and droning, and it seemed as though someone were running and stumbling over the beams.

Half of the lower storey was used as a tavern, while Terehov's family lived in the other half, so that when drunken visitors were noisy in the tavern every word they said could be heard in the rooms. Matvey lived in a room next to the kitchen, with a big stove, in which, in old days, when this had been a posting inn, bread had been baked every day. Dashutka, who had no room of her own, lived in the same room behind the stove. A cricket chirped there always at night and mice ran in and out.

Matvey lighted a candle and began reading a book which he had borrowed from the station policeman. While he was sitting over it the service ended, and they all went to bed. Dashutka lay down, too. She began snoring at once, but soon woke up and said, yawning:

"You shouldn't burn a candle for nothing, Uncle Matvey."

"It's my candle," answered Matvey; "I bought it with my own money."

Dashutka turned over a little and fell asleep again. Matvey sat up a good time longer—he was not sleepy—and when he had finished the last page he took a pencil out of a box and wrote on the book:

"I, Matvey Terehov, have read this book, and think it the very best of all the books I have read, for which I express my gratitude to the non-commissioned officer of the Police Department of Railways, Kuzma Nikolaev Zhukov, as the possessor of this priceless book."

He considered it an obligation of politeness to make such inscriptions in other people's books.

II

ON ANNUNCIATION DAY, AFTER THE mail train had been sent off, Matvey was sitting in the refreshment bar, talking and drinking tea with lemon in it.

The waiter and Zhukov the policeman were listening to him.

"I was, I must tell you," Matvey was saying, "inclined to religion from my earliest childhood. I was only twelve years old when I used to read the epistle in church, and my parents were greatly delighted, and every summer I used to go on a pilgrimage with my dear mother. Sometimes other lads would be singing songs and catching crayfish, while I would

ANTON CHEKHOV

be all the time with my mother. My elders commended me, and, indeed, I was pleased myself that I was of such good behaviour. And when my mother sent me with her blessing to the factory, I used between working hours to sing tenor there in our choir, and nothing gave me greater pleasure. I needn't say, I drank no vodka, I smoked no tobacco, and lived in chastity; but we all know such a mode of life is displeasing to the enemy of mankind, and he, the unclean spirit, once tried to ruin me and began to darken my mind, just as now with my cousin. First of all, I took a vow to fast every Monday and not to eat meat any day, and as time went on all sorts of fancies came over me. For the first week of Lent down to Saturday the holy fathers have ordained a diet of dry food, but it is no sin for the weak or those who work hard even to drink tea, yet not a crumb passed into my mouth till the Sunday, and afterwards all through Lent I did not allow myself a drop of oil, and on Wednesdays and Fridays I did not touch a morsel at all. It was the same in the lesser fasts. Sometimes in St. Peter's fast our factory lads would have fish soup, while I would sit a little apart from them and suck a dry crust. Different people have different powers, of course, but I can say of myself I did not find fast days hard, and, indeed, the greater the zeal the easier it seems. You are only hungry on the first days of the fast, and then you get used to it; it goes on getting easier, and by the end of a week you don't mind it at all, and there is a numb feeling in your legs as though you were not on earth, but in the clouds. And, besides that, I laid all sorts of penances on myself; I used to get up in the night and pray, bowing down to the ground, used to drag heavy stones from place to place, used to go out barefoot in the snow, and I even wore chains, too. Only, as time went on, you know, I was confessing one day to the priest and suddenly this reflection occurred to me: why, this priest, I thought, is married, he eats meat and smokes tobacco—how can he confess me, and what power has he to absolve my sins if he is more sinful that I? I even scruple to eat Lenten oil, while he eats sturgeon, I dare say. I went to another priest, and he, as ill luck would have it, was a fat fleshy man, in a silk cassock; he rustled like a lady, and he smelt of tobacco too. I went to fast and confess in the monastery, and my heart was not at ease even there; I kept fancying the monks were not living according to their rules. And after that I could not find a service to my mind: in one place they read the service too fast, in another they sang the wrong prayer, in a third the sacristan stammered. Sometimes, the Lord forgive me a sinner, I would stand in church and my heart would throb with anger. How could one pray, feeling like that? And I fancied that the people in the church did not cross themselves properly, did not listen properly; wherever I looked it seemed to me that they were all drunkards, that they broke the fast, smoked, lived loose lives and played cards. I was the only one who lived according to the commandments. The wily spirit did not slumber; it got worse as it went on. I gave up singing in the choir and I did not go to church at all; since my notion was that I was a righteous man and that the church did not suit me owing to its imperfections—that is, indeed, like a fallen angel, I was puffed up in my pride beyond all belief. After this I began attempting to make a church for myself. I hired from a deaf woman a tiny little room, a long way out of town near the cemetery, and made a prayer-room like my cousin's, only I had big church candlesticks, too, and a real censer. In this prayer-room of mine I kept the rules of holy Mount Athos— that is, every day my matins began at midnight without fail, and on the eve of the chief of the twelve great holy days my midnight service lasted ten hours and sometimes even twelve. Monks are allowed by rule to sit during the singing of the Psalter and the reading of the Bible, but I wanted to be better than the monks, and so I used to stand all through. I used to read and sing slowly, with tears and sighing, lifting up my hands, and I used to go straight from prayer to work without sleeping; and, indeed, I was always praying at my work, too. Well, it got all over the town 'Matvey is a saint; Matvey heals the sick and senseless.' I never had healed anyone, of course, but we all know wherever any heresy or false doctrine springs up there's no keeping the female sex away. They are just like flies on the honey. Old maids and females of all sorts came trailing to me, bowing down to my feet, kissing my hands and crying out I was a saint and all the rest of it, and one even saw a halo round my head. It was too crowded in the prayer-room. I took a bigger room, and then we had a regular tower of Babel. The devil got hold of me completely and screened the light from my eyes with his unclean hoofs. We all behaved as though we were frantic. I read, while the old maids and other females sang, and then after standing on their legs for twenty-four hours or longer without eating or drinking, suddenly a trembling would come over them as though they were in a fever; after that, one would begin screaming and then another—it was horrible! I, too, would shiver all over like a Jew in a frying-pan, I don't know myself why, and our legs began to prance about. It's a strange thing, indeed: you don't want to, but you prance about and waggle your arms; and after that, screaming and shrieking, we all danced and ran after one another—ran till we dropped; and in that way, in wild frenzy, I fell into fornication."

The policeman laughed, but, noticing that no one else was laughing, became serious and said:

"That's Molokanism. I have heard they are all like that in the Caucasus."

"But I was not killed by a thunderbolt," Matvey went on, crossing himself before the ikon and moving his lips. "My dead mother must have been praying for me in the other world. When everyone in the town looked upon me as a saint, and even the ladies and gentlemen of good family used to come to me in secret for consolation, I happened to go into our landlord, Osip Varlamitch, to ask forgiveness—it was the Day of Forgiveness—and he fastened the door with the hook, and we were left alone face to face. And he began to reprove me, and I must tell you Osip Varlamitch was a man of brains, though without education, and everyone respected and feared him, for he was a man of stern, God-fearing life and worked hard. He had been the mayor of the town, and a warden of the church for twenty years maybe, and had done a great deal of good; he had covered all the New Moscow Road with gravel, had painted the church, and had decorated the columns to look like malachite. Well, he fastened the door, and—'I have been wanting to get at you for a long time, you rascal,. . .' he said. 'You think you are a saint,' he said. 'No you are not a saint, but a backslider from God, a heretic and an evildoer!. . .' And he went on and on. . . I can't tell you how he said it, so eloquently and cleverly, as though it were all written down, and so touchingly. He talked for two hours. His words penetrated my soul; my eyes were opened. I listened, listened and—burst into sobs! 'Be an ordinary man,' he said, 'eat and drink, dress and pray like everyone else. All that is above the ordinary is of the devil. Your chains,' he said, 'are of the devil; your fasting is of the devil; your prayer-room is of the devil. It is all pride,' he said. Next day, on Monday in Holy Week, it pleased God I should fall ill. I ruptured myself and was taken to the hospital. I was terribly worried, and wept bitterly and trembled. I thought there was a straight road before me from the hospital to hell, and I almost died. I was in misery on a bed of sickness for six months, and when I was discharged the first thing I did I confessed, and took the sacrament in the regular way and became a man again. Osip Varlamitch saw me off home and exhorted me: 'Remember, Matvey, that anything above the ordinary is of the devil.' And now I eat and drink like everyone else and pray like everyone else. . . If it happens now that the priest smells of tobacco or vodka I don't venture to blame him, because the priest, too, of course, is an ordinary man. But as soon as I am told that in the town or in the village a saint has set up who does not eat for weeks, and makes rules of his own, I know whose work it is. So that is how I carried on in the past, gentlemen. Now, like Osip Varlamitch, I am continually exhorting my cousins and reproaching them, but I am a voice crying in the wilderness. God has not vouchsafed me the gift."

Matvey's story evidently made no impression whatever. Sergey Nikanoritch said nothing, but began clearing the refreshments off the counter, while the policeman began talking of how rich Matvey's cousin was.

"He must have thirty thousand at least," he said.

Zhukov the policeman, a sturdy, well-fed, red-haired man with a full face (his cheeks quivered when he walked), usually sat lolling and crossing his legs when not in the presence of his superiors. As he talked he swayed to and fro and whistled carelessly, while his face had a self-satisfied replete air, as though he had just had dinner. He was making money, and he always talked of it with the air of a connoisseur. He undertook jobs as an agent, and when anyone wanted to sell an estate, a horse or a carriage, they applied to him.

"Yes, it will be thirty thousand, I dare say," Sergey Nikanoritch assented. "Your grandfather had an immense fortune," he said, addressing Matvey. "Immense it was; all left to your father and your uncle. Your father died as a young man and your uncle got hold of it all, and afterwards, of course, Yakov Ivanitch. While you were going pilgrimages with your mama and singing tenor in the factory, they didn't let the grass grow under their feet."

"Fifteen thousand comes to your share," said the policeman swaying from side to side. "The tavern belongs to you in common, so the capital is in common. Yes. If I were in your place I should have taken it into court long ago. I would have taken it into court for one thing, and while the case was going on I'd have knocked his face to a jelly."

Yakov Ivanitch was disliked because, when anyone believes differently from others, it upsets even people who are indifferent to religion. The policeman disliked him also because he, too, sold horses and carriages.

"You don't care about going to law with your cousin because you have plenty of money of your own," said the waiter to Matvey, looking at him with envy. "It is all very well for anyone who has means, but here I shall die in this position, I suppose. . ."

Matvey began declaring that he hadn't any money at all, but Sergey Nikanoritch was not listening. Memories of the past and of the insults which he endured every day came showering upon him. His bald head began to perspire; he flushed and blinked.

"A cursed life!" he said with vexation, and he banged the sausage on the floor.

III

THE STORY RAN THAT THE tavern had been built in the time of Alexander I, by a widow who had settled here with her son; her name was Avdotya Terehov. The dark roofed-in courtyard and the gates always kept locked excited, especially on moonlight nights, a feeling of depression and unaccountable uneasiness in people who drove by with posting-horses, as though sorcerers or robbers were living in it; and the driver always looked back after he passed, and whipped up his horses. Travellers did not care to put up here, as the people of the house were always unfriendly and charged heavily. The yard was muddy even in summer; huge fat pigs used to lie there in the mud, and the horses in which the Terehovs dealt wandered about untethered, and often it happened that they ran out of the yard and dashed along the road like mad creatures, terrifying the pilgrim women. At that time there was a great deal of traffic on the road; long trains of loaded waggons trailed by, and all sorts of adventures happened, such as, for instance, that thirty years ago some waggoners got up a quarrel with a passing merchant and killed him, and a slanting cross is standing to this day half a mile from the tavern; posting-chaises with bells and the heavy *dormeuses* of country gentlemen drove by; and herds of horned cattle passed bellowing and stirring up clouds of dust.

When the railway came there was at first at this place only a platform, which was called simply a halt; ten years afterwards the present station, Progonnaya, was built. The traffic on the old posting-road almost ceased, and only local landowners and peasants drove along it now, but the working people walked there in crowds in spring and autumn. The posting-inn was transformed into a restaurant; the upper storey was destroyed by fire, the roof had grown yellow with rust, the roof over the yard had fallen by degrees, but huge fat pigs, pink and revolting, still wallowed in the mud in the yard. As before, the horses sometimes ran away and, lashing their tails dashed madly along the road. In the tavern they sold tea, hay oats and flour, as well as vodka and beer, to be drunk on the premises and also to be taken away; they sold spirituous liquors warily, for they had never taken out a licence.

The Terehovs had always been distinguished by their piety, so much so that they had even been given the nickname of the "Godlies." But perhaps because they lived apart like bears, avoided people and thought out all their ideas for themselves, they were given to dreams and to doubts and to changes of faith and almost each generation had a peculiar faith of its own. The grandmother Avdotya, who had built the inn, was an Old Believer; her son and both her grandsons (the fathers of Matvey and Yakov) went to the Orthodox church, entertained the clergy, and worshipped before the new ikons as devoutly as they had done before the old. The son in old age refused to eat meat and imposed upon himself the rule of silence, considering all conversation as sin; it was the peculiarity of the grandsons that they interpreted the Scripture not simply, but sought in it a hidden meaning, declaring that every sacred word must contain a mystery.

Avdotya's great-grandson Matvey had struggled from early childhood with all sorts of dreams and fancies and had been almost ruined by it; the other great-grandson, Yakov Ivanitch, was orthodox, but after his wife's death he gave up going to church and prayed at home. Following his example, his sister Aglaia had turned, too; she did not go to church herself, and did not let Dashutka go. Of Aglaia it was told that in her youth she used to attend the Flagellant meetings in Vedenyapino, and that she was still a Flagellant in secret, and that was why she wore a white kerchief.

Yakov Ivanitch was ten years older than Matvey—he was a very handsome tall old man with a big grey beard almost to his waist, and bushy eyebrows which gave his face a stern, even ill-natured expression. He wore a long jerkin of good cloth or a black sheepskin coat, and altogether tried to be clean and neat in dress; he wore goloshes even in dry weather. He did not go to church, because, to his thinking, the services were not properly celebrated and because the priests drank wine at unlawful times and smoked tobacco. Every day he read and sang the service at home with Aglaia. At Vedenyapino they left out the "Praises" at early matins, and had no evening service even on great holidays, but he used to read through at home everything that was laid down for every day, without hurrying or leaving out a single line, and even in his spare time read aloud the Lives of the Saints. And in everyday life he adhered strictly to the rules of the church; thus, if wine were allowed on some day in Lent "for the sake of the vigil," then he never failed to drink wine, even if he were not inclined.

He read, sang, burned incense and fasted, not for the sake of receiving blessings of some sort from God, but for the sake of good order. Man cannot live without religion, and religion ought to be expressed from year to year and from day to day in a certain order, so that every morning and every evening a man might turn to God with exactly those words and thoughts that were befitting that special day and hour. One must live, and, therefore, also pray as is pleasing to God, and so every day one must read and sing what is pleasing to God—that is, what is laid down in the rule of the church. Thus the first chapter of St. John must only be read on Easter Day, and "It is most meet" must not be sung from Easter to Ascension, and so on. The consciousness of this order and its importance afforded Yakov Ivanitch great gratification during his religious exercises. When he was forced to break this order by some necessity—to drive to town or to the bank, for instance his conscience was uneasy and he felt miserable.

When his cousin Matvey had returned unexpectedly from the factory and settled in the tavern as though it were his home, he had from the very first day disturbed his settled order. He refused to pray with them, had meals and drank tea at wrong times, got up late, drank milk on Wednesdays and Fridays on the pretext of weak health; almost every day he went into the prayer-room while they were at prayers and cried: "Think what you are doing, brother! Repent, brother!" These words threw Yakov into a fury, while Aglaia could not refrain from beginning to scold; or at night Matvey would steal into the prayer-room and say softly: "Cousin, your prayer is not pleasing to God. For it is written, First be reconciled with thy brother and then offer thy gift. You lend money at usury, you deal in vodka—repent!"

In Matvey's words Yakov saw nothing but the usual evasions of empty-headed and careless people who talk of loving your neighbour, of being reconciled with your brother, and so on, simply to avoid praying, fasting and reading holy books, and who talk contemptuously of profit and interest simply because they don't like working. Of course, to be poor, save nothing, and put by nothing was a great deal easier than being rich.

But yet he was troubled and could not pray as before. As soon as he went into the prayer-room and opened the book he began to be afraid his cousin would come in and hinder him; and, in fact, Matvey did soon appear and cry in a trembling voice: "Think what you are doing, brother! Repent, brother!" Aglaia stormed and Yakov, too, flew into a passion and shouted: "Go out of my house!" while Matvey answered him: "The house belongs to both of us."

Yakov would begin singing and reading again, but he could not regain his calm, and unconsciously fell to dreaming over his book. Though he regarded his cousin's words as nonsense, yet for some reason it had of late haunted his memory that it is hard for a rich man to enter the kingdom of heaven, that the year before last he had made a very good bargain over buying a stolen horse, that one day when his wife was alive a drunkard had died of vodka in his tavern. . .

He slept badly at nights now and woke easily, and he could hear that Matvey, too, was awake, and continually sighing and pining for his tile factory. And while Yakov turned over from one side to another at night he thought of the stolen horse and the drunken man, and what was said in the gospels about the camel.

It looked as though his dreaminess were coming over him again. And as ill-luck would have it, although it was the end of March, every day it kept snowing, and the forest roared as though it were winter, and there was no believing that spring would ever come. The weather disposed one to depression, and to quarrelling and to hatred and in the night, when the wind droned over the ceiling, it seemed as though someone were living overhead in the empty storey; little by little the broodings settled like a burden on his mind, his head burned and he could not sleep.

IV

ON THE MORNING OF THE Monday before Good Friday, Matvey heard from his room Dashutka say to Aglaia:

"Uncle Matvey said, the other day, that there is no need to fast."

Matvey remembered the whole conversation he had had the evening before with Dashutka, and he felt hurt all at once.

"Girl, don't do wrong!" he said in a moaning voice, like a sick man. "You can't do without fasting; our Lord Himself fasted forty days. I only explained that fasting does a bad man no good."

"You should just listen to the factory hands; they can teach you goodness," Aglaia said sarcastically as she washed the floor (she usually washed the floors on working days and was always angry with everyone when she did it). "We know how they keep the fasts in the factory. You had better ask that uncle of yours—ask him about his 'Darling,' how he used to guzzle milk on fast days with her, the viper. He teaches others; he forgets about his viper. But ask him who was it he left his money with—who was it?"

Matvey had carefully concealed from everyone, as though it were a foul sore, that during that period of his life when old women and unmarried girls had danced and run about with him at their prayers he had formed a connection with a working woman and had had a child by her. When he went home he had given this woman all he had saved at the factory, and had borrowed from his landlord for his journey, and now he had only a few roubles which he spent on tea and candles. The "Darling" had informed him later on that the child was dead, and asked him in a letter what she should do with the money. This letter was brought from the station by the labourer. Aglaia intercepted it and read it, and had reproached Matvey with his "Darling" every day since.

"Just fancy, nine hundred roubles," Aglaia went on. "You gave nine hundred roubles to a viper, no relation, a factory jade, blast you!" She had flown into a passion by now and was shouting shrilly: "Can't you speak? I could tear you to pieces, wretched creature! Nine hundred roubles as though it were a farthing. You might have left it to Dashutka—she is a relation, not a stranger—or else have it sent to Byelev for Marya's poor orphans. And your viper did not choke, may she be thrice accursed, the she-devil! May she never look upon the light of day!"

Yakov Ivanitch called to her: it was time to begin the "Hours." She washed, put on a white kerchief, and by now quiet and meek, went into the prayer-room to the brother she loved. When she spoke to Matvey or served peasants in the tavern with tea she was a gaunt, keen-eyed, ill-humoured old woman; in the prayer-room her face was serene and softened, she looked younger altogether, she curtsied affectedly, and even pursed up her lips.

Yakov Ivanitch began reading the service softly and dolefully, as he always did in Lent. After he had read a little he stopped to listen to the stillness that reigned through the house, and then went on reading again, with a feeling of gratification; he folded his hands in supplication, rolled his eyes, shook his head, sighed. But all at once there was the sound of voices. The policeman and Sergey Nikanoritch had come to see Matvey. Yakov Ivanitch was embarrassed at reading aloud and singing when there were strangers in the house, and now, hearing voices, he began reading in a whisper and slowly. He could hear in the prayer-room the waiter say:

"The Tatar at Shtchepovo is selling his business for fifteen hundred. He'll take five hundred down and an I.O.U. for the rest. And so, Matvey Vassilitch, be so kind as to lend me that five hundred roubles. I will pay you two per cent a month."

"What money have I got?" cried Matvey, amazed. "I have no money!"

"Two per cent a month will be a godsend to you," the policeman explained. "While lying by, your money is simply eaten by the moth, and that's all that you get from it."

Afterwards the visitors went out and a silence followed. But Yakov Ivanitch had hardly begun reading and singing again when a voice was heard outside the door:

"Brother, let me have a horse to drive to Vedenyapino."

It was Matvey. And Yakov was troubled again. "Which can you go with?" he asked after a moment's thought. "The man has gone with the sorrel to take the pig, and I am going with the little stallion to Shuteykino as soon as I have finished."

"Brother, why is it you can dispose of the horses and not I?" Matvey asked with irritation.

"Because I am not taking them for pleasure, but for work."

"Our property is in common, so the horses are in common, too, and you ought to understand that, brother."

A silence followed. Yakov did not go on praying, but waited for Matvey to go away from the door.

"Brother," said Matvey, "I am a sick man. I don't want possession— let them go; you have them, but give me a small share to keep me in my illness. Give it me and I'll go away."

Yakov did not speak. He longed to be rid of Matvey, but he could not give him money, since all the money was in the business; besides, there had never been a case of the family dividing in the whole history of the Terehovs. Division means ruin.

Yakov said nothing, but still waited for Matvey to go away, and kept looking at his sister, afraid that she would interfere, and that there would be a storm of abuse again, as there had been in the morning. When at last Matvey did go Yakov went on reading, but now he had no pleasure in it. There was a heaviness in his head and a darkness before his eyes from continually bowing down to the ground, and he was weary of the sound of his soft dejected voice. When such a depression of spirit came over him at night, he put it down to not being able to sleep; by day it frightened him, and he began to feel as though devils were sitting on his head and shoulders.

Finishing the service after a fashion, dissatisfied and ill-humoured, he set off for Shuteykino. In the previous autumn a gang of navvies had dug a boundary ditch near Progonnaya, and had run up a bill at the tavern for eighteen roubles, and now he had to find their foreman in Shuteykino and get the money from him. The road had been spoilt by the thaw and the snowstorm; it was of a dark colour and full of holes, and in parts it had given way altogether. The snow had sunk away at the sides below the road, so that he had to drive, as it were, upon a narrow causeway, and it was very difficult to turn off it when he met anything. The sky had been overcast ever since the morning and a damp wind was blowing. . .

A long train of sledges met him; peasant women were carting bricks. Yakov had to turn off the road. His horse sank into the snow up to its belly; the sledge lurched over to the right, and to avoid falling out he bent over to the left, and sat so all the time the sledges moved slowly by him. Through the wind he heard the creaking of the sledge poles and the breathing of the gaunt horses, and the women saying about him, "There's Godly coming," while one, gazing with compassion at his horse, said quickly:

"It looks as though the snow will be lying till Yegory's Day! They are worn out with it!"

Yakov sat uncomfortably huddled up, screwing up his eyes on account of the wind, while horses and red bricks kept passing before him. And perhaps because he was uncomfortable and his side ached, he felt all at once annoyed, and the business he was going about seemed to him unimportant, and he reflected that he might send the labourer next day to Shuteykino. Again, as in the previous sleepless night, he thought of the saying about the camel, and then memories of all sorts crept into his mind; of the peasant who had sold him the stolen horse, of the drunken man, of the peasant women who had brought their samovars to him to pawn. Of course, every merchant tries to get as much as he can, but Yakov felt depressed that he was in trade; he longed to get somewhere far away from this routine, and he felt dreary at the thought that he would have to read the evening service that day. The wind blew straight into his face and soughed in his collar; and it seemed as though it were whispering to him all these thoughts, bringing them from the broad white plain. . . Looking at that plain, familiar to him from childhood, Yakov remembered that he had had just this same trouble and these same thoughts in his young days when dreams and imaginings had come upon him and his faith had wavered.

He felt miserable at being alone in the open country; he turned back and drove slowly after the sledges, and the women laughed and said:

"Godly has turned back."

At home nothing had been cooked and the samovar was not heated on account of the fast, and this made the day seem very long. Yakov Ivanitch had long ago taken the horse to the stable, dispatched the flour to the station, and twice taken up the Psalms to read, and yet the evening was still far off. Aglaia has already washed all the floors, and, having nothing to do, was tidying up her chest, the lid of which was pasted over on the inside with labels off bottles. Matvey, hungry and melancholy, sat reading, or went up to the Dutch stove and slowly scrutinized the tiles which reminded him of the factory. Dashutka was asleep; then, waking up, she went to take water to the cattle. When she was getting water from the well the cord broke and the pail fell in. The labourer began looking for a boathook to get the pail out, and Dashutka, barefooted, with legs as red as a goose's, followed him about in the muddy snow, repeating: "It's too far!" She meant to say that the well was too deep for the hook to reach the bottom, but the labourer did not understand her, and evidently she bothered him, so that he suddenly turned around and abused her in unseemly language. Yakov Ivanitch, coming out that moment into the yard, heard Dashutka answer the labourer in a long rapid stream of choice abuse, which she could only have learned from drunken peasants in the tavern.

"What are you saying, shameless girl!" he cried to her, and he was positively aghast. "What language!"

And she looked at her father in perplexity, dully, not understanding why she should not use those words. He would have admonished her, but she struck him as so savage and benighted; and for the first time he realized that she had no religion. And all this life in the forest, in the snow, with drunken peasants, with coarse oaths, seemed to him as savage and benighted as this girl, and instead of giving her a lecture he only waved his hand and went back into the room.

At that moment the policeman and Sergey Nikanoritch came in again to see Matvey. Yakov Ivanitch thought that these people, too, had no religion, and that that did not trouble them in the least; and human life began to seem to him as strange, senseless and unenlightened as a dog's. Bareheaded he walked about the yard, then he went out on to the road, clenching his fists. Snow was falling in big flakes at the time. His beard was blown about in the wind. He kept shaking his head, as though there were something weighing upon his head and shoulders, as though devils were sitting on them; and it seemed to him that it was not himself walking about, but some wild beast, a huge terrible beast, and that if he were to cry out his voice would be a roar that would sound all over the forest and the plain, and would frighten everyone. . .

V

When he went back into the house the policeman was no longer there, but the waiter was sitting with Matvey, counting something on the reckoning beads. He was in the habit of coming often, almost every day, to the tavern; in old days he had come to see Yakov Ivanitch, now he came to see Matvey. He was continually reckoning on the beads, while his face perspired and looked strained, or he would ask for money or, stroking his whiskers, would describe how he had once been in a first-class station and used to prepare champagne-punch for officers, and at grand dinners served the sturgeon-soup with his own hands. Nothing in this world interested him but refreshment bars, and he could only talk about things to eat, about wines and the paraphernalia of the dinner-table. On one occasion, handing a cup of tea to a young woman who was nursing her baby and wishing to say something agreeable to her, he expressed himself in this way:

"The mother's breast is the baby's refreshment bar."

Reckoning with the beads in Matvey's room, he asked for money; said he could not go on living at Progonnaya, and several times repeated in a tone of voice that sounded as though he were just going to cry:

"Where am I to go? Where am I to go now? Tell me that, please."

Then Matvey went into the kitchen and began peeling some boiled potatoes which he had probably put away from the day before. It was quiet, and it seemed to Yakov Ivanitch that the waiter was gone. It was past the time for evening service; he called Aglaia, and, thinking there was no one else in the house sang out aloud without embarrassment. He sang and read, but was inwardly pronouncing other words, "Lord, forgive me! Lord, save me!" and, one after another, without ceasing, he made low bows to the ground as though he wanted to exhaust himself, and he kept shaking his head, so that Aglaia looked at him with wonder. He was afraid Matvey would come in, and was certain that he would come in, and felt an anger against him which he could overcome neither by prayer nor by continually bowing down to the ground.

Matvey opened the door very softly and went into the prayer-room.

"It's a sin, such a sin!" he said reproachfully, and heaved a sigh. "Repent! Think what you are doing, brother!"

Yakov Ivanitch, clenching his fists and not looking at him for fear of striking him, went quickly out of the room. Feeling himself a huge terrible wild beast, just as he had done before on the road, he crossed the passage into the grey, dirty room, reeking with smoke and fog, in which the peasants usually drank tea, and there he spent a long time walking from one corner to the other, treading heavily, so that the crockery jingled on the shelves and the tables shook. It was clear to him now that he was himself dissatisfied with his religion, and could not pray as he used to do. He must repent, he must think things over, reconsider, live and pray in some other way. But how pray? And perhaps all this was a temptation of the devil, and nothing of this was necessary?. . . How was it to be? What was he to do? Who could guide him? What helplessness! He stopped and, clutching at his head, began to think, but Matvey's being near him prevented him from reflecting calmly. And he went rapidly into the room.

Matvey was sitting in the kitchen before a bowl of potato, eating. Close by, near the stove, Aglaia and Dashutka were sitting facing one another, spinning yarn. Between the stove and the table at which Matvey was sitting was stretched an ironing-board; on it stood a cold iron.

"Sister," Matvey asked, "let me have a little oil!"

"Who eats oil on a day like this?" asked Aglaia.

"I am not a monk, sister, but a layman. And in my weak health I may take not only oil but milk."

"Yes, at the factory you may have anything."

Aglaia took a bottle of Lenten oil from the shelf and banged it angrily down before Matvey, with a malignant smile evidently pleased that he was such a sinner.

"But I tell you, you can't eat oil!" shouted Yakov.

Aglaia and Dashutka started, but Matvey poured the oil into the bowl and went on eating as though he had not heard.

"I tell you, you can't eat oil!" Yakov shouted still more loudly; he turned red all over, snatched up the bowl, lifted it higher than his head, and dashed it with all his force to the ground, so that it flew into fragments. "Don't dare to speak!" he cried in a furious voice, though Matvey had not said a word. "Don't dare!" he repeated, and struck his fist on the table.

Matvey turned pale and got up.

"Brother!" he said, still munching—"brother, think what you are about!"

"Out of my house this minute!" shouted Yakov; he loathed Matvey's wrinkled face, and his voice, and the crumbs on his moustache, and the fact that he was munching. "Out, I tell you!"

"Brother, calm yourself! The pride of hell has confounded you!"

"Hold your tongue!" (Yakov stamped.) "Go away, you devil!"

"If you care to know," Matvey went on in a loud voice, as he, too, began to get angry, "you are a backslider from God and a heretic. The accursed spirits have hidden the true light from you; your prayer is not acceptable to God. Repent before it is too late! The deathbed of the sinner is terrible! Repent, brother!"

Yakov seized him by the shoulders and dragged him away from the table, while he turned whiter than ever, and frightened and bewildered, began muttering, "What is it? What's the matter?" and, struggling and making efforts to free himself from Yakov's hands, he accidentally caught hold of his shirt near the neck and tore the collar; and it seemed to Aglaia that he was trying to beat Yakov. She uttered a shriek, snatched up the bottle of Lenten oil and with all her force brought it down straight on the skull of the cousin she hated. Matvey reeled, and in one instant his face became calm and indifferent. Yakov, breathing heavily, excited, and feeling pleasure at the gurgle the bottle had made, like a living thing, when it had struck the head, kept him from falling and several times (he remembered this very distinctly) motioned Aglaia towards the iron with his finger; and only when the blood began trickling through his hands and he heard Dashutka's loud wail, and when the ironing-board fell with a crash, and Matvey rolled heavily on it, Yakov left off feeling anger and understood what had happened.

"Let him rot, the factory buck!" Aglaia brought out with repulsion, still keeping the iron in her hand. The white bloodstained kerchief slipped on to her shoulders and her grey hair fell in disorder. "He's got what he deserved!"

Everything was terrible. Dashutka sat on the floor near the stove with the yarn in her hands, sobbing, and continually bowing down, uttering at each bow a gasping sound. But nothing was so terrible to Yakov as the potato in the blood, on which he was afraid of stepping, and there was something else terrible which weighed upon him like a bad dream and seemed the worst danger, though he could not take it in for the first minute. This was the waiter, Sergey Nikanoritch, who was standing in the doorway with the reckoning beads in his hands, very pale, looking with horror at what was happening in the kitchen. Only when he turned and went quickly into the passage and from there outside, Yakov grasped who it was and followed him.

Wiping his hands on the snow as he went, he reflected. The idea flashed through his mind that their labourer had gone away long before and had asked leave to stay the night at home in the village; the day before they had killed a pig, and there were huge bloodstains in the snow and on the sledge, and even one side of the top of the well was splattered with blood, so that it could not have seemed suspicious even if the whole of Yakov's family had been stained with blood. To conceal the murder would be agonizing, but for the policeman, who would whistle and smile ironically, to come from the station, for the peasants to arrive and bind Yakov's and Aglaia's hands, and take them solemnly to the district courthouse and from there to the town, while everyone on the way would point at them and say mirthfully, "They are taking the Godlies!"—this seemed to Yakov more agonizing than anything, and he longed to lengthen out the time somehow, so as to endure this shame not now, but later, in the future.

"I can lend you a thousand roubles,. . ." he said, overtaking Sergey Nikanoritch. "If you tell anyone, it will do no good. . . There's no bringing the man back, anyway;" and with difficulty keeping up with the waiter, who did not look round, but tried to walk away faster than ever, he went on: "I can give you fifteen hundred. . ."

He stopped because he was out of breath, while Sergey Nikanoritch walked on as quickly as ever, probably afraid that he would be killed, too. Only after passing the railway crossing and going half the way from the crossing to the station, he furtively looked round and walked more slowly. Lights, red and green, were already gleaming in the station and along the line; the wind had fallen, but flakes of snow were still coming down and the road had turned white again. But just at the station

Sergey Nikanoritch stopped, thought a minute, and turned resolutely back. It was growing dark.

"Oblige me with the fifteen hundred, Yakov Ivanitch," he said, trembling all over. "I agree."

VI

YAKOV IVANITCH'S MONEY WAS IN the bank of the town and was invested in second mortgages; he only kept a little at home, Just what was wanted for necessary expenses. Going into the kitchen he felt for the matchbox, and while the sulphur was burning with a blue light he had time to make out the figure of Matvey, which was still lying on the floor near the table, but now it was covered with a white sheet, and nothing could be seen but his boots. A cricket was chirruping. Aglaia and Dashutka were not in the room, they were both sitting behind the counter in the tea-room, spinning yarn in silence. Yakov Ivanitch crossed to his own room with a little lamp in his hand, and pulled from under the bed a little box in which he kept his money. This time there were in it four hundred and twenty one-rouble notes and silver to the amount of thirty-five roubles; the notes had an unpleasant heavy smell. Putting the money together in his cap, Yakov Ivanitch went out into the yard and then out of the gate. He walked, looking from side to side, but there was no sign of the waiter.

"Hi!" cried Yakov.

A dark figure stepped out from the barrier at the railway crossing and came irresolutely towards him.

"Why do you keep walking about?" said Yakov with vexation, as he recognized the waiter. "Here you are; there is a little less than five hundred. . . I've no more in the house."

"Very well;. . . very grateful to you," muttered Sergey Nikanoritch, taking the money greedily and stuffing it into his pockets. He was trembling all over, and that was perceptible in spite of the darkness. "Don't worry yourself, Yakov Ivanitch. . . What should I chatter for: I came and went away, that's all I've had to do with it. As the saying is, I know nothing and I can tell nothing. . ." And at once he added with a sigh "Cursed life!"

For a minute they stood in silence, without looking at each other.

"So it all came from a trifle, goodness knows how,. . ." said the waiter, trembling. "I was sitting counting to myself when all at once a noise. . .

I looked through the door, and just on account of Lenten oil you. . . Where is he now?"

"Lying there in the kitchen."

"You ought to take him somewhere. . . Why put it off?"

Yakov accompanied him to the station without a word, then went home again and harnessed the horse to take Matvey to Limarovo. He had decided to take him to the forest of Limarovo, and to leave him there on the road, and then he would tell everyone that Matvey had gone off to Vedenyapino and had not come back, and then everyone would think that he had been killed by someone on the road. He knew there was no deceiving anyone by this, but to move, to do something, to be active, was not as agonizing as to sit still and wait. He called Dashutka, and with her carried Matvey out. Aglaia stayed behind to clean up the kitchen.

When Yakov and Dashutka turned back they were detained at the railway crossing by the barrier being let down. A long goods train was passing, dragged by two engines, breathing heavily, and flinging puffs of crimson fire out of their funnels.

The foremost engine uttered a piercing whistle at the crossing in sight of the station.

"It's whistling,. . ." said Dashutka.

The train had passed at last, and the signalman lifted the barrier without haste.

"Is that you, Yakov Ivanitch? I didn't know you, so you'll be rich."

And then when they had reached home they had to go to bed.

Aglaia and Dashutka made themselves a bed in the tea-room and lay down side by side, while Yakov stretched himself on the counter. They neither said their prayers nor lighted the ikon lamp before lying down to sleep. All three lay awake till morning, but did not utter a single word, and it seemed to them that all night someone was walking about in the empty storey overhead.

Two days later a police inspector and the examining magistrate came from the town and made a search, first in Matvey's room and then in the whole tavern. They questioned Yakov first of all, and he testified that on the Monday Matvey had gone to Vedenyapino to confess, and that he must have been killed by the sawyers who were working on the line.

And when the examining magistrate had asked him how it had happened that Matvey was found on the road, while his cap had turned up at home—surely he had not gone to Vedenyapino without his cap?—and why they had not found a single drop of blood beside him in the snow on the road, though his head was smashed in and his face and chest were black with blood, Yakov was confused, lost his head and answered:

"I cannot tell."

And just what Yakov had so feared happened: the policeman came, the district police officer smoked in the prayer-room and Aglaia fell upon him with abuse and was rude to the police inspector; and afterwards when Yakov and Aglaia were led out to the yard, the peasants crowded at the gates and said, "They are taking the Godlies!" and it seemed that they were all glad.

At the inquiry the policeman stated positively that Yakov and Aglaia had killed Matvey in order not to share with him, and that Matvey had money of his own, and that if it was not found at the search evidently Yakov and Aglaia had got hold of it. And Dashutka was questioned. She said that Uncle Matvey and Aunt Aglaia quarrelled and almost fought every day over money, and that Uncle Matvey was rich, so much so that he had given someone—"his Darling"—nine hundred roubles.

Dashutka was left alone in the tavern. No one came now to drink tea or vodka, and she divided her time between cleaning up the rooms, drinking mead and eating rolls; but a few days later they questioned the signalman at the railway crossing, and he said that late on Monday evening he had seen Yakov and Dashutka driving from Limarovo. Dashutka, too, was arrested, taken to the town and put in prison. It soon became known, from what Aglaia said, that Sergey Nikanoritch had been present at the murder. A search was made in his room, and money was found in an unusual place, in his snowboots under the stove, and the money was all in small change, three hundred one-rouble notes. He swore he had made this money himself, and that he hadn't been in the tavern for a year, but witnesses testified that he was poor and had been in great want of money of late, and that he used to go every day to the tavern to borrow from Matvey; and the policeman described how on the day of the murder he had himself gone twice to the tavern with the waiter to help him to borrow. It was recalled at this juncture that on Monday evening Sergey Nikanoritch had not been there to meet the passenger train, but had gone off somewhere. And he, too, was arrested and taken to the town.

The trial took place eleven months later.

Yakov Ivanitch looked much older and much thinner, and spoke in a low voice like a sick man. He felt weak, pitiful, lower in stature that anyone else, and it seemed as though his soul, too, like his body, had grown older and wasted, from the pangs of his conscience and from the dreams and imaginings which never left him all the while he was in prison. When it came out that he did not go to church the president of the court asked him:

"Are you a dissenter?"

"I can't tell," he answered.

He had no religion at all now; he knew nothing and understood nothing; and his old belief was hateful to him now, and seemed to him darkness and folly. Aglaia was not in the least subdued, and she still went on abusing the dead man, blaming him for all their misfortunes. Sergey Nikanoritch had grown a beard instead of whiskers. At the trial he was red and perspiring, and was evidently ashamed of his grey prison coat and of sitting on the same bench with humble peasants. He defended himself awkwardly, and, trying to prove that he had not been to the tavern for a whole year, got into an altercation with every witness, and the spectators laughed at him. Dashutka had grown fat in prison. At the trial she did not understand the questions put to her, and only said that when they killed Uncle Matvey she was dreadfully frightened, but afterwards she did not mind.

All four were found guilty of murder with mercenary motives. Yakov Ivanitch was sentenced to penal servitude for twenty years; Aglaia for thirteen and a half; Sergey Nikanoritch to ten; Dashutka to six.

VII

LATE ONE EVENING A FOREIGN steamer stopped in the roads of Dué in Sahalin and asked for coal. The captain was asked to wait till morning, but he did not want to wait over an hour, saying that if the weather changed for the worse in the night there would be a risk of his having to go off without coal. In the Gulf of Tartary the weather is liable to violent changes in the course of half an hour, and then the shores of Sahalin are dangerous. And already it had turned fresh, and there was a considerable sea running.

A gang of convicts were sent to the mine from the Voevodsky prison, the grimmest and most forbidding of all the prisons in Sahalin. The coal had to be loaded upon barges, and then they had to be towed by a steam-cutter alongside the steamer which was anchored more than a quarter of a mile from the coast, and then the unloading and reloading had to begin—an exhausting task when the barge kept rocking against the steamer and the men could scarcely keep on their legs for sea-sickness. The convicts, only just roused from their sleep, still drowsy, went along the shore, stumbling in the darkness and clanking their fetters. On the left, scarcely visible, was a tall, steep, extremely gloomy-looking cliff, while on the right there was a thick impenetrable mist, in which the sea moaned with a prolonged monotonous sound, "Ah!. . . ah!. . . ah!. . . ah!. . ." And it was only when the overseer was lighting his pipe, casting as he did so a passing ray of light on the escort with a gun and on the coarse faces of two or three of the nearest convicts, or when he went with his lantern close to the water that the white crests of the foremost waves could be discerned.

One of this gang was Yakov Ivanitch, nicknamed among the convicts the "Brush," on account of his long beard. No one had addressed him by his name or his father's name for a long time now; they called him simply Yashka.

He was here in disgrace, as, three months after coming to Siberia, feeling an intense irresistible longing for home, he had succumbed to temptation and run away; he had soon been caught, had been sentenced to penal servitude for life and given forty lashes. Then he was punished by flogging twice again for losing his prison clothes, though on each occasion they were stolen from him. The longing for home had begun from the very time he had been brought to Odessa, and the convict train had stopped in the night at Progonnaya; and Yakov, pressing to the window, had tried to see his own home, and could see nothing in the darkness. He had no one with whom to talk of home. His sister Aglaia had been sent right across Siberia, and he did not know where she was now. Dashutka was in Sahalin, but she had been sent to live with some ex-convict in a far away settlement; there was no news of her except that once a settler who had come to the Voevodsky Prison told Yakov that Dashutka had three children. Sergey Nikanoritch was serving as a footman at a government official's at Dué, but he could not reckon on ever seeing him, as he was ashamed of being acquainted with convicts of the peasant class.

The gang reached the mine, and the men took their places on the quay. It was said there would not be any loading, as the weather kept getting worse and the steamer was meaning to set off. They could see three lights. One of them was moving: that was the steam-cutter going to the steamer, and it seemed to be coming back to tell them whether the work was to be done or not. Shivering with the autumn cold and the damp sea mist, wrapping himself in his short torn coat, Yakov Ivanitch looked intently without blinking in the direction in which lay his home. Ever since he had lived in prison together with men banished here from all ends of the earth—with Russians, Ukrainians, Tatars, Georgians, Chinese, Gypsies, Jews—and ever since he had listened to their talk and watched their sufferings, he had begun to turn again to God, and it seemed to him at last that he had learned the true faith for which all his family, from his grandmother Avdotya down, had so thirsted, which they had sought so long and which they had never found. He knew it all now and understood where God was, and how He was to be served, and the only thing he could not understand was why men's destinies were so diverse, why this simple faith which other men receive from God for nothing and together with their lives, had cost him such a price that his arms and legs trembled like a drunken man's from all the horrors and agonies which as far as he could see would go on without a break to the day of his death. He looked with strained eyes into the darkness, and it seemed to him that through the thousand miles of that mist he could see home, could see his native province, his district, Progonnaya, could see the darkness, the savagery, the heartlessness, and the dull, sullen, animal indifference of the men he had left there. His eyes were dimmed with tears; but still he gazed into the distance where the pale lights of the steamer faintly gleamed, and his heart ached with yearning for home, and he longed to live, to go back home to tell them there of his new faith and to save from ruin if only one man, and to live without suffering if only for one day.

The cutter arrived, and the overseer announced in a loud voice that there would be no loading.

"Back!" he commanded. "Steady!"

They could hear the hoisting of the anchor chain on the steamer. A strong piercing wind was blowing by now; somewhere on the steep cliff overhead the trees were creaking. Most likely a storm was coming.

Uprooted

An Incident of My Travels

I was on my way back from evening service. The clock in the belfry of the Svyatogorsky Monastery pealed out its soft melodious chimes by way of prelude and then struck twelve. The great courtyard of the monastery stretched out at the foot of the Holy Mountains on the banks of the Donets, and, enclosed by the high hostel buildings as by a wall, seemed now in the night, when it was lighted up only by dim lanterns, lights in the windows, and the stars, a living hotch-potch full of movement, sound, and the most original confusion. From end to end, so far as the eye could see, it was all choked up with carts, old-fashioned coaches and chaises, vans, tilt-carts, about which stood crowds of horses, dark and white, and horned oxen, while people bustled about, and black long-skirted lay brothers threaded their way in and out in all directions. Shadows and streaks of light cast from the windows moved over the carts and the heads of men and horses, and in the dense twilight this all assumed the most monstrous capricious shapes: here the tilted shafts stretched upwards to the sky, here eyes of fire appeared in the face of a horse, there a lay brother grew a pair of black wings. . . There was the noise of talk, the snorting and munching of horses, the creaking of carts, the whimpering of children. Fresh crowds kept walking in at the gate and belated carts drove up.

The pines which were piled up on the overhanging mountain, one above another, and leaned towards the roof of the hostel, gazed into the courtyard as into a deep pit, and listened in wonder; in their dark thicket the cuckoos and nightingales never ceased calling. . . Looking at the confusion, listening to the uproar, one fancied that in this living hotch-potch no one understood anyone, that everyone was looking for something and would not find it, and that this multitude of carts, chaises and human beings could not ever succeed in getting off.

More than ten thousand people flocked to the Holy Mountains for the festivals of St. John the Divine and St. Nikolay the wonder-worker. Not only the hostel buildings, but even the bakehouse, the tailoring room, the carpenter's shop, the carriage house, were filled to overflowing. . . Those who had arrived towards night clustered like flies in autumn, by the walls, round the wells in the yard, or in the narrow passages of the hostel, waiting to be shown a resting-place for the night. The lay brothers, young and old, were in an incessant movement, with no rest or hope of being relieved. By day or late at night they produced the same impression of men hastening somewhere and agitated by something, yet, in spite of their extreme exhaustion, their faces remained full of courage and kindly welcome, their voices friendly, their movements rapid. . . For everyone who came they had to find a place to sleep, and to provide food and drink; to those who were deaf, slow to understand, or profuse in questions, they had to give long and wearisome explanations, to tell them why there were no empty rooms, at what o'clock the service was to be where holy bread was sold, and so on. They had to run, to carry, to talk incessantly, but more than that, they had to be polite, too, to be tactful, to try to arrange that the Greeks from Mariupol, accustomed to live more comfortably than the Little Russians, should be put with other Greeks, that some shopkeeper from Bahmut or Lisitchansk, dressed like a lady, should not be offended by being put with peasants. There were continual cries of: "Father, kindly give us some kvass! Kindly give us some hay!" or "Father, may I drink water after confession?" And the lay brother would have to give out kvass or hay or to answer: "Address yourself to the priest, my good woman, we have not the authority to give permission." Another question would follow, "Where is the priest then?" and the lay brother would have to explain where was the priest's cell. With all this bustling activity, he yet had to make time to go to service in the church, to serve in the part devoted to the gentry, and to give full answers to the mass of necessary and unnecessary questions which pilgrims of the educated class are fond of showering about them. Watching them during the course of twenty-four hours, I found it hard to imagine when these black moving figures sat down and when they slept.

When, coming back from the evening service, I went to the hostel in which a place had been assigned me, the monk in charge of the sleeping quarters was standing in the doorway, and beside him, on the steps, was a group of several men and women dressed like townsfolk.

"Sir," said the monk, stopping me, "will you be so good as to allow this young man to pass the night in your room? If you would do us the favour! There are so many people and no place left—it is really dreadful!"

And he indicated a short figure in a light overcoat and a straw hat. I consented, and my chance companion followed me. Unlocking the little padlock on my door, I was always, whether I wanted to or not, obliged to look at the picture that hung on the doorpost on a level with my face. This picture with the title, "A Meditation on Death," depicted a monk on his knees, gazing at a coffin and at a skeleton laying in it. Behind the man's back stood another skeleton, somewhat more solid and carrying a scythe.

"There are no bones like that," said my companion, pointing to the place in the skeleton where there ought to have been a pelvis. "Speaking generally, you know, the spiritual fare provided for the people is not of the first quality," he added, and heaved through his nose a long and very melancholy sigh, meant to show me that I had to do with a man who really knew something about spiritual fare.

While I was looking for the matches to light a candle he sighed once more and said:

"When I was in Harkov I went several times to the anatomy theatre and saw the bones there; I have even been in the mortuary. Am I not in your way?"

My room was small and poky, with neither table nor chairs in it, but quite filled up with a chest of drawers by the window, the stove and two little wooden sofas which stood against the walls, facing one another, leaving a narrow space to walk between them. Thin rusty-looking little mattresses lay on the little sofas, as well as my belongings. There were two sofas, so this room was evidently intended for two, and I pointed out the fact to my companion.

"They will soon be ringing for mass, though," he said, "and I shan't have to be in your way very long."

Still under the impression that he was in my way and feeling awkward, he moved with a guilty step to his little sofa, sighed guiltily and sat down. When the tallow candle with its dim, dilatory flame had left off flickering and burned up sufficiently to make us both visible, I could make out what he was like. He was a young man of two-and-twenty, with a round and pleasing face, dark childlike eyes, dressed like a townsman in grey cheap clothes, and as one could judge from his complexion and narrow shoulders, not used to manual labour. He was of a very indefinite type; one could take him neither for a student nor for a man in trade, still less for a workman. But looking at his attractive face and childlike friendly eyes, I was unwilling to believe he was one of those vagabond impostors with whom every conventual establishment where they give food and lodging is flooded, and who give themselves out as divinity students, expelled for standing up for justice, or for church singers who have lost their voice. . . There was something characteristic, typical, very familiar in his face, but what exactly, I could not remember nor make out.

For a long time he sat silent, pondering. Probably because I had not shown appreciation of his remarks about bones and the mortuary, he thought that I was ill-humoured and displeased at his presence. Pulling a sausage out of his pocket, he turned it about before his eyes and said irresolutely:

"Excuse my troubling you,. . . have you a knife?"

I gave him a knife.

"The sausage is disgusting," he said, frowning and cutting himself off a little bit. "In the shop here they sell you rubbish and fleece you horribly. . . I would offer you a piece, but you would scarcely care to consume it. Will you have some?"

In his language, too, there was something typical that had a very great deal in common with what was characteristic in his face, but what it was exactly I still could not decide. To inspire confidence and to show that I was not ill-humoured, I took some of the proffered sausage. It certainly was horrible; one needed the teeth of a good house-dog to deal with it. As we worked our jaws we got into conversation; we began complaining to each other of the lengthiness of the service.

"The rule here approaches that of Mount Athos," I said; "but at Athos the night services last ten hours, and on great feast-days—fourteen! You should go there for prayers!"

"Yes," answered my companion, and he wagged his head, "I have been here for three weeks. And you know, every day services, every day services. On ordinary days at midnight they ring for matins, at five o'clock for early mass, at nine o'clock for late mass. Sleep is utterly out of the question. In the daytime there are hymns of praise, special prayers, vespers. . . And when I was preparing for the sacrament I was simply dropping from exhaustion." He sighed and went on: "And it's awkward not to go to church. . . The monks give one a room, feed one, and, you know, one is ashamed not to go. One wouldn't mind standing it for a day or two, perhaps, but three weeks is too much—much too much! Are you here for long?"

"I am going to-morrow evening."

"But I am staying another fortnight."

"But I thought it was not the rule to stay for so long here?" I said.

"Yes, that's true: if anyone stays too long, sponging on the monks, he is asked to go. Judge for yourself, if the proletariat were allowed to stay on here as long as they liked there would never be a room vacant, and they would eat up the whole monastery. That's true. But the monks make an exception for me, and I hope they won't turn me out for some time. You know I am a convert."

"You mean?"

"I am a Jew baptized. . . Only lately I have embraced orthodoxy."

Now I understood what I had before been utterly unable to understand from his face: his thick lips, and his way of twitching up the right corner of his mouth and his right eyebrow, when he was talking, and that peculiar oily brilliance of his eyes which is only found in Jews. I understood, too, his phraseology. . . From further conversation I learned that his name was Alexandr Ivanitch, and had in the past been Isaac, that he was a native of the Mogilev province, and that he had come to the Holy Mountains from Novotcherkassk, where he had adopted the orthodox faith.

Having finished his sausage, Alexandr Ivanitch got up, and, raising his right eyebrow, said his prayer before the ikon. The eyebrow remained up when he sat down again on the little sofa and began giving me a brief account of his long biography.

"From early childhood I cherished a love for learning," he began in a tone which suggested he was not speaking of himself, but of some great man of the past. "My parents were poor Hebrews; they exist by buying and selling in a small way; they live like beggars, you know, in filth. In fact, all the people there are poor and superstitious; they don't like education, because education, very naturally, turns a man away from religion. . . They are fearful fanatics. . . Nothing would induce my parents to let me be educated, and they wanted me to take to trade, too, and to know nothing but the Talmud. . . But you will agree, it is not everyone who can spend his whole life struggling for a crust of bread, wallowing in filth, and mumbling the Talmud. At times officers and country gentlemen would put up at papa's inn, and they used to talk a great deal of things which in those days I had never dreamed of; and, of course, it was alluring and moved me to envy. I used to cry and entreat them to send me to school, but they taught me to read Hebrew and nothing more. Once I found a Russian newspaper, and took it home with me to make a kite of it. I was beaten for it, though I couldn't read Russian. Of course, fanaticism is inevitable, for every people instinctively strives to preserve its nationality, but I did not know that then and was very indignant. . ."

Having made such an intellectual observation, Isaac, as he had been, raised his right eyebrow higher than ever in his satisfaction and looked at me, as it were, sideways, like a cock at a grain of corn, with an air as though he would say: "Now at last you see for certain that I am an intellectual man, don't you?" After saying something more about fanaticism and his irresistible yearning for enlightenment, he went on:

"What could I do? I ran away to Smolensk. And there I had a cousin who relined saucepans and made tins. Of course, I was glad to work under him, as I had nothing to live upon; I was barefoot and in rags. . . I thought I could work by day and study at night and on Saturdays. And so I did, but the police found out I had no passport and sent me back by stages to my father. . ."

Alexandr Ivanitch shrugged one shoulder and sighed.

"What was one to do?" he went on, and the more vividly the past rose up before his mind, the more marked his Jewish accent became. "My parents punished me and handed me over to my grandfather, a fanatical old Jew, to be reformed. But I went off at night to Shklov. And when my uncle tried to catch me in Shklov, I went off to Mogilev; there I stayed two days and then I went off to Starodub with a comrade."

Later on he mentioned in his story Gonel, Kiev, Byelaya, Tserkov, Uman, Balt, Bendery and at last reached Odessa.

"In Odessa I wandered about for a whole week, out of work and hungry, till I was taken in by some Jews who went about the town buying second-hand clothes. I knew how to read and write by then, and had done arithmetic up to fractions, and I wanted to go to study somewhere, but I had not the means. What was I to do? For six months I went about Odessa buying old clothes, but the Jews paid me no wages, the rascals. I resented it and left them. Then I went by steamer to Perekop."

"What for?"

"Oh, nothing. A Greek promised me a job there. In short, till I was sixteen I wandered about like that with no definite work and no roots till I got to Poltava. There a student, a Jew, found out that I wanted to study, and gave me a letter to the Harkov students. Of course, I went to Harkov. The students consulted together and began to prepare me for the technical school. And, you know, I must say the students that I met there were such that I shall never forget them to the day of my death. To say nothing of their giving me food and lodging, they set me on the right path, they made me think, showed me the object of life. Among them were intellectual remarkable people who by now are celebrated. For instance, you have heard of Grumaher, haven't you?"

"No, I haven't."

"You haven't! He wrote very clever articles in the *Harkov Gazette*, and was preparing to be a professor. Well, I read a great deal and attended the student's societies, where you hear nothing that is commonplace. I was working up for six months, but as one has to have been through the whole high-school course of mathematics to enter the technical school, Grumaher advised me to try for the veterinary institute, where they admit high-school boys from the sixth form. Of course, I began working for it. I did not want to be a veterinary surgeon but they told me that after finishing the course at the veterinary institute I should be admitted to the faculty of medicine without examination. I learnt all Kühner; I could read Cornelius Nepos, *à livre ouvert*; and in Greek I read through almost all Curtius. But, you know, one thing and another,... the students leaving and the uncertainty of my position, and then I heard that my mamma had come and was looking for me all over Harkov. Then I went away. What was I to do? But luckily I learned that there was a school of mines here on the Donets line. Why should I not enter that? You know the school of mines qualifies one as a mining foreman—a splendid berth. I know of mines where the foremen get a salary of fifteen hundred a year. Capital... I entered it..."

With an expression of reverent awe on his face Alexandr Ivanitch enumerated some two dozen abstruse sciences in which instruction was given at the school of mines; he described the school itself, the construction of the shafts, and the condition of the miners... Then he told me a terrible story which sounded like an invention, though I could not help believing it, for his tone in telling it was too genuine and the expression of horror on his Semitic face was too evidently sincere.

"While I was doing the practical work, I had such an accident one day!" he said, raising both eyebrows. "I was at a mine here in the Donets district. You have seen, I dare say, how people are let down into the mine. You remember when they start the horse and set the gates moving one bucket on the pulley goes down into the mine, while the other comes up; when the first begins to come up, then the second goes down—exactly like a well with two pails. Well, one day I got into the bucket, began going down, and can you fancy, all at once I heard, Trrr! The chain had broken and I flew to the devil together with the bucket and the broken bit of chain... I fell from a height of twenty feet, flat on my chest and stomach, while the bucket, being heavier, reached the bottom before me, and I hit this shoulder here against its edge. I lay, you know, stunned. I thought I was killed, and all at once I saw a fresh calamity: the other bucket, which was going up, having lost the counter-balancing weight, was coming down with a crash straight upon me... What was I to do? Seeing the position, I squeezed closer to the wall, crouching and waiting for the bucket to come full crush next minute on my head. I thought of papa and mamma and Mogilev and Grumaher... I prayed... But happily... it frightens me even to think of it..."

Alexandr Ivanitch gave a constrained smile and rubbed his forehead with his hand.

"But happily it fell beside me and only caught this side a little... It tore off coat, shirt and skin, you know, from this side... The force of it was terrific. I was unconscious after it. They got me out and sent me to the hospital. I was there four months, and the doctors there said I should go into consumption. I always have a cough now and a pain in my chest. And my psychic condition is terrible... When I am alone in a room I feel overcome with terror. Of course, with my health in that state, to be a mining foreman is out of the question. I had to give up the school of mines..."

"And what are you doing now?" I asked.

"I have passed my examination as a village schoolmaster. Now I belong to the orthodox church, and I have a right to be a teacher. In Novotcherkassk, where I was baptized, they took a great interest in me and promised me a place in a church parish school. I am going there in a fortnight, and shall ask again."

Alexandr Ivanitch took off his overcoat and remained in a shirt with an embroidered Russian collar and a worsted belt.

"It is time for bed," he said, folding his overcoat for a pillow, and yawning. "Till lately, you know, I had no knowledge of God at all. I was an atheist. When I was lying in the hospital I thought of religion, and began reflecting on that subject. In my opinion, there is only one religion possible for a thinking man, and that is the Christian religion. If you don't believe in Christ, then there is nothing else to believe in,... is there? Judaism has outlived its day, and is preserved only owing to the peculiarities of the Jewish race. When civilization reaches the Jews there will not be a trace of Judaism left. All young Jews are atheists now, observe. The New Testament is the natural continuation of the Old, isn't it?"

I began trying to find out the reasons which had led him to take so grave and bold a step as the change of religion, but he kept repeating the same, "The New Testament is the natural continuation of the Old"—a formula obviously not his own, but acquired—which did not explain the question in the least. In spite of my efforts and artifices, the reasons remained obscure. If one could believe that he had embraced Orthodoxy from conviction, as he said he had done, what was the nature and foundation of this conviction it was impossible to grasp from his words. It was equally impossible to assume that he had changed his religion from interested motives: his cheap shabby clothes, his going on living at the expense of the convent, and the uncertainty of his future, did not look like interested motives. There was nothing for it but to accept the idea that my companion had been impelled to change his religion by the same restless spirit which had flung him like a chip of wood from town to town, and which he, using the generally accepted formula, called the craving for enlightenment.

Before going to bed I went into the corridor to get a drink of water. When I came back my companion was standing in the middle of the room, and he looked at me with a scared expression. His face looked a greyish white, and there were drops of perspiration on his forehead.

"My nerves are in an awful state," he muttered with a sickly smile," awful! It's acute psychological disturbance. But that's of no consequence."

And he began reasoning again that the New Testament was a natural continuation of the Old, that Judaism has outlived its day. . . Picking out his phrases, he seemed to be trying to put together the forces of his conviction and to smother with them the uneasiness of his soul, and to prove to himself that in giving up the religion of his fathers he had done nothing dreadful or peculiar, but had acted as a thinking man free from prejudice, and that therefore he could boldly remain in a room all alone with his conscience. He was trying to convince himself, and with his eyes besought my assistance.

Meanwhile a big clumsy wick had burned up on our tallow candle. It was by now getting light. At the gloomy little window, which was turning blue, we could distinctly see both banks of the Donets River and the oak copse beyond the river. It was time to sleep.

"It will be very interesting here to-morrow," said my companion when I put out the candle and went to bed. "After early mass, the procession will go in boats from the Monastery to the Hermitage."

Raising his right eyebrow and putting his head on one side, he prayed before the ikons, and, without undressing, lay down on his little sofa.

"Yes," he said, turning over on the other side.

"Why yes?" I asked.

"When I accepted orthodoxy in Novotcherkassk my mother was looking for me in Rostov. She felt that I meant to change my religion," he sighed, and went on: "It is six years since I was there in the province of Mogilev. My sister must be married by now."

After a short silence, seeing that I was still awake, he began talking quietly of how they soon, thank God, would give him a job, and that at last he would have a home of his own, a settled position, his daily bread secure. . . And I was thinking that this man would never have a home of his own, nor a settled position, nor his daily bread secure. He dreamed aloud of a village school as of the Promised Land; like the majority of people, he had a prejudice against a wandering life, and regarded it as something exceptional, abnormal and accidental, like an illness, and was looking for salvation in ordinary workaday life. The tone of his voice betrayed that he was conscious of his abnormal position and regretted it. He seemed as it were apologizing and justifying himself.

Not more than a yard from me lay a homeless wanderer; in the rooms of the hostels and by the carts in the courtyard among the pilgrims some hundreds of such homeless wanderers were waiting for the morning, and further away, if one could picture to oneself the whole of Russia, a vast multitude of such uprooted creatures was pacing at that moment along highroads and side-tracks, seeking something better, or were waiting for the dawn, asleep in wayside inns and little taverns, or on the grass under the open sky. . . As I fell asleep I imagined how amazed and perhaps even overjoyed all these people would have been if reasoning and words could be found to prove to them that their life was as little in need of justification as any other. In my sleep I heard a bell ring outside as plaintively as though shedding bitter tears, and the lay brother calling out several times:

"Lord Jesus Christ, Son of God, have mercy upon us! Come to mass!"

When I woke up my companion was not in the room. It was sunny and there was a murmur of the crowds through the window. Going out, I learned that mass was over and that the procession had set off for the Hermitage some time before. The people were wandering in crowds upon the river bank and, feeling at liberty, did not know what to do with themselves: they could not eat or drink, as the late mass was not yet over at the Hermitage; the Monastery shops where pilgrims are so fond of crowding and asking prices were still shut. In spite of their exhaustion, many of them from sheer boredom were trudging to the Hermitage. The path from the Monastery to the Hermitage, towards which I directed my steps, twined like a snake along the high steep bank, going up and down and threading in and out among the oaks and pines. Below, the Donets gleamed, reflecting the sun; above, the rugged chalk cliff stood up white with bright green on the top from the young foliage of oaks and pines, which, hanging one above another, managed somehow to grow on the vertical cliff without falling. The pilgrims trailed along the path in single file, one behind another. The majority of them were Little Russians from the neighbouring districts, but there were many from a distance, too, who had come on foot from the provinces of Kursk and Orel; in the long string of varied colours there were Greek settlers, too, from Mariupol, strongly built, sedate and friendly people, utterly unlike their weakly and degenerate compatriots who fill our southern seaside towns. There were men from the Donets, too, with red stripes on their breeches, and emigrants from the Tavritchesky province. There were a good many pilgrims of a nondescript class, like my Alexandr Ivanitch; what sort of people they were and where they came from it was impossible to tell from their faces, from their clothes, or from their speech. The path ended at the little landing-stage, from which a narrow road went to the left to the Hermitage, cutting its way through the mountain. At the landing-stage stood two heavy big boats of a forbidding aspect, like the New Zealand pirogues which one may see in the works of Jules Verne. One boat with rugs on the seats was destined for the clergy and the singers, the other without rugs for the public. When the procession was returning I found myself among the elect who had succeeded in squeezing themselves into the second. There were so many of the elect that the boat scarcely moved, and one had to stand all the way without stirring and to be careful that one's hat was not crushed. The route was lovely. Both banks—one high, steep and white, with overhanging pines and oaks, with the crowds hurrying back along the path, and the other shelving, with green meadows and an oak copse bathed in sunshine—looked as happy and rapturous as though the May morning owed its charm only to them. The reflection of the sun in the rapidly flowing Donets quivered and raced away in all directions, and its long rays played on the chasubles, on the banners and on the drops splashed up by the oars. The singing of the Easter hymns, the ringing of the bells, the splash of the oars in the water, the calls of the birds, all mingled in the air into something tender and harmonious. The boat with the priests and the banners led the way; at its helm the black figure of a lay brother stood motionless as a statue.

When the procession was getting near the Monastery, I noticed Alexandr Ivanitch among the elect. He was standing in front of them all, and, his mouth wide open with pleasure and his right eyebrow cocked up, was gazing at the procession. His face was beaming; probably at such moments, when there were so many people round him and it was so bright, he was satisfied with himself, his new religion, and his conscience.

When a little later we were sitting in our room, drinking tea, he still beamed with satisfaction; his face showed that he was satisfied both with the tea and with me, that he fully appreciated my being an intellectual, but that he would know how to play his part with credit if any intellectual topic turned up. . .

"Tell me, what psychology ought I to read?" he began an intellectual conversation, wrinkling up his nose.

"Why, what do you want it for?"

"One cannot be a teacher without a knowledge of psychology. Before teaching a boy I ought to understand his soul."

I told him that psychology alone would not be enough to make one understand a boy's soul, and moreover psychology for a teacher who had not yet mastered the technical methods of instruction in reading, writing, and arithmetic would be a luxury as superfluous as the higher mathematics. He readily agreed with me, and began describing how hard and responsible was the task of a teacher, how hard it was to eradicate in the boy the habitual tendency to evil and superstition, to make him think honestly and independently, to instil into him true religion, the ideas of personal dignity, of freedom, and so on. In answer to this I said something to him. He agreed again. He agreed very readily, in fact. Obviously his brain had not a very firm grasp of all these "intellectual subjects."

Up to the time of my departure we strolled together about the Monastery, whiling away the long hot day. He never left my side a minute; whether he had taken a fancy to me or was afraid of solitude, God only knows! I remember we sat together under a clump of yellow acacia in one of the little gardens that are scattered on the mountain side.

"I am leaving here in a fortnight," he said; "it is high time."

"Are you going on foot?"

"From here to Slavyansk I shall walk, then by railway to Nikitovka; from Nikitovka the Donets line branches off, and along that branch line I shall walk as far as Hatsepetovka, and there a railway guard, I know, will help me on my way."

I thought of the bare, deserted steppe between Nikitovka and Hatsepetovka, and pictured to myself Alexandr Ivanitch striding along it, with his doubts, his homesickness, and his fear of solitude... He read boredom in my face, and sighed.

"And my sister must be married by now," he said, thinking aloud, and at once, to shake off melancholy thoughts, pointed to the top of the rock and said:

"From that mountain one can see Izyum."

As we were walking up the mountain he had a little misfortune. I suppose he stumbled, for he slit his cotton trousers and tore the sole of his shoe.

"Tss!" he said, frowning as he took off a shoe and exposed a bare foot without a stocking. "How unpleasant!... That's a complication, you know, which... Yes!"

Turning the shoe over and over before his eyes, as though unable to believe that the sole was ruined for ever, he spent a long time frowning, sighing, and clicking with his tongue.

I had in my trunk a pair of boots, old but fashionable, with pointed toes and laces. I had brought them with me in case of need, and only wore them in wet weather. When we got back to our room I made up a phrase as diplomatic as I could and offered him these boots. He accepted them and said with dignity:

"I should thank you, but I know that you consider thanks a convention."

He was pleased as a child with the pointed toes and the laces, and even changed his plans.

"Now I shall go to Novotcherkassk in a week, and not in a fortnight," he said, thinking aloud. "In shoes like these I shall not be ashamed to show myself to my godfather. I was not going away from here just because I hadn't any decent clothes..."

When the coachman was carrying out my trunk, a lay brother with a good ironical face came in to sweep out the room. Alexandr Ivanitch seemed flustered and embarrassed and asked him timidly:

"Am I to stay here or go somewhere else?"

He could not make up his mind to occupy a whole room to himself, and evidently by now was feeling ashamed of living at the expense of the Monastery. He was very reluctant to part from me; to put off being lonely as long as possible, he asked leave to see me on my way.

The road from the Monastery, which had been excavated at the cost of no little labour in the chalk mountain, moved upwards, going almost like a spiral round the mountain, over roots and under sullen overhanging pines. . .

The Donets was the first to vanish from our sight, after it the Monastery yard with its thousands of people, and then the green roofs. . . Since I was mounting upwards everything seemed vanishing into a pit. The cross on the church, burnished by the rays of the setting sun, gleamed brightly in the abyss and vanished. Nothing was left but the oaks, the pines, and the white road. But then our carriage came out on a level country, and that was all left below and behind us. Alexandr Ivanitch jumped out and, smiling mournfully, glanced at me for the last time with his childish eyes, and vanished from me for ever. . .

The impressions of the Holy Mountains had already become memories, and I saw something new: the level plain, the whitish-brown distance, the way side copse, and beyond it a windmill which stood without moving, and seemed bored at not being allowed to wave its sails because it was a holiday.

THE STEPPE

The Story of a Journey

I

EARLY ONE MORNING IN JULY a shabby covered chaise, one of those antediluvian chaises without springs in which no one travels in Russia nowadays, except merchant's clerks, dealers and the less well-to-do among priests, drove out of N., the principal town of the province of Z., and rumbled noisily along the posting-track. It rattled and creaked at every movement; the pail, hanging on behind, chimed in gruffly, and from these sounds alone and from the wretched rags of leather hanging loose about its peeling body one could judge of its decrepit age and readiness to drop to pieces.

Two of the inhabitants of N. were sitting in the chaise; they were a merchant of N. called Ivan Ivanitch Kuzmitchov, a man with a shaven face wearing glasses and a straw hat, more like a government clerk than a merchant, and Father Christopher Sireysky, the priest of the Church of St. Nikolay at N., a little old man with long hair, in a grey canvas cassock, a wide-brimmed top-hat and a coloured embroidered girdle. The former was absorbed in thought, and kept tossing his head to shake off drowsiness; in his countenance an habitual business-like reserve was struggling with the genial expression of a man who has just said good-bye to his relatives and has had a good drink at parting. The latter gazed with moist eyes wonderingly at God's world, and his smile was so broad that it seemed to embrace even the brim of his hat; his face was red and looked frozen. Both of them, Father Christopher as well as Kuzmitchov, were going to sell wool. At parting with their families they had just eaten heartily of pastry puffs and cream, and although it was so early in the morning had had a glass or two. . . Both were in the best of humours.

Apart from the two persons described above and the coachman Deniska, who lashed the pair of frisky bay horses, there was another figure in the chaise—a boy of nine with a sunburnt face, wet with tears. This was Yegorushka, Kuzmitchov's nephew. With the sanction of his uncle and the blessing of Father Christopher, he was now on his way to go to school. His mother, Olga Ivanovna, the widow of a collegiate secretary, and Kuzmitchov's sister, who was fond of educated people and refined society, had entreated her brother to take Yegorushka with him when he went to sell wool and to put him to school; and now the boy was sitting on the box beside the coachman Deniska, holding on to his elbow to keep from falling off, and dancing up and down like a kettle on the hob, with no notion where he was going or what he was going for. The rapid motion through the air blew out his red shirt like a balloon on his back and made his new hat with a peacock's feather in it, like a coachman's, keep slipping on to the back of his head. He felt himself an intensely unfortunate person, and had an inclination to cry.

When the chaise drove past the prison, Yegorushka glanced at the sentinels pacing slowly by the high white walls, at the little barred windows, at the cross shining on the roof, and remembered how the week before, on the day of the Holy Mother of Kazan, he had been with his mother to the prison church for the Dedication Feast, and how before that, at Easter, he had gone to the prison with Deniska and Ludmila the cook, and had taken the prisoners Easter bread, eggs, cakes and roast beef. The prisoners had thanked them and made the sign of the cross, and one of them had given Yegorushka a pewter buckle of his own making.

The boy gazed at the familiar places, while the hateful chaise flew by and left them all behind. After the prison he caught glimpses of black grimy foundries, followed by the snug green cemetery surrounded by a wall of cobblestones; white crosses and tombstones, nestling among green cherry-trees and looking in the distance like patches of white, peeped out gaily from behind the wall. Yegorushka remembered that when the cherries were in blossom those white patches melted with the flowers into a sea of white; and that when the cherries were ripe the white tombstones and crosses were dotted with splashes of red like bloodstains. Under the cherry trees in the cemetery Yegorushka's father and granny, Zinaida Danilovna, lay sleeping day and night. When Granny had died she had been put in a long narrow coffin and two pennies had been put upon her eyes, which would not keep shut. Up to the time of her death she had been brisk, and used to bring soft rolls covered with poppy seeds from the market. Now she did nothing but sleep and sleep. . .

Beyond the cemetery came the smoking brickyards. From under the long roofs of reeds that looked as though pressed flat to the ground, a thick black smoke rose in great clouds and floated lazily upwards.

The sky was murky above the brickyards and the cemetery, and great shadows from the clouds of smoke crept over the fields and across the roads. Men and horses covered with red dust were moving about in the smoke near the roofs.

The town ended with the brickyards and the open country began. Yegorushka looked at the town for the last time, pressed his face against Deniska's elbow, and wept bitterly.

"Come, not done howling yet, cry-baby!" cried Kuzmitchov. "You are blubbering again, little milksop! If you don't want to go, stay behind; no one is taking you by force!

"Never mind, never mind, Yegor boy, never mind," Father Christopher muttered rapidly—"never mind, my boy. . . Call upon God. . . You are not going for your harm, but for your good. Learning is light, as the saying is, and ignorance is darkness. . . That is so, truly."

"Do you want to go back?" asked Kuzmitchov.

"Yes,. . . yes,. . ." answered Yegorushka, sobbing.

"Well, you'd better go back then. Anyway, you are going for nothing; it's a day's journey for a spoonful of porridge."

"Never mind, never mind, my boy," Father Christopher went on. "Call upon God. . . Lomonosov set off with the fishermen in the same way, and he became a man famous all over Europe. Learning in conjunction with faith brings forth fruit pleasing to God. What are the words of the prayer? For the glory of our Maker, for the comfort of our parents, for the benefit of our Church and our country. . . Yes, indeed!"

"The benefit is not the same in all cases," said Kuzmitchov, lighting a cheap cigar; "some will study twenty years and get no sense from it."

"That does happen."

"Learning is a benefit to some, but others only muddle their brains. My sister is a woman who does not understand; she is set upon refinement, and wants to turn Yegorka into a learned man, and she does not understand that with my business I could settle Yegorka happily for the rest of his life. I tell you this, that if everyone were to go in for being learned and refined there would be no one to sow the corn and do the trading; they would all die of hunger."

"And if all go in for trading and sowing corn there will be no one to acquire learning."

And considering that each of them had said something weighty and convincing, Kuzmitchov and Father Christopher both looked serious and cleared their throats simultaneously.

Deniska, who had been listening to their conversation without understanding a word of it, shook his head and, rising in his seat, lashed at both the bays. A silence followed.

Meanwhile a wide boundless plain encircled by a chain of low hills lay stretched before the travellers' eyes. Huddling together and peeping out from behind one another, these hills melted together into rising ground, which stretched right to the very horizon and disappeared into the lilac distance; one drives on and on and cannot discern where it begins or where it ends. . . The sun had already peeped out from beyond the town behind them, and quietly, without fuss, set to its accustomed task. At first in the distance before them a broad, bright, yellow streak of light crept over the ground where the earth met the sky, near the little barrows and the windmills, which in the distance looked like tiny men waving their arms. A minute later a similar streak gleamed a little nearer, crept to the right and embraced the hills. Something warm touched Yegorushka's spine; the streak of light, stealing up from behind, darted between the chaise and the horses, moved to meet the other streak, and soon the whole wide steppe flung off the twilight of early morning, and was smiling and sparkling with dew.

The cut rye, the coarse steppe grass, the milkwort, the wild hemp, all withered from the sultry heat, turned brown and half dead, now washed by the dew and caressed by the sun, revived, to fade again. Arctic petrels flew across the road with joyful cries; marmots called to one another in the grass. Somewhere, far away to the left, lapwings uttered their plaintive notes. A covey of partridges, scared by the chaise, fluttered up and with their soft "trrrr!" flew off to the hills. In the grass crickets, locusts and grasshoppers kept up their churring, monotonous music.

But a little time passed, the dew evaporated, the air grew stagnant, and the disillusioned steppe began to wear its jaded July aspect. The grass drooped, everything living was hushed. The sun-baked hills, brownish-green and lilac in the distance, with their quiet shadowy tones, the plain with the misty distance and, arched above them, the sky, which seems terribly deep and transparent in the steppes, where there are no woods or high hills, seemed now endless, petrified with dreariness. . .

How stifling and oppressive it was! The chaise raced along, while Yegorushka saw always the same—the sky, the plain, the low hills. . . The music in the grass was hushed, the petrels had flown away, the partridges were out of sight, rooks hovered idly over the withered grass; they were all alike and made the steppe even more monotonous.

A hawk flew just above the ground, with an even sweep of its wings, suddenly halted in the air as though pondering on the dreariness of life, then fluttered its wings and flew like an arrow over the steppe, and there was no telling why it flew off and what it wanted. In the distance a windmill waved its sails. . .

Now and then a glimpse of a white potsherd or a heap of stones broke the monotony; a grey stone stood out for an instant or a parched willow with a blue crow on its top branch; a marmot would run across the road and—again there flitted before the eyes only the high grass, the low hills, the rooks. . .

But at last, thank God, a waggon loaded with sheaves came to meet them; a peasant wench was lying on the very top. Sleepy, exhausted by the heat, she lifted her head and looked at the travellers. Deniska gaped, looking at her; the horses stretched out their noses towards the sheaves; the chaise, squeaking, kissed the waggon, and the pointed ears passed over Father Christopher's hat like a brush.

"You are driving over folks, fatty!" cried Deniska. "What a swollen lump of a face, as though a bumble-bee had stung it!"

The girl smiled drowsily, and moving her lips lay down again; then a solitary poplar came into sight on the low hill. Someone had planted it, and God only knows why it was there. It was hard to tear the eyes away from its graceful figure and green drapery. Was that lovely creature happy? Sultry heat in summer, in winter frost and snowstorms, terrible nights in autumn when nothing is to be seen but darkness and nothing is to be heard but the senseless angry howling wind, and, worst of all, alone, alone for the whole of life. . . Beyond the poplar stretches of wheat extended like a bright yellow carpet from the road to the top of the hills. On the hills the corn was already cut and laid up in sheaves, while at the bottom they were still cutting. . . Six mowers were standing in a row swinging their scythes, and the scythes gleamed gaily and uttered in unison together "Vzhee, vzhee!" From the movements of the peasant women binding the sheaves, from the faces of the mowers, from the glitter of the scythes, it could be seen that the sultry heat was baking and stifling. A black dog with its tongue hanging out ran from the mowers to meet the chaise, probably with the intention of barking, but stopped halfway and stared indifferently at Deniska, who shook his whip at him; it was too hot to bark! One peasant woman got up and, putting both hands to her aching back, followed Yegorushka's red shirt with her eyes. Whether it was that the colour pleased her or that he reminded her of her children, she stood a long time motionless staring after him.

But now the wheat, too, had flashed by; again the parched plain, the sunburnt hills, the sultry sky stretched before them; again a hawk hovered over the earth. In the distance, as before, a windmill whirled its sails, and still it looked like a little man waving his arms. It was wearisome to watch, and it seemed as though one would never reach it, as though it were running away from the chaise.

Father Christopher and Kuzmitchov were silent. Deniska lashed the horses and kept shouting to them, while Yegorushka had left off crying, and gazed about him listlessly. The heat and the tedium of the steppes overpowered him. He felt as though he had been travelling and jolting up and down for a very long time, that the sun had been baking his back a long time. Before they had gone eight miles he began to feel "It must be time to rest." The geniality gradually faded out of his uncle's face and nothing else was left but the air of business reserve; and to a gaunt shaven face, especially when it is adorned with spectacles and the nose and temples are covered with dust, this reserve gives a relentless, inquisitorial appearance. Father Christopher never left off gazing with wonder at God's world, and smiling. Without speaking, he brooded over something pleasant and nice, and a kindly, genial smile remained imprinted on his face. It seemed as though some nice and pleasant thought were imprinted on his brain by the heat.

"Well, Deniska, shall we overtake the waggons to-day?" asked Kuzmitchov.

Deniska looked at the sky, rose in his seat, lashed at his horses and then answered:

"By nightfall, please God, we shall overtake them."

There was a sound of dogs barking. Half a dozen steppe sheep-dogs, suddenly leaping out as though from ambush, with ferocious howling barks, flew to meet the chaise. All of them, extraordinarily furious, surrounded the chaise, with their shaggy spider-like muzzles and their eyes red with anger, and jostling against one another in their anger, raised a hoarse howl. They were filled with passionate hatred of the horses, of the chaise, and of the human beings, and seemed ready to tear them into pieces. Deniska, who was fond of teasing and beating, was delighted at the chance of it, and with a malignant expression bent

ANTON CHEKHOV

over and lashed at the sheep-dogs with his whip. The brutes growled more than ever, the horses flew on; and Yegorushka, who had difficulty in keeping his seat on the box, realized, looking at the dogs' eyes and teeth, that if he fell down they would instantly tear him to bits; but he felt no fear and looked at them as malignantly as Deniska, and regretted that he had no whip in his hand.

The chaise came upon a flock of sheep.

"Stop!" cried Kuzmitchov. "Pull up! Woa!"

Deniska threw his whole body backwards and pulled up the horses.

"Come here!" Kuzmitchov shouted to the shepherd. "Call off the dogs, curse them!"

The old shepherd, tattered and barefoot, wearing a fur cap, with a dirty sack round his loins and a long crook in his hand—a regular figure from the Old Testament—called off the dogs, and taking off his cap, went up to the chaise. Another similar Old Testament figure was standing motionless at the other end of the flock, staring without interest at the travellers.

"Whose sheep are these?" asked Kuzmitchov.

"Varlamov's," the old man answered in a loud voice.

"Varlamov's," repeated the shepherd standing at the other end of the flock.

"Did Varlamov come this way yesterday or not?"

"He did not; his clerk came. . ."

"Drive on!"

The chaise rolled on and the shepherds, with their angry dogs, were left behind. Yegorushka gazed listlessly at the lilac distance in front, and it began to seem as though the windmill, waving its sails, were getting nearer. It became bigger and bigger, grew quite large, and now he could distinguish clearly its two sails. One sail was old and patched, the other had only lately been made of new wood and glistened in the sun. The chaise drove straight on, while the windmill, for some reason, began retreating to the left. They drove on and on, and the windmill kept moving away to the left, and still did not disappear.

"A fine windmill Boltva has put up for his son," observed Deniska.

"And how is it we don't see his farm?"

"It is that way, beyond the creek."

Boltva's farm, too, soon came into sight, but yet the windmill did not retreat, did not drop behind; it still watched Yegorushka with its shining sail and waved. What a sorcerer!

II

Towards midday the chaise turned off the road to the right; it went on a little way at walking pace and then stopped. Yegorushka heard a soft, very caressing gurgle, and felt a different air breathe on his face with a cool velvety touch. Through a little pipe of hemlock stuck there by some unknown benefactor, water was running in a thin trickle from a low hill, put together by nature of huge monstrous stones. It fell to the ground, and limpid, sparkling gaily in the sun, and softly murmuring as though fancying itself a great tempestuous torrent, flowed swiftly away to the left. Not far from its source the little stream spread itself out into a pool; the burning sunbeams and the parched soil greedily drank it up and sucked away its strength; but a little further on it must have mingled with another rivulet, for a hundred paces away thick reeds showed green and luxuriant along its course, and three snipe flew up from them with a loud cry as the chaise drove by.

The travellers got out to rest by the stream and feed the horses. Kuzmitchov, Father Christopher and Yegorushka sat down on a mat in the narrow strip of shade cast by the chaise and the unharnessed horses. The nice pleasant thought that the heat had imprinted in Father Christopher's brain craved expression after he had had a drink of water and eaten a hard-boiled egg. He bent a friendly look upon Yegorushka, munched, and began:

"I studied too, my boy; from the earliest age God instilled into me good sense and understanding, so that while I was just such a lad as you I was beyond others, a comfort to my parents and preceptors by my good sense. Before I was fifteen I could speak and make verses in Latin, just as in Russian. I was the crosier-bearer to his Holiness Bishop Christopher. After mass one day, as I remember it was the patron saint's day of His Majesty Tsar Alexandr Pavlovitch of blessed memory, he unrobed at the altar, looked kindly at me and asked, 'Puer bone, quam appelaris?' And I answered, 'Christopherus sum;' and he said, 'Ergo connominati sumus'—that is, that we were namesakes. . . Then he asked in Latin, 'Whose son are you?' To which I answered, also in Latin, that I was the son of deacon Sireysky of the village of Lebedinskoe. Seeing my readiness and the clearness of my answers, his Holiness blessed me and said, 'Write to your father that I will not forget him, and that I will keep you in view.' The holy priests and fathers who were standing round the altar, hearing our discussion in Latin, were not a little surprised, and everyone expressed his pleasure in praise of me. Before I had moustaches, my boy, I could read Latin, Greek, and French; I knew philosophy, mathematics, secular history, and all the sciences. The Lord gave me a marvellous memory. Sometimes, if I read a thing once or twice, I knew it by heart. My preceptors and patrons were amazed, and so they expected I should make a learned man, a luminary of the Church. I did think of going to Kiev to continue my studies, but my parents did not approve. 'You'll be studying all your life,' said my father; 'when shall we see you finished?' Hearing such words, I gave up study and took a post. . . Of course, I did not become a learned man, but then I did not disobey my parents; I was a comfort to them in their old age and gave them a creditable funeral. Obedience is more than fasting and prayer.

"I suppose you have forgotten all your learning?" observed Kuzmitchov.

"I should think so! Thank God, I have reached my eightieth year! Something of philosophy and rhetoric I do remember, but languages and mathematics I have quite forgotten."

Father Christopher screwed up his eyes, thought a minute and said in an undertone:

"What is a substance? A creature is a self-existing object, not requiring anything else for its completion."

He shook his head and laughed with feeling.

"Spiritual nourishment!" he said. "Of a truth matter nourishes the flesh and spiritual nourishment the soul!"

"Learning is all very well," sighed Kuzmitchov, "but if we don't overtake Varlamov, learning won't do much for us."

"A man isn't a needle—we shall find him. He must be going his rounds in these parts."

Among the sedge were flying the three snipe they had seen before, and in their plaintive cries there was a note of alarm and vexation at having been driven away from the stream. The horses were steadily munching and snorting. Deniska walked about by them and, trying to appear indifferent to the cucumbers, pies, and eggs that the gentry were eating, he concentrated himself on the gadflies and horseflies that were fastening upon the horses' backs and bellies; he squashed his victims apathetically, emitting a peculiar, fiendishly triumphant, guttural sound, and when he missed them cleared his throat with an air of vexation and looked after every lucky one that escaped death.

"Deniska, where are you? Come and eat," said Kuzmitchov, heaving a deep sigh, a sign that he had had enough.

Deniska diffidently approached the mat and picked out five thick and yellow cucumbers (he did not venture to take the smaller and fresher ones), took two hard-boiled eggs that looked dark and were cracked, then irresolutely, as though afraid he might get a blow on his outstretched hand, touched a pie with his finger.

"Take them, take them," Kuzmitchov urged him on.

Deniska took the pies resolutely, and, moving some distance away, sat down on the grass with his back to the chaise. At once there was such a sound of loud munching that even the horses turned round to look suspiciously at Deniska.

After his meal Kuzmitchov took a sack containing something out of the chaise and said to Yegorushka:

"I am going to sleep, and you mind that no one takes the sack from under my head."

Father Christopher took off his cassock, his girdle, and his full coat, and Yegorushka, looking at him, was dumb with astonishment. He had never imagined that priests wore trousers, and Father Christopher had on real canvas trousers thrust into high boots, and a short striped jacket. Looking at him, Yegorushka thought that in this costume, so unsuitable to his dignified position, he looked with his long hair and beard very much like Robinson Crusoe. After taking off their outer garments Kuzmitchov and Father Christopher lay down in the shade under the chaise, facing one another, and closed their eyes. Deniska, who had finished munching, stretched himself out on his back and also closed his eyes.

"You look out that no one takes away the horses!" he said to Yegorushka, and at once fell asleep.

Stillness reigned. There was no sound except the munching and snorting of the horses and the snoring of the sleepers; somewhere far away a lapwing wailed, and from time to time there sounded the shrill cries of the three snipe who had flown up to see whether their uninvited visitors had gone away; the rivulet babbled, lisping softly, but all these sounds did not break the stillness, did not stir the stagnation, but, on the contrary, lulled all nature to slumber.

Yegorushka, gasping with the heat, which was particularly oppressive after a meal, ran to the sedge and from there surveyed the country. He saw exactly the same as he had in the morning: the plain, the low hills, the sky, the lilac distance; only the hills stood nearer; and he could not see the windmill, which had been left far behind. From behind the rocky hill from which the stream flowed rose another, smoother and broader; a little hamlet of five or six homesteads clung to it. No people, no trees, no shade were to be seen about the huts; it looked as though the hamlet had expired in the burning air and was dried up. To while away the time Yegorushka caught a grasshopper in the grass, held it in his closed hand to his ear, and spent a long time listening to the creature playing on its instrument. When he was weary of its music he ran after a flock of yellow butterflies who were flying towards the sedge on the watercourse, and found himself again beside the chaise, without noticing how he came there. His uncle and Father Christopher were sound asleep; their sleep would be sure to last two or three hours till the horses had rested. . . How was he to get through that long time, and where was he to get away from the heat? A hard problem. . . Mechanically Yegorushka put his lips to the trickle that ran from the waterpipe; there was a chilliness in his mouth and there was the smell of hemlock. He drank at first eagerly, then went on with effort till the sharp cold had run from his mouth all over his body and the water was spilt on his shirt. Then he went up to the chaise and began looking at the sleeping figures. His uncle's face wore, as before, an expression of business-like reserve. Fanatically devoted to his work, Kuzmitchov always, even in his sleep and at church when they were singing, "Like the cherubim," thought about his business and could never forget it for a moment; and now he was probably dreaming about bales of wool, waggons, prices, Varlamov. . . Father Christopher, now, a soft, frivolous and absurd person, had never all his life been conscious of anything which could, like a boa-constrictor, coil about his soul and hold it tight. In all the numerous enterprises he had undertaken in his day what attracted him was not so much the business itself, but the bustle and the contact with other people involved in every undertaking. Thus, in the present expedition, he was not so much interested in wool, in Varlamov, and in prices, as in the long journey, the conversations on the way, the sleeping under a chaise, and the meals at odd times. . . And now, judging from his face, he must have been dreaming of Bishop Christopher, of the Latin discussion, of his wife, of puffs and cream and all sorts of things that Kuzmitchov could not possibly dream of.

While Yegorushka was watching their sleeping faces he suddenly heard a soft singing; somewhere at a distance a woman was singing, and it was difficult to tell where and in what direction. The song was subdued, dreary and melancholy, like a dirge, and hardly audible, and seemed to come first from the right, then from the left, then from above, and then from underground, as though an unseen spirit were hovering over the steppe and singing. Yegorushka looked about him, and could not make out where the strange song came from. Then as he listened he began to fancy that the grass was singing; in its song, withered and half-dead, it was without words, but plaintively and passionately, urging that it was not to blame, that the sun was burning it for no fault of its own; it urged that it ardently longed to live, that it was young and might have been beautiful but for the heat and the drought; it was guiltless, but yet it prayed forgiveness and protested that it was in anguish, sad and sorry for itself. . .

Yegorushka listened for a little, and it began to seem as though this dreary, mournful song made the air hotter, more suffocating and more stagnant. . . To drown the singing he ran to the sedge, humming to himself and trying to make a noise with his feet. From there he looked about in all directions and found out who was singing. Near the furthest hut in the hamlet stood a peasant woman in a short petticoat, with long thin legs like a heron. She was sowing something. A white dust floated languidly from her sieve down the hillock. Now it was evident that she was singing. A couple of yards from her a little bare-headed boy in nothing but a smock was standing motionless. As though fascinated by the song, he stood stock-still, staring away into the distance, probably at Yegorushka's crimson shirt.

The song ceased. Yegorushka sauntered back to the chaise, and to while away the time went again to the trickle of water.

And again there was the sound of the dreary song. It was the same long-legged peasant woman in the hamlet over the hill. Yegorushka's boredom came back again. He left the pipe and looked upwards. What he saw was so unexpected that he was a little frightened. Just above his head on one of the big clumsy stones stood a chubby little boy, wearing nothing but a shirt, with a prominent stomach and thin legs, the same boy who had been standing before by the peasant woman. He was gazing with open mouth and unblinking eyes at Yegorushka's crimson shirt and at the chaise, with a look of blank astonishment and even fear, as though he saw before him creatures of another world. The red colour of the shirt charmed and allured him. But the chaise and the men sleeping under it excited his curiosity; perhaps he had not noticed how the agreeable red colour and curiosity had attracted him down from the hamlet, and now probably he was surprised at his own boldness. For a long while Yegorushka stared at him, and he at Yegorushka. Both were silent and conscious of some awkwardness. After a long silence Yegorushka asked:

"What's your name?"

The stranger's cheeks puffed out more than ever; he pressed his back against the rock, opened his eyes wide, moved his lips, and answered in a husky bass: "Tit!"

The boys said not another word to each other; after a brief silence, still keeping his eyes fixed on Yegorushka, the mysterious Tit kicked up one leg, felt with his heel for a niche and clambered up the rock; from that point he ascended to the next rock, staggering backwards and looking intently at Yegorushka, as though afraid he might hit him from behind, and so made his way upwards till he disappeared altogether behind the crest of the hill.

After watching him out of sight, Yegorushka put his arms round his knees and leaned his head on them. . . The burning sun scorched the back of his head, his neck, and his spine. The melancholy song died away, then floated again on the stagnant stifling air. The rivulet gurgled monotonously, the horses munched, and time dragged on endlessly, as though it, too, were stagnant and had come to a standstill. It seemed as though a hundred years had passed since the morning. Could it be that God's world, the chaise and the horses would come to a standstill in that air, and, like the hills, turn to stone and remain for ever in one spot? Yegorushka raised his head, and with smarting eyes looked before him; the lilac distance, which till then had been motionless, began heaving, and with the sky floated away into the distance. . . It drew after it the brown grass, the sedge, and with extraordinary swiftness Yegorushka floated after the flying distance. Some force noiselessly drew him onwards, and the heat and the wearisome song flew after in pursuit. Yegorushka bent his head and shut his eyes. . .

Deniska was the first to wake up. Something must have bitten him, for he jumped up, quickly scratched his shoulder and said:

"Plague take you, cursed idolater!"

Then he went to the brook, had a drink and slowly washed. His splashing and puffing roused Yegorushka from his lethargy. The boy looked at his wet face with drops of water and big freckles which made it look like marble, and asked:

"Shall we soon be going?"

Deniska looked at the height of the sun and answered:

"I expect so."

He dried himself with the tail of his shirt and, making a very serious face, hopped on one leg.

"I say, which of us will get to the sedge first?" he said.

Yegorushka was exhausted by the heat and drowsiness, but he raced off after him all the same. Deniska was in his twentieth year, was a coachman and going to be married, but he had not left off being a boy. He was very fond of flying kites, chasing pigeons, playing knuckle-bones, running races, and always took part in children's games and disputes. No sooner had his master turned his back or gone to sleep than Deniska would begin doing something such as hopping on one leg or throwing stones. It was hard for any grown-up person, seeing the genuine enthusiasm with which he frolicked about in the society of children, to resist saying, "What a baby!" Children, on the other hand, saw nothing strange in the invasion of their domain by the big coachman. "Let him play," they thought, "as long as he doesn't fight!" In the same way little dogs see nothing strange in it when a simple-hearted big dog joins their company uninvited and begins playing with them.

Deniska outstripped Yegorushka, and was evidently very much pleased at having done so. He winked at him, and to show that he could hop on one leg any distance, suggested to Yegorushka that he should hop with him along the road and from there, without resting, back to the chaise. Yegorushka declined this suggestion, for he was very much out of breath and exhausted.

All at once Deniska looked very grave, as he did not look even when Kuzmitchov gave him a scolding or threatened him with a stick; listening intently, he dropped quietly on one knee and an expression of sternness and alarm came into his face, such as one sees in people who hear heretical talk. He fixed his eyes on one spot, raised his hand curved into a hollow, and suddenly fell on his stomach on the ground and slapped the hollow of his hand down upon the grass.

"Caught!" he wheezed triumphantly, and, getting up, lifted a big grasshopper to Yegorushka's eyes.

The two boys stroked the grasshopper's broad green back with their fingers and touched his antenna, supposing that this would please the creature. Then Deniska caught a fat fly that had been sucking blood and offered it to the grasshopper. The latter moved his huge jaws, that were like the visor of a helmet, with the utmost unconcern, as though he had been long acquainted with Deniska, and bit off the fly's stomach. They let him go. With a flash of the pink lining of his wings, he flew down into the grass and at once began his churring notes again. They let the fly go, too. It preened its wings, and without its stomach flew off to the horses.

A loud sigh was heard from under the chaise. It was Kuzmitchov waking up. He quickly raised his head, looked uneasily into the distance, and from that look, which passed by Yegorushka and Deniska without sympathy or interest, it could be seen that his thought on awaking was of the wool and of Varlamov.

"Father Christopher, get up; it is time to start," he said anxiously. "Wake up; we've slept too long as it is! Deniska, put the horses in."

Father Christopher woke up with the same smile with which he had fallen asleep; his face looked creased and wrinkled from sleep, and seemed only half the size. After washing and dressing, he proceeded without haste to take out of his pocket a little greasy psalter; and standing with his face towards the east, began in a whisper repeating the psalms of the day and crossing himself.

"Father Christopher," said Kuzmitchov reproachfully, "it's time to start; the horses are ready, and here are you,. . . upon my word."

"In a minute, in a minute," muttered Father Christopher. "I must read the psalms. . . I haven't read them to-day."

"The psalms can wait."

"Ivan Ivanitch, that is my rule every day. . . I can't. . ."

"God will overlook it."

For a full quarter of an hour Father Christopher stood facing the east and moving his lips, while Kuzmitchov looked at him almost with hatred and impatiently shrugged his shoulders. He was particularly irritated when, after every "Hallelujah," Father Christopher drew a long breath, rapidly crossed himself and repeated three times, intentionally raising his voice so that the others might cross themselves, "Hallelujah, hallelujah, hallelujah! Glory be to Thee, O Lord!" At last he smiled, looked upwards at the sky, and, putting the psalter in his pocket, said:

"Finis!"

A minute later the chaise had started on the road. As though it were going backwards and not forwards, the travellers saw the same scene as they had before midday.

The low hills were still plunged in the lilac distance, and no end could be seen to them. There were glimpses of high grass and heaps of stones; strips of stubble land passed by them and still the same rooks, the same hawk, moving its wings with slow dignity, moved over the steppe. The air was more sultry than ever; from the sultry heat and the stillness submissive nature was spellbound into silence. . . No wind, no fresh cheering sound, no cloud.

But at last, when the sun was beginning to sink into the west, the steppe, the hills and the air could bear the oppression no longer, and, driven out of all patience, exhausted, tried to fling off the yoke. A fleecy ashen-grey cloud unexpectedly appeared behind the hills. It exchanged glances with the steppe, as though to say, "Here I am," and frowned. Suddenly something burst in the stagnant air; there was a violent squall of wind which whirled round and round, roaring and whistling over the steppe. At once a murmur rose from the grass and last year's dry herbage, the dust curled in spiral eddies over the road, raced over the steppe, and carrying with it straws, dragon flies and feathers, rose up in a whirling black column towards the sky and darkened the sun. Prickly uprooted plants ran stumbling and leaping in all directions over the steppe, and one of them got caught in the whirlwind, turned round and round like a bird, flew towards the sky, and turning into a little black speck, vanished from sight. After it flew another, and then a third, and Yegorushka saw two of them meet in the blue height and clutch at one another as though they were wrestling.

A bustard flew up by the very road. Fluttering his wings and his tail, he looked, bathed in the sunshine, like an angler's glittering tin fish or a waterfly flashing so swiftly over the water that its wings cannot be told from its antenna, which seem to be growing before, behind and on all sides. . . Quivering in the air like an insect with a shimmer of bright colours, the bustard flew high up in a straight line, then, probably frightened by a cloud of dust, swerved to one side, and for a long time the gleam of his wings could be seen. . .

Then a corncrake flew up from the grass, alarmed by the hurricane and not knowing what was the matter. It flew with the wind and not against it, like all the other birds, so that all its feathers were ruffled up and it was puffed out to the size of a hen and looked very angry and impressive. Only the rooks who had grown old on the steppe and were accustomed to its vagaries hovered calmly over the grass, or taking no notice of anything, went on unconcernedly pecking with their stout beaks at the hard earth.

There was a dull roll of thunder beyond the hills; there came a whiff

ANTON CHEKHOV

of fresh air. Deniska gave a cheerful whistle and lashed his horses. Father Christopher and Kuzmitchov held their hats and looked intently towards the hills. . . How pleasant a shower of rain would have been!

One effort, one struggle more, and it seemed the steppe would have got the upper hand. But the unseen oppressive force gradually riveted its fetters on the wind and the air, laid the dust, and the stillness came back again as though nothing had happened, the cloud hid, the sun-baked hills frowned submissively, the air grew calm, and only somewhere the troubled lapwings wailed and lamented their destiny. . .

Soon after that the evening came on.

III

IN THE DUSK OF EVENING a big house of one storey, with a rusty iron roof and with dark windows, came into sight. This house was called a posting-inn, though it had nothing like a stableyard, and it stood in the middle of the steppe, with no kind of enclosure round it. A little to one side of it a wretched little cherry orchard shut in by a hurdle fence made a dark patch, and under the windows stood sleepy sunflowers drooping their heavy heads. From the orchard came the clatter of a little toy windmill, set there to frighten away hares by the rattle. Nothing more could be seen near the house, and nothing could be heard but the steppe. The chaise had scarcely stopped at the porch with an awning over it, when from the house there came the sound of cheerful voices, one a man's, another a woman's; there was the creak of a swing-door, and in a flash a tall gaunt figure, swinging its arms and fluttering its coat, was standing by the chaise. This was the innkeeper, Moisey Moisevitch, a man no longer young, with a very pale face and a handsome beard as black as charcoal. He was wearing a threadbare black coat, which hung flapping on his narrow shoulders as though on a hatstand, and fluttered its skirts like wings every time Moisey Moisevitch flung up his hands in delight or horror. Besides his coat the innkeeper was wearing full white trousers, not stuck into his boots, and a velvet waistcoat with brown flowers on it that looked like gigantic bugs.

Moisey Moisevitch was at first dumb with excess of feeling on recognizing the travellers, then he clasped his hands and uttered a moan. His coat swung its skirts, his back bent into a bow, and his pale face twisted into a smile that suggested that to see the chaise was not merely a pleasure to him, but actually a joy so sweet as to be painful.

"Oh dear! oh dear!" he began in a thin sing-song voice, breathless, fussing about and preventing the travellers from getting out of the chaise by his antics. "What a happy day for me! Oh, what am I to do now? Ivan Ivanitch! Father Christopher! What a pretty little gentleman sitting on the box, God strike me dead! Oh, my goodness! why am I standing here instead of asking the visitors indoors? Please walk in, I humbly beg you. . . You are kindly welcome! Give me all your things. . . Oh, my goodness me!"

Moisey Moisevitch, who was rummaging in the chaise and assisting the travellers to alight, suddenly turned back and shouted in a voice as frantic and choking as though he were drowning and calling for help:

"Solomon! Solomon!"

"Solomon! Solomon!" a woman's voice repeated indoors.

The swing-door creaked, and in the doorway appeared a rather short young Jew with a big beak-like nose, with a bald patch surrounded by rough red curly hair; he was dressed in a short and very shabby reefer jacket, with rounded lappets and short sleeves, and in short serge trousers, so that he looked skimpy and short-tailed like an unfledged bird. This was Solomon, the brother of Moisey Moisevitch. He went up to the chaise, smiling rather queerly, and did not speak or greet the travellers.

"Ivan Ivanitch and Father Christopher have come," said Moisey Moisevitch in a tone as though he were afraid his brother would not believe him. "Dear, dear! What a surprise! Such honoured guests to have come us so suddenly! Come, take their things, Solomon. Walk in, honoured guests."

A little later Kuzmitchov, Father Christopher, and Yegorushka were sitting in a big gloomy empty room at an old oak table. The table was almost in solitude, for, except a wide sofa covered with torn American leather and three chairs, there was no other furniture in the room. And, indeed, not everybody would have given the chairs that name. They were a pitiful semblance of furniture, covered with American leather that had seen its best days, and with backs bent backwards at an unnaturally acute angle, so that they looked like children's sledges. It was hard to imagine what had been the unknown carpenter's object in bending the chairbacks so mercilessly, and one was tempted to imagine that it was not the carpenter's fault, but that some athletic visitor had bent the chairs like this as a feat, then had tried to bend them back

ANTON CHEKHOV

again and had made them worse. The room looked gloomy, the walls were grey, the ceilings and the cornices were grimy; on the floor were chinks and yawning holes that were hard to account for (one might have fancied they were made by the heel of the same athlete), and it seemed as though the room would still have been dark if a dozen lamps had hung in it. There was nothing approaching an ornament on the walls or the windows. On one wall, however, there hung a list of regulations of some sort under a two-headed eagle in a grey wooden frame, and on another wall in the same sort of frame an engraving with the inscription, "The Indifference of Man." What it was to which men were indifferent it was impossible to make out, as the engraving was very dingy with age and was extensively flyblown. There was a smell of something decayed and sour in the room.

As he led the visitors into the room, Moisey Moisevitch went on wriggling, gesticulating, shrugging and uttering joyful exclamations; he considered these antics necessary in order to seem polite and agreeable.

"When did our waggons go by?" Kuzmitchov asked.

"One party went by early this morning, and the other, Ivan Ivanitch, put up here for dinner and went on towards evening."

"Ah!. . . Has Varlamov been by or not?"

"No, Ivan Ivanitch. His clerk, Grigory Yegoritch, went by yesterday morning and said that he had to be to-day at the Molokans' farm."

"Good! so we will go after the waggons directly and then on to the Molokans'."

"Mercy on us, Ivan Ivanitch!" Moisey Moisevitch cried in horror, flinging up his hands. "Where are you going for the night? You will have a nice little supper and stay the night, and to-morrow morning, please God, you can go on and overtake anyone you like."

"There is no time for that. . . Excuse me, Moisey Moisevitch, another time; but now I must make haste. We'll stay a quarter of an hour and then go on; we can stay the night at the Molokans'."

"A quarter of an hour!" squealed Moisey Moisevitch. "Have you no fear of God, Ivan Ivanitch? You will compel me to hide your caps and lock the door! You must have a cup of tea and a snack of something, anyway."

"We have no time for tea," said Kuzmitchov.

Moisey Moisevitch bent his head on one side, crooked his knees, and put his open hands before him as though warding off a blow, while with a smile of agonized sweetness he began imploring:

"Ivan Ivanitch! Father Christopher! Do be so good as to take a cup of tea with me. Surely I am not such a bad man that you can't even drink tea in my house? Ivan Ivanitch!"

"Well, we may just as well have a cup of tea," said Father Christopher, with a sympathetic smile; "that won't keep us long."

"Very well," Kuzmitchov assented.

Moisey Moisevitch, in a fluster uttered an exclamation of joy, and shrugging as though he had just stepped out of cold weather into warm, ran to the door and cried in the same frantic voice in which he had called Solomon:

"Rosa! Rosa! Bring the samovar!"

A minute later the door opened, and Solomon came into the room carrying a large tray in his hands. Setting the tray on the table, he looked away sarcastically with the same queer smile as before. Now, by the light of the lamp, it was possible to see his smile distinctly; it was very complex, and expressed a variety of emotions, but the predominant element in it was undisguised contempt. He seemed to be thinking of something ludicrous and silly, to be feeling contempt and dislike, to be pleased at something and waiting for the favourable moment to turn something into ridicule and to burst into laughter. His long nose, his thick lips, and his sly prominent eyes seemed tense with the desire to laugh. Looking at his face, Kuzmitchov smiled ironically and asked:

"Solomon, why did you not come to our fair at N. this summer, and act some Jewish scenes?"

Two years before, as Yegorushka remembered very well, at one of the booths at the fair at N., Solomon had performed some scenes of Jewish life, and his acting had been a great success. The allusion to this made no impression whatever upon Solomon. Making no answer, he went out and returned a little later with the samovar.

When he had done what he had to do at the table he moved a little aside, and, folding his arms over his chest and thrusting out one leg, fixed his sarcastic eyes on Father Christopher. There was something defiant, haughty, and contemptuous in his attitude, and at the same time it was comic and pitiful in the extreme, because the more impressive his attitude the more vividly it showed up his short trousers, his bobtail coat, his caricature of a nose, and his bird-like plucked-looking little figure.

Moisey Moisevitch brought a footstool from the other room and sat down a little way from the table.

ANTON CHEKHOV

"I wish you a good appetite! Tea and sugar!" he began, trying to entertain his visitors. "I hope you will enjoy it. Such rare guests, such rare ones; it is years since I last saw Father Christopher. And will no one tell me who is this nice little gentleman?" he asked, looking tenderly at Yegorushka.

"He is the son of my sister, Olga Ivanovna," answered Kuzmitchov.

"And where is he going?"

"To school. We are taking him to a high school."

In his politeness, Moisey Moisevitch put on a look of wonder and wagged his head expressively.

"Ah, that is a fine thing," he said, shaking his finger at the samovar. "That's a fine thing. You will come back from the high school such a gentleman that we shall all take off our hats to you. You will be wealthy and wise and so grand that your mamma will be delighted. Oh, that's a fine thing!"

He paused a little, stroked his knees, and began again in a jocose and deferential tone.

"You must excuse me, Father Christopher, but I am thinking of writing to the bishop to tell him you are robbing the merchants of their living. I shall take a sheet of stamped paper and write that I suppose Father Christopher is short of pence, as he has taken up with trade and begun selling wool."

"H'm, yes. . . it's a queer notion in my old age," said Father Christopher, and he laughed. "I have turned from priest to merchant, brother. I ought to be at home now saying my prayers, instead of galloping about the country like a Pharaoh in his chariot. . . Vanity!"

"But it will mean a lot of pence!"

"Oh, I dare say! More kicks than halfpence, and serve me right. The wool's not mine, but my son-in-law Mikhail's!"

"Why doesn't he go himself?"

"Why, because. . . His mother's milk is scarcely dry upon his lips. He can buy wool all right, but when it comes to selling, he has no sense; he is young yet. He has wasted all his money; he wanted to grow rich and cut a dash, but he tried here and there, and no one would give him his price. And so the lad went on like that for a year, and then he came to me and said, 'Daddy, you sell the wool for me; be kind and do it! I am no good at the business!' And that is true enough. As soon as there is anything wrong then it's 'Daddy,' but till then they could get on without their dad. When he was buying he did not consult me, but now when he is in difficulties it's Daddy's turn. And what does his dad know about it? If it were not for Ivan Ivanitch, his dad could do nothing. I have a lot of worry with them."

"Yes; one has a lot of worry with one's children, I can tell you that," sighed Moisey Moisevitch. "I have six of my own. One needs schooling, another needs doctoring, and a third needs nursing, and when they grow up they are more trouble still. It is not only nowadays, it was the same in Holy Scripture. When Jacob had little children he wept, and when they grew up he wept still more bitterly."

"H'm, yes. . ." Father Christopher assented pensively, looking at his glass. "I have no cause myself to rail against the Lord. I have lived to the end of my days as any man might be thankful to live. . . I have married my daughters to good men, my sons I have set up in life, and now I am free; I have done my work and can go where I like. I live in peace with my wife. I eat and drink and sleep and rejoice in my grandchildren, and say my prayers and want nothing more. I live on the fat of the land, and don't need to curry favour with anyone. I have never had any trouble from childhood, and now suppose the Tsar were to ask me, 'What do you need? What would you like?' why, I don't need anything. I have everything I want and everything to be thankful for. In the whole town there is no happier man than I am. My only trouble is I have so many sins, but there—only God is without sin. That's right, isn't it?"

"No doubt it is."

"I have no teeth, of course; my poor old back aches; there is one thing and another,. . . asthma and that sort of thing. . . I ache. . . The flesh is weak, but then think of my age! I am in the eighties! One can't go on for ever; one mustn't outstay one's welcome."

Father Christopher suddenly thought of something, spluttered into his glass and choked with laughter. Moisey Moisevitch laughed, too, from politeness, and he, too, cleared his throat.

"So funny!" said Father Christopher, and he waved his hand. "My eldest son Gavrila came to pay me a visit. He is in the medical line, and is a district doctor in the province of Tchernigov. . . 'Very well. . .' I said to him, 'here I have asthma and one thing and another. . . You are a doctor; cure your father!' He undressed me on the spot, tapped me, listened, and all sorts of tricks,. . . kneaded my stomach, and then he said, 'Dad, you ought to be treated with compressed air.'" Father Christopher laughed convulsively, till the tears came into his eyes, and got up.

ANTON CHEKHOV

"And I said to him, 'God bless your compressed air!'" he brought out through his laughter, waving both hands. "God bless your compressed air!"

Moisey Moisevitch got up, too, and with his hands on his stomach, went off into shrill laughter like the yap of a lap-dog.

"God bless the compressed air!" repeated Father Christopher, laughing.

Moisey Moisevitch laughed two notes higher and so violently that he could hardly stand on his feet.

"Oh dear!" he moaned through his laughter. "Let me get my breath. . . You'll be the death of me."

He laughed and talked, though at the same time he was casting timorous and suspicious looks at Solomon. The latter was standing in the same attitude and still smiling. To judge from his eyes and his smile, his contempt and hatred were genuine, but that was so out of keeping with his plucked-looking figure that it seemed to Yegorushka as though he were putting on his defiant attitude and biting sarcastic smile to play the fool for the entertainment of their honoured guests.

After drinking six glasses of tea in silence, Kuzmitchov cleared a space before him on the table, took his bag, the one which he kept under his head when he slept under the chaise, untied the string and shook it. Rolls of paper notes were scattered out of the bag on the table.

"While we have the time, Father Christopher, let us reckon up," said Kuzmitchov.

Moisey Moisevitch was embarrassed at the sight of the money. He got up, and, as a man of delicate feeling unwilling to pry into other people's secrets, he went out of the room on tiptoe, swaying his arms. Solomon remained where he was.

"How many are there in the rolls of roubles?" Father Christopher began.

"The rouble notes are done up in fifties,. . . the three-rouble notes in nineties, the twenty-five and hundred roubles in thousands. You count out seven thousand eight hundred for Varlamov, and I will count out for Gusevitch. And mind you don't make a mistake. . ."

Yegorushka had never in his life seen so much money as was lying on the table before him. There must have been a great deal of money, for the roll of seven thousand eight hundred, which Father Christopher put aside for Varlamov, seemed very small compared with the whole heap. At any other time such a mass of money would have impressed Yegorushka, and would have moved him to reflect how many cracknels, buns and poppy-cakes could be bought for that money. Now he looked at it listlessly, only conscious of the disgusting smell of kerosene and rotten apples that came from the heap of notes. He was exhausted by the jolting ride in the chaise, tired out and sleepy. His head was heavy, his eyes would hardly keep open and his thoughts were tangled like threads. If it had been possible he would have been relieved to lay his head on the table, so as not to see the lamp and the fingers moving over the heaps of notes, and to have let his tired sleepy thoughts go still more at random. When he tried to keep awake, the light of the lamp, the cups and the fingers grew double, the samovar heaved and the smell of rotten apples seemed even more acrid and disgusting.

"Ah, money, money!" sighed Father Christopher, smiling. "You bring trouble! Now I expect my Mihailo is asleep and dreaming that I am going to bring him a heap of money like this."

"Your Mihailo Timofevitch is a man who doesn't understand business," said Kuzmitchov in an undertone; "he undertakes what isn't his work, but you understand and can judge. You had better hand over your wool to me, as I have said already, and I would give you half a rouble above my own price—yes, I would, simply out of regard for you. . ."

"No, Ivan Ivanitch." Father Christopher sighed. "I thank you for your kindness. . . Of course, if it were for me to decide, I shouldn't think twice about it; but as it is, the wool is not mine, as you know. . ."

Moisey Moisevitch came in on tiptoe. Trying from delicacy not to look at the heaps of money, he stole up to Yegorushka and pulled at his shirt from behind.

"Come along, little gentleman," he said in an undertone, "come and see the little bear I can show you! Such a queer, cross little bear. Oo-oo!"

The sleepy boy got up and listlessly dragged himself after Moisey Moisevitch to see the bear. He went into a little room, where, before he saw anything, he felt he could not breathe from the smell of something sour and decaying, which was much stronger here than in the big room and probably spread from this room all over the house. One part of the room was occupied by a big bed, covered with a greasy quilt and another by a chest of drawers and heaps of rags of all kinds from a woman's stiff petticoat to children's little breeches and braces. A tallow candle stood on the chest of drawers.

Instead of the promised bear, Yegorushka saw a big fat Jewess with her hair hanging loose, in a red flannel skirt with black sprigs on it;

she turned with difficulty in the narrow space between the bed and the chest of drawers and uttered drawn-out moaning as though she had toothache. On seeing Yegorushka, she made a doleful, woe-begone face, heaved a long drawn-out sigh, and before he had time to look round, put to his lips a slice of bread smeared with honey.

"Eat it, dearie, eat it!" she said. "You are here without your mamma, and no one to look after you. Eat it up."

Yegorushka did eat it, though after the goodies and poppy-cakes he had every day at home, he did not think very much of the honey, which was mixed with wax and bees' wings. He ate while Moisey Moisevitch and the Jewess looked at him and sighed.

"Where are you going, dearie?" asked the Jewess.

"To school," answered Yegorushka.

"And how many brothers and sisters have you got?"

"I am the only one; there are no others."

"O-oh!" sighed the Jewess, and turned her eyes upward. "Poor mamma, poor mamma! How she will weep and miss you! We are going to send our Nahum to school in a year. O-oh!"

"Ah, Nahum, Nahum!" sighed Moisey Moisevitch, and the skin of his pale face twitched nervously. "And he is so delicate."

The greasy quilt quivered, and from beneath it appeared a child's curly head on a very thin neck; two black eyes gleamed and stared with curiosity at Yegorushka. Still sighing, Moisey Moisevitch and the Jewess went to the chest of drawers and began talking in Yiddish. Moisey Moisevitch spoke in a low bass undertone, and altogether his talk in Yiddish was like a continual "ghaal-ghaal-ghaal-ghaal,. . ." while his wife answered him in a shrill voice like a turkeycock's, and the whole effect of her talk was something like "Too-too-too-too!" While they were consulting, another little curly head on a thin neck peeped out of the greasy quilt, then a third, then a fourth. . . If Yegorushka had had a fertile imagination he might have imagined that the hundred-headed hydra was hiding under the quilt.

"Ghaal-ghaal-ghaal-ghaal!" said Moisey Moisevitch.

"Too-too-too-too!" answered the Jewess.

The consultation ended in the Jewess's diving with a deep sigh into the chest of drawers, and, unwrapping some sort of green rag there, she took out a big rye cake made in the shape of a heart.

"Take it, dearie," she said, giving Yegorushka the cake; "you have no mamma now—no one to give you nice things."

Yegorushka stuck the cake in his pocket and staggered to the door, as he could not go on breathing the foul, sour air in which the innkeeper and his wife lived. Going back to the big room, he settled himself more comfortably on the sofa and gave up trying to check his straying thoughts.

As soon as Kuzmitchov had finished counting out the notes he put them back into the bag. He did not treat them very respectfully and stuffed them into the dirty sack without ceremony, as indifferently as though they had not been money but waste paper.

Father Christopher was talking to Solomon.

"Well, Solomon the Wise!" he said, yawning and making the sign of the cross over his mouth. "How is business?"

"What sort of business are you talking about?" asked Solomon, and he looked as fiendish, as though it were a hint of some crime on his part.

"Oh, things in general. What are you doing?"

"What am I doing?" Solomon repeated, and he shrugged his shoulders. "The same as everyone else. . . You see, I am a menial, I am my brother's servant; my brother's the servant of the visitors; the visitors are Varlamov's servants; and if I had ten millions, Varlamov would be my servant."

"Why would he be your servant?"

"Why, because there isn't a gentleman or millionaire who isn't ready to lick the hand of a scabby Jew for the sake of making a kopeck. Now, I am a scabby Jew and a beggar. Everybody looks at me as though I were a dog, but if I had money Varlamov would play the fool before me just as Moisey does before you."

Father Christopher and Kuzmitchov looked at each other. Neither of them understood Solomon. Kuzmitchov looked at him sternly and dryly, and asked:

"How can you compare yourself with Varlamov, you blockhead?"

"I am not such a fool as to put myself on a level with Varlamov," answered Solomon, looking sarcastically at the speaker. "Though Varlamov is a Russian, he is at heart a scabby Jew; money and gain are all he lives for, but I threw my money in the stove! I don't want money, or land, or sheep, and there is no need for people to be afraid of me and to take off their hats when I pass. So I am wiser than your Varlamov and more like a man!"

A little later Yegorushka, half asleep, heard Solomon in a hoarse hollow voice choked with hatred, in hurried stuttering phrases, talking about the Jews. At first he talked correctly in Russian, then he fell into the tone of a Jewish recitation, and began speaking as he had done at the fair with an exaggerated Jewish accent.

"Stop!. . ." Father Christopher said to him. "If you don't like your religion you had better change it, but to laugh at it is a sin; it is only the lowest of the low who will make fun of his religion."

"You don't understand," Solomon cut him short rudely. "I am talking of one thing and you are talking of something else. . ."

"One can see you are a foolish fellow," sighed Father Christopher. "I admonish you to the best of my ability, and you are angry. I speak to you like an old man quietly, and you answer like a turkeycock: 'Bla—bla—bla!' You really are a queer fellow. . ."

Moisey Moisevitch came in. He looked anxiously at Solomon and at his visitors, and again the skin on his face quivered nervously. Yegorushka shook his head and looked about him; he caught a passing glimpse of Solomon's face at the very moment when it was turned three-quarters towards him and when the shadow of his long nose divided his left cheek in half; the contemptuous smile mingled with that shadow; the gleaming sarcastic eyes, the haughty expression, and the whole plucked-looking little figure, dancing and doubling itself before Yegorushka's eyes, made him now not like a buffoon, but like something one sometimes dreams of, like an evil spirit.

"What a ferocious fellow you've got here, Moisey Moisevitch! God bless him!" said Father Christopher with a smile. "You ought to find him a place or a wife or something. . . There's no knowing what to make of him. . ."

Kuzmitchov frowned angrily. Moisey Moisevitch looked uneasily and inquiringly at his brother and the visitors again.

"Solomon, go away!" he said shortly. "Go away!" and he added something in Yiddish. Solomon gave an abrupt laugh and went out.

"What was it?" Moisey Moisevitch asked Father Christopher anxiously.

"He forgets himself," answered Kuzmitchov. "He's rude and thinks too much of himself."

"I knew it!" Moisey Moisevitch cried in horror, clasping his hands. "Oh dear, oh dear!" he muttered in a low voice. "Be so kind as to excuse it, and don't be angry. He is such a queer fellow, such a queer fellow! Oh dear, oh dear! He is my own brother, but I have never had anything but trouble from him. You know he's. . ."

Moisey Moisevitch crooked his finger by his forehead and went on:

"He is not in his right mind;. . . he's hopeless. And I don't know what I am to do with him! He cares for nobody, he respects nobody, and is afraid of nobody. . . You know he laughs at everybody, he says silly things, speaks familiarly to anyone. You wouldn't believe it, Varlamov came here one day and Solomon said such things to him that he gave us both a taste of his whip. . . But why whip me? Was it my fault? God has robbed him of his wits, so it is God's will, and how am I to blame?"

Ten minutes passed and Moisey Moisevitch was still muttering in an undertone and sighing:

"He does not sleep at night, and is always thinking and thinking and thinking, and what he is thinking about God only knows. If you go to him at night he is angry and laughs. He doesn't like me either. . . And there is nothing he wants! When our father died he left us each six thousand roubles. I bought myself an inn, married, and now I have children; and he burnt all his money in the stove. Such a pity, such a pity! Why burn it? If he didn't want it he could give it to me, but why burn it?"

Suddenly the swing-door creaked and the floor shook under footsteps. Yegorushka felt a draught of cold air, and it seemed to him as though some big black bird had passed by him and had fluttered its wings close in his face. He opened his eyes. . . His uncle was standing by the sofa with his sack in his hands ready for departure; Father Christopher, holding his broad-brimmed top-hat, was bowing to someone and smiling—not his usual soft kindly smile, but a respectful forced smile which did not suit his face at all—while Moisey Moisevitch looked as though his body had been broken into three parts, and he were balancing and doing his utmost not to drop to pieces. Only Solomon stood in the corner with his arms folded, as though nothing had happened, and smiled contemptuously as before.

"Your Excellency must excuse us for not being tidy," moaned Moisey Moisevitch with the agonizingly sweet smile, taking no more notice of Kuzmitchov or Father Christopher, but swaying his whole person so as to avoid dropping to pieces. "We are plain folks, your Excellency."

Yegorushka rubbed his eyes. In the middle of the room there really was standing an Excellency, in the form of a young plump and very beautiful woman in a black dress and a straw hat. Before Yegorushka had time to examine her features the image of the solitary graceful poplar he had seen that day on the hill for some reason came into his mind.

"Has Varlamov been here to-day?" a woman's voice inquired.

"No, your Excellency," said Moisey Moisevitch.

"If you see him to-morrow, ask him to come and see me for a minute."

All at once, quite unexpectedly, Yegorushka saw half an inch from his eyes velvety black eyebrows, big brown eyes, delicate feminine cheeks with dimples, from which smiles seemed radiating all over the face like sunbeams. There was a glorious scent.

"What a pretty boy!" said the lady. "Whose boy is it? Kazimir Mihalovitch, look what a charming fellow! Good heavens, he is asleep!"

And the lady kissed Yegorushka warmly on both cheeks, and he smiled and, thinking he was asleep, shut his eyes. The swing-door squeaked, and there was the sound of hurried footsteps, coming in and going out.

"Yegorushka, Yegorushka!" he heard two bass voices whisper. "Get up; it is time to start."

Somebody, it seemed to be Deniska, set him on his feet and led him by the arm. On the way he half-opened his eyes and once more saw the beautiful lady in the black dress who had kissed him. She was standing in the middle of the room and watched him go out, smiling at him and nodding her head in a friendly way. As he got near the door he saw a handsome, stoutly built, dark man in a bowler hat and in leather gaiters. This must have been the lady's escort.

"Woa!" he heard from the yard.

At the front door Yegorushka saw a splendid new carriage and a pair of black horses. On the box sat a groom in livery, with a long whip in his hands. No one but Solomon came to see the travellers off. His face was tense with a desire to laugh; he looked as though he were waiting impatiently for the visitors to be gone, so that he might laugh at them without restraint.

"The Countess Dranitsky," whispered Father Christopher, clambering into the chaise.

"Yes, Countess Dranitsky," repeated Kuzmitchov, also in a whisper.

The impression made by the arrival of the countess was probably very great, for even Deniska spoke in a whisper, and only ventured to lash his bays and shout when the chaise had driven a quarter of a mile away and nothing could be seen of the inn but a dim light.

IV

WHO WAS THIS ELUSIVE, MYSTERIOUS Varlamov of whom people talked so much, whom Solomon despised, and whom even the beautiful countess needed? Sitting on the box beside Deniska, Yegorushka, half asleep, thought about this person. He had never seen him. But he had often heard of him and pictured him in his imagination. He knew that Varlamov possessed several tens of thousands of acres of land, about a hundred thousand sheep, and a great deal of money. Of his manner of life and occupation Yegorushka knew nothing, except that he was always "going his rounds in these parts," and he was always being looked for.

At home Yegorushka had heard a great deal of the Countess Dranitsky, too. She, too, had some tens of thousands of acres, a great many sheep, a stud farm and a great deal of money, but she did not "go rounds," but lived at home in a splendid house and grounds, about which Ivan Ivanitch, who had been more than once at the countess's on business, and other acquaintances told many marvellous tales; thus, for instance, they said that in the countess's drawing-room, where the portraits of all the kings of Poland hung on the walls, there was a big table-clock in the form of a rock, on the rock a gold horse with diamond eyes, rearing, and on the horse the figure of a rider also of gold, who brandished his sword to right and to left whenever the clock struck. They said, too, that twice a year the countess used to give a ball, to which the gentry and officials of the whole province were invited, and to which even Varlamov used to come; all the visitors drank tea from silver samovars, ate all sorts of extraordinary things (they had strawberries and raspberries, for instance, in winter at Christmas), and danced to a band which played day and night. . .

"And how beautiful she is," thought Yegorushka, remembering her face and smile.

Kuzmitchov, too, was probably thinking about the countess. For when the chaise had driven a mile and a half he said:

"But doesn't that Kazimir Mihalovitch plunder her right and left! The year before last when, do you remember, I bought some wool from her, he made over three thousand from my purchase alone."

"That is just what you would expect from a Pole," said Father Christopher.

"And little does it trouble her. Young and foolish, as they say, her head is full of nonsense."

Yegorushka, for some reason, longed to think of nothing but Varlamov and the countess, particularly the latter. His drowsy brain utterly refused ordinary thoughts, was in a cloud and retained only fantastic fairy-tale images, which have the advantage of springing into the brain of themselves without any effort on the part of the thinker, and completely vanishing of themselves at a mere shake of the head; and, indeed, nothing that was around him disposed to ordinary thoughts. On the right there were the dark hills which seemed to be screening something unseen and terrible; on the left the whole sky about the horizon was covered with a crimson glow, and it was hard to tell whether there was a fire somewhere, or whether it was the moon about to rise. As by day the distance could be seen, but its tender lilac tint had gone, quenched by the evening darkness, in which the whole steppe was hidden like Moisey Moisevitch's children under the quilt.

Corncrakes and quails do not call in the July nights, the nightingale does not sing in the woodland marsh, and there is no scent of flowers, but still the steppe is lovely and full of life. As soon as the sun goes down and the darkness enfolds the earth, the day's weariness is forgotten, everything is forgiven, and the steppe breathes a light sigh from its broad bosom. As though because the grass cannot see in the dark that it has grown old, a gay youthful twitter rises up from it, such as is not heard by day; chirruping, twittering, whistling, scratching, the basses, tenors and sopranos of the steppe all mingle in an incessant, monotonous roar of sound in which it is sweet to brood on memories and sorrows. The monotonous twitter soothes to sleep like a lullaby; you drive and feel you are falling asleep, but suddenly there comes the abrupt agitated cry of a wakeful bird, or a vague sound like a voice crying out in wonder "A-ah, a-ah!" and slumber closes one's eyelids again. Or you drive by a little creek where there are bushes and hear the bird, called by the steppe dwellers "the sleeper," call "Asleep, asleep, asleep!" while another laughs or breaks into trills of hysterical weeping—that is the owl. For whom do they call and who hears them on that plain, God only knows, but there is deep sadness and lamentation in their cry. . . There is a scent of hay and dry grass and belated flowers, but the scent is heavy, sweetly mawkish and soft.

Everything can be seen through the mist, but it is hard to make out the colours and the outlines of objects. Everything looks different from what it is. You drive on and suddenly see standing before you right in the roadway a dark figure like a monk; it stands motionless, waiting, holding something in its hands. . . Can it be a robber? The figure comes closer, grows bigger; now it is on a level with the chaise, and you see it is not a man, but a solitary bush or a great stone. Such motionless expectant figures stand on the low hills, hide behind the old barrows, peep out from the high grass, and they all look like human beings and arouse suspicion.

And when the moon rises the night becomes pale and dim. The mist seems to have passed away. The air is transparent, fresh and warm; one can see well in all directions and even distinguish the separate stalks of grass by the wayside. Stones and bits of pots can be seen at a long distance. The suspicious figures like monks look blacker against the light background of the night, and seem more sinister. More and more often in the midst of the monotonous chirruping there comes the sound of the "A-ah, a-ah!" of astonishment troubling the motionless air, and the cry of a sleepless or delirious bird. Broad shadows move across the plain like clouds across the sky, and in the inconceivable distance, if you look long and intently at it, misty monstrous shapes rise up and huddle one against another. . . It is rather uncanny. One glances at the pale green, star-spangled sky on which there is no cloudlet, no spot, and understands why the warm air is motionless, why nature is on her guard, afraid to stir: she is afraid and reluctant to lose one instant of life. Of the unfathomable depth and infinity of the sky one can only form a conception at sea and on the steppe by night when the moon is shining. It is terribly lonely and caressing; it looks down languid and alluring, and its caressing sweetness makes one giddy.

You drive on for one hour, for a second. . . You meet upon the way a silent old barrow or a stone figure put up God knows when and by whom; a nightbird floats noiselessly over the earth, and little by little those legends of the steppes, the tales of men you have met, the stories of some old nurse from the steppe, and all the things you have managed to see and treasure in your soul, come back to your mind. And then in the churring of insects, in the sinister figures, in the ancient barrows, in the blue sky, in the moonlight, in the flight of the nightbird, in everything you see and hear, triumphant beauty, youth, the fulness of power, and the passionate thirst for life begin to be apparent; the soul responds to the call of her lovely austere fatherland, and longs to fly over the steppes with the nightbird. And in the triumph of beauty, in the exuberance of happiness you are conscious of yearning and grief, as though the steppe knew she was solitary, knew that her wealth and her inspiration were wasted for the world, not glorified in song, not wanted by anyone; and through the joyful clamour one hears her mournful, hopeless call for singers, singers!

"Woa! Good-evening, Panteley! Is everything all right?"

"First-rate, Ivan Ivanitch!"

"Haven't you seen Varlamov, lads?"

"No, we haven't."

Yegorushka woke up and opened his eyes. The chaise had stopped. On the right the train of waggons stretched for a long way ahead on the road, and men were moving to and fro near them. All the waggons being loaded up with great bales of wool looked very high and fat, while the horses looked short-legged and little.

"Well, then, we shall go on to the Molokans'!" Kuzmitchov said aloud. "The Jew told us that Varlamov was putting up for the night at the Molokans'. So good-bye, lads! Good luck to you!"

"Good-bye, Ivan Ivanitch," several voices replied.

"I say, lads," Kuzmitchov cried briskly, "you take my little lad along with you! Why should he go jolting off with us for nothing? You put him on the bales, Panteley, and let him come on slowly, and we shall overtake you. Get down, Yegor! Go on; it's all right. . ."

Yegorushka got down from the box-seat. Several hands caught him, lifted him high into the air, and he found himself on something big, soft, and rather wet with dew. It seemed to him now as though the sky were quite close and the earth far away.

"Hey, take his little coat!" Deniska shouted from somewhere far below.

His coat and bundle flung up from far below fell close to Yegorushka. Anxious not to think of anything, he quickly put his bundle under his head and covered himself with his coat, and stretching his legs out and shrinking a little from the dew, he laughed with content.

"Sleep, sleep, sleep,. . ." he thought.

"Don't be unkind to him, you devils!" he heard Deniska's voice below.

"Good-bye, lads; good luck to you," shouted Kuzmitchov. "I rely upon you!"

"Don't you be uneasy, Ivan Ivanitch!"

Deniska shouted to the horses, the chaise creaked and started, not along the road, but somewhere off to the side. For two minutes there was silence, as though the waggons were asleep and there was no sound except the clanking of the pails tied on at the back of the chaise as it slowly died away in the distance. Then someone at the head of the waggons shouted:

"Kiruha! Sta-art!"

The foremost of the waggons creaked, then the second, then the third. . . Yegorushka felt the waggon he was on sway and creak also. The waggons were moving. Yegorushka took a tighter hold of the cord with which the bales were tied on, laughed again with content, shifted the cake in his pocket, and fell asleep just as he did in his bed at home. . .

When he woke up the sun had risen, it was screened by an ancient barrow, and, trying to shed its light upon the earth, it scattered its beams in all directions and flooded the horizon with gold. It seemed to Yegorushka that it was not in its proper place, as the day before it had risen behind his back, and now it was much more to his left. . . And the whole landscape was different. There were no hills now, but on all sides, wherever one looked, there stretched the brown cheerless plain; here and there upon it small barrows rose up and rooks flew as they had done the day before. The belfries and huts of some village showed white in the distance ahead; as it was Sunday the Little Russians were at home baking and cooking—that could be seen by the smoke which rose from every chimney and hung, a dark blue transparent veil, over the village. In between the huts and beyond the church there were blue glimpses of a river, and beyond the river a misty distance. But nothing was so different from yesterday as the road. Something extraordinarily broad, spread out and titanic, stretched over the steppe by way of a road. It was a grey streak well trodden down and covered with dust, like all roads. Its width puzzled Yegorushka and brought thoughts of fairy tales to his mind. Who travelled along that road? Who needed so much space? It was strange and unintelligible. It might have been supposed that giants with immense strides, such as Ilya Muromets and Solovy the Brigand, were still surviving in Russia, and that their gigantic steeds were still alive. Yegorushka, looking at the road, imagined some half a dozen high chariots racing along side by side, like some he used to see in pictures in his Scripture history; these chariots were each drawn by six wild furious horses, and their great wheels raised a cloud of dust to the sky, while the horses were driven by men such as one may see in one's dreams or in imagination brooding over fairy tales. And if those figures had existed, how perfectly in keeping with the steppe and the road they would have been!

Telegraph-poles with two wires on them stretched along the right side of the road to its furthermost limit. Growing smaller and smaller they disappeared near the village behind the huts and green trees, and then again came into sight in the lilac distance in the form of very small thin sticks that looked like pencils stuck into the ground. Hawks, falcons, and crows sat on the wires and looked indifferently at the moving waggons.

Yegorushka was lying in the last of the waggons, and so could see the whole string. There were about twenty waggons, and there was a driver to every three waggons. By the last waggon, the one in which Yegorushka was, there walked an old man with a grey beard, as short and lean as Father Christopher, but with a sunburnt, stern and brooding face. It is very possible that the old man was not stern and not brooding, but his red eyelids and his sharp long nose gave his face a stern frigid expression such as is common with people in the habit of continually thinking of serious things in solitude. Like Father Christopher he was wearing a wide-brimmed top-hat, not like a gentleman's, but made of brown felt, and in shape more like a cone with the top cut off than a real top-hat. Probably from a habit acquired in cold winters, when he must more than once have been nearly frozen as he trudged beside the waggons, he kept slapping his thighs and stamping with his feet as he walked. Noticing that Yegorushka was awake, he looked at him and said, shrugging his shoulders as though from the cold:

"Ah, you are awake, youngster! So you are the son of Ivan Ivanitch?"

"No; his nephew. . ."

"Nephew of Ivan Ivanitch? Here I have taken off my boots and am hopping along barefoot. My feet are bad; they are swollen, and it's easier without my boots. . . easier, youngster. . . without boots, I mean. . . So you are his nephew? He is a good man; no harm in him. . . God give him health. . . No harm in him. . . I mean Ivan Ivanitch. . . He has gone to the Molokans'. . . O Lord, have mercy upon us!"

The old man talked, too, as though it were very cold, pausing and not opening his mouth properly; and he mispronounced the labial consonants, stuttering over them as though his lips were frozen. As he talked to Yegorushka he did not once smile, and he seemed stern.

Two waggons ahead of them there walked a man wearing a long reddish-brown coat, a cap and high boots with sagging bootlegs and carrying a whip in his hand. This was not an old man, only about forty. When he looked round Yegorushka saw a long red face with a scanty goat-beard and a spongy looking swelling under his right eye. Apart from this very ugly swelling, there was another peculiar thing about him which caught the eye at once: in his left hand he carried a whip, while he waved the right as though he were conducting an unseen choir; from time to time he put the whip under his arm, and then he conducted with both hands and hummed something to himself.

The next driver was a long rectilinear figure with extremely sloping shoulders and a back as flat as a board. He held himself as stiffly erect as though he were marching or had swallowed a yard measure. His hands did not swing as he walked, but hung down as if they were straight sticks, and he strode along in a wooden way, after the manner of toy soldiers, almost without bending his knees, and trying to take as long steps as possible. While the old man or the owner of the spongy swelling were taking two steps he succeeded in taking only one, and so it seemed as though he were walking more slowly than any of them, and would drop behind. His face was tied up in a rag, and on his head something stuck up that looked like a monk's peaked cap; he was dressed in a short Little Russian coat, with full dark blue trousers and bark shoes.

Yegorushka did not even distinguish those that were farther on. He lay on his stomach, picked a little hole in the bale, and, having nothing better to do, began twisting the wool into a thread. The old man trudging along below him turned out not to be so stern as one might have supposed from his face. Having begun a conversation, he did not let it drop.

"Where are you going?" he asked, stamping with his feet.

"To school," answered Yegorushka.

"To school? Aha!. . . Well, may the Queen of Heaven help you. Yes. One brain is good, but two are better. To one man God gives one brain, to another two brains, and to another three. . . To another three, that is true. . . One brain you are born with, one you get from learning, and a third with a good life. So you see, my lad, it is a good thing if a man has three brains. Living is easier for him, and, what's more, dying is, too. Dying is, too. . . And we shall all die for sure."

The old man scratched his forehead, glanced upwards at Yegorushka with his red eyes, and went on:

"Maxim Nikolaitch, the gentleman from Slavyanoserbsk, brought a little lad to school, too, last year. I don't know how he is getting on there in studying the sciences, but he was a nice good little lad. . . God give them help, they are nice gentlemen. Yes, he, too, brought his boy to school. . . In Slavyanoserbsk there is no establishment, I suppose, for study. No. . . But it is a nice town. . . There's an ordinary school for simple folks, but for the higher studies there is nothing. No, that's true. What's your name?. . ."

"Yegorushka."

"Yegory, then. . . The holy martyr Yegory, the Bearer of Victory, whose day is the twenty-third of April. And my christian name is Panteley,. . . Panteley Zaharov Holodov. . . We are Holodovs. . . I am a native of—maybe you've heard of it—Tim in the province of Kursk. My brothers are artisans and work at trades in the town, but I am a peasant. . . I have remained a peasant. Seven years ago I went there—home, I mean. I went to the village and to the town. . . To Tim, I mean. Then, thank God, they were all alive and well;. . . but now I don't know. . . Maybe some of them are dead. . . And it's time they did die, for some of them are older than I am. Death is all right; it is good so long, of course, as one does not die without repentance. There is no worse evil than an impenitent death; an impenitent death is a joy to the devil. And if you want to die penitent, so that you may not be forbidden to enter the mansions of the Lord, pray to the holy martyr Varvara. She is the intercessor. She is, that's the truth. . . For God has given her such a place in the heavens that everyone has the right to pray to her for penitence."

Panteley went on muttering, and apparently did not trouble whether Yegorushka heard him or not. He talked listlessly, mumbling to himself, without raising or dropping his voice, but succeeded in telling him a great deal in a short time. All he said was made up of fragments that had very little connection with one another, and quite uninteresting for Yegorushka. Possibly he talked only in order to reckon over his thoughts aloud after the night spent in silence, in order to see if they were all there. After talking of repentance, he spoke about a certain Maxim Nikolaitch from Slavyanoserbsk.

"Yes, he took his little lad;. . . he took him, that's true. . ."

One of the waggoners walking in front darted from his place, ran to one side and began lashing on the ground with his whip. He was a stalwart, broad-shouldered man of thirty, with curly flaxen hair and a look of great health and vigour. Judging from the movements of his shoulders and the whip, and the eagerness expressed in his attitude, he was beating something alive. Another waggoner, a short stubby little man with a bushy black beard, wearing a waistcoat and a shirt outside his trousers, ran up to him. The latter broke into a deep guffaw of laughter and coughing and said: "I say, lads, Dymov has killed a snake!"

There are people whose intelligence can be gauged at once by their voice and laughter. The man with the black beard belonged to that class of fortunate individuals; impenetrable stupidity could be felt in his voice and laugh. The flaxen-headed Dymov had finished, and lifting from the ground with his whip something like a cord, flung it with a laugh into the cart.

"That's not a viper; it's a grass snake!" shouted someone.

The man with the wooden gait and the bandage round his face strode up quickly to the dead snake, glanced at it and flung up his stick-like arms.

"You jail-bird!" he cried in a hollow wailing voice. "What have you killed a grass snake for? What had he done to you, you damned brute? Look, he has killed a grass snake; how would you like to be treated so?"

"Grass snakes ought not to be killed, that's true," Panteley muttered placidly, "they ought not. . . They are not vipers; though it looks like a snake, it is a gentle, innocent creature. . . It's friendly to man, the grass snake is."

Dymov and the man with the black beard were probably ashamed, for they laughed loudly, and not answering, slouched lazily back to their waggons. When the hindmost waggon was level with the spot where the dead snake lay, the man with his face tied up standing over it turned to Panteley and asked in a tearful voice:

"Grandfather, what did he want to kill the grass snake for?"

His eyes, as Yegorushka saw now, were small and dingy looking; his face was grey, sickly and looked somehow dingy too while his chin was red and seemed very much swollen.

"Grandfather, what did he kill it for?" he repeated, striding along beside Panteley.

"A stupid fellow. His hands itch to kill, and that is why he does it," answered the old man; "but he oughtn't to kill a grass snake, that's true. . . Dymov is a ruffian, we all know, he kills everything he comes across, and Kiruha did not interfere. He ought to have taken its part, but instead of that, he goes off into 'Ha-ha-ha!' and 'Ho-ho-ho!'. . . But don't be angry, Vassya. . . Why be angry? They've killed it—well, never mind them. Dymov is a ruffian and Kiruha acted from foolishness—never mind. . . They are foolish people without understanding—but there, don't mind them. Emelyan here never touches what he shouldn't;

he never does;. . . that is true,. . . because he is a man of education, while they are stupid. . . Emelyan, he doesn't touch things."

The waggoner in the reddish-brown coat and the spongy swelling on his face, who was conducting an unseen choir, stopped. Hearing his name, and waiting till Panteley and Vassya came up to him, he walked beside them.

"What are you talking about?" he asked in a husky muffled voice.

"Why, Vassya here is angry," said Panteley. "So I have been saying things to him to stop his being angry. . . Oh, how my swollen feet hurt! Oh, oh! They are more inflamed than ever for Sunday, God's holy day!"

"It's from walking," observed Vassya.

"No, lad, no. It's not from walking. When I walk it seems easier; when I lie down and get warm,. . . it's deadly. Walking is easier for me."

Emelyan, in his reddish-brown coat, walked between Panteley and Vassya and waved his arms, as though they were going to sing. After waving them a little while he dropped them, and croaked out hopelessly:

"I have no voice. It's a real misfortune. All last night and this morning I have been haunted by the trio 'Lord, have Mercy' that we sang at the wedding at Marionovsky's. It's in my head and in my throat. It seems as though I could sing it, but I can't; I have no voice."

He paused for a minute, thinking, then went on:

"For fifteen years I was in the choir. In all the Lugansky works there was, maybe, no one with a voice like mine. But, confound it, I bathed two years ago in the Donets, and I can't get a single note true ever since. I took cold in my throat. And without a voice I am like a workman without hands."

"That's true," Panteley agreed.

"I think of myself as a ruined man and nothing more."

At that moment Vassya chanced to catch sight of Yegorushka. His eyes grew moist and smaller than ever.

"There's a little gentleman driving with us," and he covered his nose with his sleeve as though he were bashful. "What a grand driver! Stay with us and you shall drive the waggons and sell wool."

The incongruity of one person being at once a little gentleman and a waggon driver seemed to strike him as very queer and funny, for he burst into a loud guffaw, and went on enlarging upon the idea. Emelyan glanced upwards at Yegorushka, too, but coldly and cursorily. He was absorbed in his own thoughts, and had it not been for Vassya, would not have noticed Yegorushka's presence. Before five minutes had passed he was waving his arms again, then describing to his companions the beauties of the wedding anthem, "Lord, have Mercy," which he had remembered in the night. He put the whip under his arm and waved both hands.

A mile from the village the waggons stopped by a well with a crane. Letting his pail down into the well, black-bearded Kiruha lay on his stomach on the framework and thrust his shaggy head, his shoulders, and part of his chest into the black hole, so that Yegorushka could see nothing but his short legs, which scarcely touched the ground. Seeing the reflection of his head far down at the bottom of the well, he was delighted and went off into his deep bass stupid laugh, and the echo from the well answered him. When he got up his neck and face were as red as beetroot. The first to run up and drink was Dymov. He drank laughing, often turning from the pail to tell Kiruha something funny, then he turned round, and uttered aloud, to be heard all over the steppe, five very bad words. Yegorushka did not understand the meaning of such words, but he knew very well they were bad words. He knew the repulsion his friends and relations silently felt for such words. He himself, without knowing why, shared that feeling and was accustomed to think that only drunk and disorderly people enjoy the privilege of uttering such words aloud. He remembered the murder of the grass snake, listened to Dymov's laughter, and felt something like hatred for the man. And as ill-luck would have it, Dymov at that moment caught sight of Yegorushka, who had climbed down from the waggon and gone up to the well. He laughed aloud and shouted:

"I say, lads, the old man has been brought to bed of a boy in the night!"

Kiruha laughed his bass laugh till he coughed. Someone else laughed too, while Yegorushka crimsoned and made up his mind finally that Dymov was a very wicked man.

With his curly flaxen head, with his shirt opened on his chest and no hat on, Dymov looked handsome and exceptionally strong; in every movement he made one could see the reckless dare-devil and athlete, knowing his value. He shrugged his shoulders, put his arms akimbo, talked and laughed louder than any of the rest, and looked as though he were going to lift up something very heavy with one hand and astonish the whole world by doing so. His mischievous mocking eyes glided over the road, the waggons, and the sky without resting on anything, and seemed looking for someone to kill, just as a pastime, and something

ANTON CHEKHOV

to laugh at. Evidently he was afraid of no one, would stick at nothing, and most likely was not in the least interested in Yegorushka's opinion of him. . . Yegorushka meanwhile hated his flaxen head, his clear face, and his strength with his whole heart, listened with fear and loathing to his laughter, and kept thinking what word of abuse he could pay him out with.

Panteley, too, went up to the pail. He took out of his pocket a little green glass of an ikon lamp, wiped it with a rag, filled it from the pail and drank from it, then filled it again, wrapped the little glass in the rag, and then put it back into his pocket.

"Grandfather, why do you drink out of a lamp?" Yegorushka asked him, surprised.

"One man drinks out of a pail and another out of a lamp," the old man answered evasively. "Every man to his own taste. . . You drink out of the pail—well, drink, and may it do you good. . ."

"You darling, you beauty!" Vassya said suddenly, in a caressing, plaintive voice. "You darling!"

His eyes were fixed on the distance; they were moist and smiling, and his face wore the same expression as when he had looked at Yegorushka.

"Who is it you are talking to?" asked Kiruha.

"A darling fox,. . . lying on her back, playing like a dog."

Everyone began staring into the distance, looking for the fox, but no one could see it, only Vassya with his grey muddy-looking eyes, and he was enchanted by it. His sight was extraordinarily keen, as Yegorushka learnt afterwards. He was so long-sighted that the brown steppe was for him always full of life and interest. He had only to look into the distance to see a fox, a hare, a bustard, or some other animal keeping at a distance from men. There was nothing strange in seeing a hare running away or a flying bustard—everyone crossing the steppes could see them; but it was not vouchsafed to everyone to see wild animals in their own haunts when they were not running nor hiding, nor looking about them in alarm. Yet Vassya saw foxes playing, hares washing themselves with their paws, bustards preening their wings and hammering out their hollow nests. Thanks to this keenness of sight, Vassya had, besides the world seen by everyone, another world of his own, accessible to no one else, and probably a very beautiful one, for when he saw something and was in raptures over it it was impossible not to envy him.

When the waggons set off again, the church bells were ringing for service.

V

THE TRAIN OF WAGGONS DREW up on the bank of a river on one side of a village. The sun was blazing, as it had been the day before; the air was stagnant and depressing. There were a few willows on the bank, but the shade from them did not fall on the earth, but on the water, where it was wasted; even in the shade under the waggon it was stifling and wearisome. The water, blue from the reflection of the sky in it, was alluring.

Styopka, a waggoner whom Yegorushka noticed now for the first time, a Little Russian lad of eighteen, in a long shirt without a belt, and full trousers that flapped like flags as he walked, undressed quickly, ran along the steep bank and plunged into the water. He dived three times, then swam on his back and shut his eyes in his delight. His face was smiling and wrinkled up as though he were being tickled, hurt and amused.

On a hot day when there is nowhere to escape from the sultry, stifling heat, the splash of water and the loud breathing of a man bathing sounds like good music to the ear. Dymov and Kiruha, looking at Styopka, undressed quickly and one after the other, laughing loudly in eager anticipation of their enjoyment, dropped into the water, and the quiet, modest little river resounded with snorting and splashing and shouting. Kiruha coughed, laughed and shouted as though they were trying to drown him, while Dymov chased him and tried to catch him by the leg.

"Ha-ha-ha!" he shouted. "Catch him! Hold him!"

Kiruha laughed and enjoyed himself, but his expression was the same as it had been on dry land, stupid, with a look of astonishment on it as though someone had, unnoticed, stolen up behind him and hit him on the head with the butt-end of an axe. Yegorushka undressed, too, but did not let himself down by the bank, but took a run and a flying leap from the height of about ten feet. Describing an arc in the air, he fell into the water, sank deep, but did not reach the bottom; some force, cold and pleasant to the touch, seemed to hold him up and bring him back to the surface. He popped out and, snorting and blowing bubbles, opened his eyes; but the sun was reflected in the water quite close to his face. At first blinding spots of light, then rainbow colours and dark patches, flitted before his eyes. He made haste to dive again, opened his eyes in the water and saw something cloudy-green like a sky on a moonlight night. Again the same force would not let him touch the bottom and stay in the coolness, but lifted him to the surface. He popped out and heaved a sigh so deep that he had a feeling of space and freshness, not only in his chest, but in his stomach. Then, to get from the water everything he possibly could get, he allowed himself every luxury; he lay on his back and basked, splashed, frolicked, swam on his face, on his side, on his back and standing up—just as he pleased till he was exhausted. The other bank was thickly overgrown with reeds; it was golden in the sun, and the flowers of the reeds hung drooping to the water in lovely tassels. In one place the reeds were shaking and nodding, with their flowers rustling—Styopka and Kiruha were hunting crayfish.

"A crayfish, look, lads! A crayfish!" Kiruha cried triumphantly and actually showed a crayfish.

Yegorushka swam up to the reeds, dived, and began fumbling among their roots. Burrowing in the slimy, liquid mud, he felt something sharp and unpleasant—perhaps it really was a crayfish. But at that minute someone seized him by the leg and pulled him to the surface. Spluttering and coughing, Yegorushka opened his eyes and saw before him the wet grinning face of the dare-devil Dymov. The impudent fellow was breathing hard, and from a look in his eyes he seemed inclined for further mischief. He held Yegorushka tight by the leg, and was lifting his hand to take hold of his neck. But Yegorushka tore himself away with repulsion and terror, as though disgusted at being touched and afraid that the bully would drown him, and said:

"Fool! I'll punch you in the face."

Feeling that this was not sufficient to express his hatred, he thought a minute and added:

"You blackguard! You son of a bitch!"

But Dymov, as though nothing were the matter, took no further notice of Yegorushka, but swam off to Kiruha, shouting:

"Ha-ha-ha! Let us catch fish! Mates, let us catch fish."

"To be sure," Kiruha agreed; "there must be a lot of fish here."

"Styopka, run to the village and ask the peasants for a net!"

"They won't give it to me."

"They will, you ask them. Tell them that they should give it to us for Christ's sake, because we are just the same as pilgrims."

"That's true."

Styopka clambered out of the water, dressed quickly, and without a cap on he ran, his full trousers flapping, to the village. The water lost all its charm for Yegorushka after his encounter with Dymov. He got out and began dressing. Panteley and Vassya were sitting on the steep bank, with their legs hanging down, looking at the bathers. Emelyan was standing naked, up to his knees in the water, holding on to the grass with one hand to prevent himself from falling while the other stroked his body. With his bony shoulder-blades, with the swelling under his eye, bending down and evidently afraid of the water, he made a ludicrous figure. His face was grave and severe. He looked angrily at the water, as though he were just going to upbraid it for having given him cold in the Donets and robbed him of his voice.

"And why don't you bathe?" Yegorushka asked Vassya.

"Oh, I don't care for it,. . ." answered Vassya.

"How is it your chin is swollen?"

"It's bad. . . I used to work at the match factory, little sir. . . The doctor used to say that it would make my jaw rot. The air is not healthy there. There were three chaps beside me who had their jaws swollen, and with one of them it rotted away altogether."

Styopka soon came back with the net. Dymov and Kiruha were already turning blue and getting hoarse by being so long in the water, but they set about fishing eagerly. First they went to a deep place beside the reeds; there Dymov was up to his neck, while the water went over squat Kiruha's head. The latter spluttered and blew bubbles, while Dymov stumbling on the prickly roots, fell over and got caught in the net; both flopped about in the water, and made a noise, and nothing but mischief came of their fishing.

"It's deep," croaked Kiruha. "You won't catch anything."

"Don't tug, you devil!" shouted Dymov trying to put the net in the proper position. "Hold it up."

"You won't catch anything here," Panteley shouted from the bank. "You are only frightening the fish, you stupids! Go more to the left! It's shallower there!"

Once a big fish gleamed above the net; they all drew a breath, and Dymov struck the place where it had vanished with his fist, and his face expressed vexation.

"Ugh!" cried Panteley, and he stamped his foot. "You've let the perch slip! It's gone!"

Moving more to the left, Dymov and Kiruha picked out a shallower place, and then fishing began in earnest. They had wandered off some hundred paces from the waggons; they could be seen silently trying to go as deep as they could and as near the reeds, moving their legs a little at a time, drawing out the nets, beating the water with their fists to drive them towards the nets. From the reeds they got to the further bank; they drew the net out, then, with a disappointed air, lifting their knees high as they walked, went back into the reeds. They were talking about something, but what it was no one could hear. The sun was scorching their backs, the flies were stinging them, and their bodies had turned from purple to crimson. Styopka was walking after them with a pail in his hands; he had tucked his shirt right up under his armpits, and was holding it up by the hem with his teeth. After every successful catch he lifted up some fish, and letting it shine in the sun, shouted:

"Look at this perch! We've five like that!"

Every time Dymov, Kiruha and Styopka pulled out the net they could be seen fumbling about in the mud in it, putting some things into the pail and throwing other things away; sometimes they passed something that was in the net from hand to hand, examined it inquisitively, then threw that, too, away.

"What is it?" they shouted to them from the bank.

Styopka made some answer, but it was hard to make out his words. Then he climbed out of the water and, holding the pail in both hands, forgetting to let his shirt drop, ran to the waggons.

"It's full!" he shouted, breathing hard. "Give us another!"

Yegorushka looked into the pail: it was full. A young pike poked its ugly nose out of the water, and there were swarms of crayfish and little fish round about it. Yegorushka put his hand down to the bottom and stirred up the water; the pike vanished under the crayfish and a perch and a tench swam to the surface instead of it. Vassya, too, looked into the pail. His eyes grew moist and his face looked as caressing as before when he saw the fox. He took something out of the pail, put it to his mouth and began chewing it.

"Mates," said Styopka in amazement, "Vassya is eating a live gudgeon! Phoo!"

"It's not a gudgeon, but a minnow," Vassya answered calmly, still munching.

He took a fish's tail out of his mouth, looked at it caressingly, and put it back again. While he was chewing and crunching with his teeth it seemed to Yegorushka that he saw before him something not human. Vassya's swollen chin, his lustreless eyes, his extraordinary sharp sight, the fish's tail in his mouth, and the caressing friendliness with which he crunched the gudgeon made him like an animal.

Yegorushka felt dreary beside him. And the fishing was over, too. He walked about beside the waggons, thought a little, and, feeling bored, strolled off to the village.

Not long afterwards he was standing in the church, and with his forehead leaning on somebody's back, listened to the singing of the choir. The service was drawing to a close. Yegorushka did not understand church singing and did not care for it. He listened a little, yawned, and began looking at the backs and heads before him. In one head, red and wet from his recent bathe, he recognized Emelyan. The back of his head had been cropped in a straight line higher than is usual; the hair in front had been cut unbecomingly high, and Emelyan's ears stood out like two dock leaves, and seemed to feel themselves out of place. Looking at the back of his head and his ears, Yegorushka, for some reason, thought that Emelyan was probably very unhappy. He remembered the way he conducted with his hands, his husky voice, his timid air when he was bathing, and felt intense pity for him. He longed to say something friendly to him.

"I am here, too," he said, putting out his hand.

People who sing tenor or bass in the choir, especially those who have at any time in their lives conducted, are accustomed to look with a stern and unfriendly air at boys. They do not give up this habit, even when they leave off being in a choir. Turning to Yegorushka, Emelyan looked at him from under his brows and said:

"Don't play in church!"

Then Yegorushka moved forwards nearer to the ikon-stand. Here he saw interesting people. On the right side, in front of everyone, a lady and a gentleman were standing on a carpet. There were chairs behind them. The gentleman was wearing newly ironed shantung trousers; he stood as motionless as a soldier saluting, and held high his bluish shaven chin. There was a very great air of dignity in his stand-up collar, in his blue chin, in his small bald patch and his cane. His neck was so strained from excess of dignity, and his chin was drawn up so tensely, that it looked as though his head were ready to fly off and soar upwards any minute. The lady, who was stout and elderly and wore a white silk shawl, held her head on one side and looked as though she had done someone a favour, and wanted to say: "Oh, don't trouble yourself to thank me; I don't like it. . ." A thick wall of Little Russian heads stood all round the carpet.

Yegorushka went up to the ikon-stand and began kissing the local ikons. Before each image he slowly bowed down to the ground, without getting up, looked round at the congregation, then got up and kissed the ikon. The contact of his forehead with the cold floor afforded him great satisfaction. When the beadle came from the altar with a pair of long snuffers to put out the candles, Yegorushka jumped up quickly from the floor and ran up to him.

"Have they given out the holy bread?" he asked.

"There is none; there is none," the beadle muttered gruffly. "It is no use your. . ."

The service was over; Yegorushka walked out of the church in a leisurely way, and began strolling about the market-place. He had seen a good many villages, market-places, and peasants in his time, and everything that met his eyes was entirely without interest for him. At a loss for something to do, he went into a shop over the door of which hung a wide strip of red cotton. The shop consisted of two roomy, badly lighted parts; in one half they sold drapery and groceries, in the other there were tubs of tar, and there were horse-collars hanging from the ceiling; from both came the savoury smell of leather and tar. The floor of the shop had been watered; the man who watered it must have been a very whimsical and original person, for it was sprinkled in patterns and mysterious symbols. The shopkeeper, an overfed-looking man with a broad face and round beard, apparently a Great Russian, was standing, leaning his person over the counter. He was nibbling a piece of sugar as he drank his tea, and heaved a deep sigh at every sip. His face expressed complete indifference, but each sigh seemed to be saying:

"Just wait a minute; I will give it you."

"Give me a farthing's worth of sunflower seeds," Yegorushka said, addressing him.

The shopkeeper raised his eyebrows, came out from behind the counter, and poured a farthing's worth of sunflower seeds into Yegorushka's pocket, using an empty pomatum pot as a measure. Yegorushka did not want to go away. He spent a long time in examining the box of cakes, thought a little and asked, pointing to some little cakes covered with the mildew of age:

"How much are these cakes?"

"Two for a farthing."

Yegorushka took out of his pocket the cake given him the day before by the Jewess, and asked him:

"And how much do you charge for cakes like this?"

The shopman took the cake in his hands, looked at it from all sides, and raised one eyebrow.

"Like that?" he asked.

Then he raised the other eyebrow, thought a minute, and answered:

"Two for three farthings. . ."

A silence followed.

"Whose boy are you?" the shopman asked, pouring himself out some tea from a red copper teapot.

"The nephew of Ivan Ivanitch."

"There are all sorts of Ivan Ivanitchs," the shopkeeper sighed. He looked over Yegorushka's head towards the door, paused a minute and asked:

"Would you like some tea?"

"Please. . ." Yegorushka assented not very readily, though he felt an intense longing for his usual morning tea.

The shopkeeper poured him out a glass and gave him with it a bit of sugar that looked as though it had been nibbled. Yegorushka sat down on the folding chair and began drinking it. He wanted to ask the price of a pound of sugar almonds, and had just broached the subject when a customer walked in, and the shopkeeper, leaving his glass of tea, attended to his business. He led the customer into the other half, where there was a smell of tar, and was there a long time discussing something with him. The customer, a man apparently very obstinate and pig-headed, was continually shaking his head to signify his disapproval, and retreating towards the door. The shopkeeper tried to persuade him of something and began pouring some oats into a big sack for him.

"Do you call those oats?" the customer said gloomily. "Those are not oats, but chaff. It's a mockery to give that to the hens; enough to make the hens laugh. . . No, I will go to Bondarenko."

When Yegorushka went back to the river a small camp fire was smoking on the bank. The waggoners were cooking their dinner. Styopka was standing in the smoke, stirring the cauldron with a big notched spoon. A little on one side Kiruha and Vassya, with eyes reddened from the smoke, were sitting cleaning the fish. Before them lay the net covered with slime and water weeds, and on it lay gleaming fish and crawling crayfish.

Emelyan, who had not long been back from the church, was sitting beside Panteley, waving his arm and humming just audibly in a husky voice: "To Thee we sing. . ." Dymov was moving about by the horses.

When they had finished cleaning them, Kiruha and Vassya put the fish and the living crayfish together in the pail, rinsed them, and from the pail poured them all into the boiling water.

"Shall I put in some fat?" asked Styopka, skimming off the froth.

"No need. The fish will make its own gravy," answered Kiruha.

Before taking the cauldron off the fire Styopka scattered into the water three big handfuls of millet and a spoonful of salt; finally he tried it, smacked his lips, licked the spoon, and gave a self-satisfied grunt, which meant that the grain was done.

All except Panteley sat down near the cauldron and set to work with their spoons.

"You there! Give the little lad a spoon!" Panteley observed sternly. "I dare say he is hungry too!"

"Ours is peasant fare," sighed Kiruha.

"Peasant fare is welcome, too, when one is hungry."

They gave Yegorushka a spoon. He began eating, not sitting, but standing close to the cauldron and looking down into it as in a hole. The grain smelt of fish and fish-scales were mixed up with the millet. The crayfish could not be hooked out with a spoon, and the men simply picked them out of the cauldron with their hands; Vassya did so particularly freely, and wetted his sleeves as well as his hands in the mess. But yet the stew seemed to Yegorushka very nice, and reminded him of the crayfish soup which his mother used to make at home on fast-days. Panteley was sitting apart munching bread.

"Grandfather, why aren't you eating?" Emelyan asked him.

"I don't eat crayfish. . . Nasty things," the old man said, and turned away with disgust.

While they were eating they all talked. From this conversation Yegorushka gathered that all his new acquaintances, in spite of the differences of their ages and their characters, had one point in common which made them all alike: they were all people with a splendid past and a very poor present. Of their past they all—every one of them— spoke with enthusiasm; their attitude to the present was almost one of contempt. The Russian loves recalling life, but he does not love living. Yegorushka did not yet know that, and before the stew had been all eaten he firmly believed that the men sitting round the cauldron were the injured victims of fate. Panteley told them that in the past, before there were railways, he used to go with trains of waggons to Moscow and to Nizhni, and used to earn so much that he did not know what to do with his money; and what merchants there used to be in those days! what fish! how cheap everything was! Now the roads were shorter, the merchants were stingier, the peasants were poorer, the bread was dearer, everything had shrunk and was on a smaller scale. Emelyan told them that in old days he had been in the choir in the Lugansky works, and that he had a remarkable voice and read music splendidly, while now he had become a peasant and lived on the charity of his brother, who sent him out with his horses and took half his earnings. Vassya had once worked in a match factory; Kiruha had been a coachman in a good family, and had been reckoned the smartest driver of a three-in-hand in the whole district. Dymov, the son of a well-to-do peasant, lived at ease, enjoyed himself and had known no trouble till he was twenty, when his stern harsh father, anxious to train him to work, and afraid he would be spoiled at home, had sent him to a carrier's to work as a hired labourer. Styopka was the only one who said nothing, but from his beardless face it was evident that his life had been a much better one in the past.

Thinking of his father, Dymov frowned and left off eating. Sullenly from under his brows he looked round at his companions and his eye rested upon Yegorushka.

"You heathen, take off your cap," he said rudely. "You can't eat with your cap on, and you a gentleman too!"

Yegorushka took off his hat and did not say a word, but the stew lost all savour for him, and he did not hear Panteley and Vassya intervening on his behalf. A feeling of anger with the insulting fellow was rankling oppressively in his breast, and he made up his mind that he would do him some injury, whatever it cost him.

After dinner everyone sauntered to the waggons and lay down in the shade.

"Are we going to start soon, grandfather?" Yegorushka asked Panteley.

"In God's good time we shall set off. There's no starting yet; it is too hot. . . O Lord, Thy will be done. Holy Mother. . . Lie down, little lad."

Soon there was a sound of snoring from under the waggons. Yegorushka meant to go back to the village, but on consideration, yawned and lay down by the old man.

VI

THE WAGGONS REMAINED BY THE river the whole day, and set off again when the sun was setting.

Yegorushka was lying on the bales again; the waggon creaked softly and swayed from side to side. Panteley walked below, stamping his feet, slapping himself on his thighs and muttering. The air was full of the churring music of the steppes, as it had been the day before.

Yegorushka lay on his back, and, putting his hands under his head, gazed upwards at the sky. He watched the glow of sunset kindle, then fade away; guardian angels covering the horizon with their gold wings disposed themselves to slumber. The day had passed peacefully; the quiet peaceful night had come, and they could stay tranquilly at home in heaven. . . Yegorushka saw the sky by degrees grow dark and the mist fall over the earth—saw the stars light up, one after the other. . .

When you gaze a long while fixedly at the deep sky thoughts and feelings for some reason merge in a sense of loneliness. One begins to feel hopelessly solitary, and everything one used to look upon as near and akin becomes infinitely remote and valueless; the stars that have looked down from the sky thousands of years already, the mists and the incomprehensible sky itself, indifferent to the brief life of man, oppress the soul with their silence when one is left face to face with them and tries to grasp their significance. One is reminded of the solitude awaiting each one of us in the grave, and the reality of life seems awful. . . full of despair. . .

Yegorushka thought of his grandmother, who was sleeping now under the cherry-trees in the cemetery. He remembered how she lay in her coffin with pennies on her eyes, how afterwards she was shut in and let down into the grave; he even recalled the hollow sound of the clods of earth on the coffin lid. . . He pictured his granny in the dark and narrow coffin, helpless and deserted by everyone. His imagination pictured his granny suddenly awakening, not understanding where she was, knocking upon the lid and calling for help, and in the end swooning with horror and dying again. He imagined his mother dead, Father Christopher, Countess Dranitsky, Solomon. But however much he tried to imagine himself in the dark tomb, far from home, outcast, helpless and dead, he could not succeed; for himself personally he could not admit the possibility of death, and felt that he would never die. . .

Panteley, for whom death could not be far away, walked below and went on reckoning up his thoughts.

"All right. . . Nice gentlefolk,. . ." he muttered. "Took his little lad to school—but how he is doing now I haven't heard say—in Slavyanoserbsk. I say there is no establishment for teaching them to be very clever. . . No, that's true—a nice little lad, no harm in him. . . He'll grow up and be a help to his father. . . You, Yegory, are little now, but you'll grow big and will keep your father and mother. . . So it is ordained of God, 'Honour your father and your mother.'. . . I had children myself, but they were burnt. . . My wife was burnt and my children,. . . that's true. . . The hut caught fire on the night of Epiphany. . . I was not at home, I was driving in Oryol. In Oryol. . . Marya dashed out into the street, but remembering that the children were asleep in the hut, ran back and was burnt with her children. . . Next day they found nothing but bones."

About midnight Yegorushka and the waggoners were again sitting round a small camp fire. While the dry twigs and stems were burning up, Kiruha and Vassya went off somewhere to get water from a creek; they vanished into the darkness, but could be heard all the time talking and clinking their pails; so the creek was not far away. The light from the fire lay a great flickering patch on the earth; though the moon was bright, yet everything seemed impenetrably black beyond that red patch. The light was in the waggoners' eyes, and they saw only part of the great road; almost unseen in the darkness the waggons with the bales and the horses looked like a mountain of undefined shape. Twenty paces from the camp fire at the edge of the road stood a wooden cross that had fallen aslant. Before the camp fire had been lighted, when he could still see things at a distance, Yegorushka had noticed that there was a similar old slanting cross on the other side of the great road.

Coming back with the water, Kiruha and Vassya filled the cauldron and fixed it over the fire. Styopka, with the notched spoon in his hand, took his place in the smoke by the cauldron, gazing dreamily into the water for the scum to rise. Panteley and Emelyan were sitting side by side in silence, brooding over something. Dymov was lying on his stomach, with his head propped on his fists, looking into the fire. . . Styopka's shadow was dancing over him, so that his handsome face was at one minute covered with darkness, at the next lighted up. . . Kiruha and Vassya were wandering about at a little distance gathering dry grass and bark for the fire. Yegorushka, with his hands in his pockets, was standing by Panteley, watching how the fire devoured the grass.

All were resting, musing on something, and they glanced cursorily at the cross over which patches of red light were dancing. There is something melancholy, pensive, and extremely poetical about a solitary tomb; one feels its silence, and the silence gives one the sense of the presence of the soul of the unknown man who lies under the cross. Is that soul at peace on the steppe? Does it grieve in the moonlight? Near the tomb the steppe seems melancholy, dreary and mournful; the grass seems more sorrowful, and one fancies the grasshoppers chirrup less freely, and there is no passer-by who would not remember that lonely soul and keep looking back at the tomb, till it was left far behind and hidden in the mists. . .

"Grandfather, what is that cross for?" asked Yegorushka.

Panteley looked at the cross and then at Dymov and asked:

"Nikola, isn't this the place where the mowers killed the merchants?"

Dymov not very readily raised himself on his elbow, looked at the road and said:

"Yes, it is. . ."

A silence followed. Kiruha broke up some dry stalks, crushed them up together and thrust them under the cauldron. The fire flared up brightly; Styopka was enveloped in black smoke, and the shadow cast by the cross danced along the road in the dusk beside the waggons.

"Yes, they were killed," Dymov said reluctantly. "Two merchants, father and son, were travelling, selling holy images. They put up in the inn not far from here that is now kept by Ignat Fomin. The old man had a drop too much, and began boasting that he had a lot of money with him. We all know merchants are a boastful set, God preserve us. . . They can't resist showing off before the likes of us. And at the time some mowers were staying the night at the inn. So they overheard what the merchants said and took note of it."

"O Lord!. . . Holy Mother!" sighed Panteley.

"Next day, as soon as it was light," Dymov went on, "the merchants were preparing to set off and the mowers tried to join them. 'Let us go together, your worships. It will be more cheerful and there will be less danger, for this is an out-of-the-way place. . .' The merchants had to travel at a walking pace to avoid breaking the images, and that just suited the mowers. . ."

Dymov rose into a kneeling position and stretched.

"Yes," he went on, yawning. "Everything went all right till they reached this spot, and then the mowers let fly at them with their scythes. The son, he was a fine young fellow, snatched the scythe from one of them, and he used it, too. . . Well, of course, they got the best of it because there were eight of them. They hacked at the merchants so that there was not a sound place left on their bodies; when they had finished they dragged both of them off the road, the father to one side and the son to the other. Opposite that cross there is another cross on this side. . . Whether it is still standing, I don't know. . . I can't see from here. . ."

"It is," said Kiruha.

"They say they did not find much money afterwards."

"No," Panteley confirmed; "they only found a hundred roubles."

"And three of them died afterwards, for the merchant had cut them badly with the scythe, too. They died from loss of blood. One had his hand cut off, so that they say he ran three miles without his hand, and they found him on a mound close to Kurikovo. He was squatting on his heels, with his head on his knees, as though he were lost in thought, but when they looked at him there was no life in him and he was dead. . ."

"They found him by the track of blood," said Panteley.

Everyone looked at the cross, and again there was a hush. From somewhere, most likely from the creek, floated the mournful cry of the bird: "Sleep! sleep! sleep!"

"There are a great many wicked people in the world," said Emelyan.

"A great many," assented Panteley, and he moved up closer to the fire as though he were frightened. "A great many," he went on in a low voice. "I've seen lots and lots of them. . . Wicked people!. . . I have seen a great many holy and just, too. . . Queen of Heaven, save us and have mercy on us. I remember once thirty years ago, or maybe more, I was driving a merchant from Morshansk. The merchant was a jolly handsome fellow, with money, too. . . the merchant was. . . a nice man, no harm in him. . . So we put up for the night at an inn. And in Russia the inns are not what they are in these parts. There the yards are roofed in and look like the ground floor, or let us say like barns in good farms. Only a barn would be a bit higher. So we put up there and were all right. My merchant was in a room, while I was with the horses, and everything was as it should be. So, lads, I said my prayers before going to sleep and began walking about the yard. And it was a dark night, I couldn't see anything; it was no good trying. So I walked about a bit up to the waggons, or nearly, when I saw a light gleaming. What could it mean? I thought the people of the inn had gone to bed long ago, and besides the merchant and me there were no other guests in the inn. . . Where could the light have come from? I felt suspicious. . . I went closer. . . towards the light. . . The Lord have mercy upon me! and save me, Queen of Heaven! I looked and there was a little window with a grating,. . . close to the ground, in the house. . . I lay down on the ground and looked in; as soon as I looked in a cold chill ran all down me. . ."

Kiruha, trying not to make a noise, thrust a handful of twigs into the fire. After waiting for it to leave off crackling and hissing, the old man went on:

"I looked in and there was a big cellar, black and dark. . . There was a lighted lantern on a tub. In the middle of the cellar were about a dozen men in red shirts with their sleeves turned up, sharpening long knives. . . Ugh! So we had fallen into a nest of robbers. . . What's to be done? I ran to the merchant, waked him up quietly, and said: 'Don't be frightened, merchant,' said I, 'but we are in a bad way. We have fallen into a nest of robbers,' I said. He turned pale and asked: 'What are we to do now, Panteley? I have a lot of money that belongs to orphans. As for my life,' he said, 'that's in God's hands. I am not afraid to die, but it's dreadful to lose the orphans' money,' said he. . . What were we to do? The gates were locked; there was no getting out. If there had been a fence one could have climbed over it, but with the yard shut up!. . . 'Come, don't be frightened, merchant,' said I; 'but pray to God. Maybe the Lord will not let the orphans suffer. Stay still.' said I, 'and make no sign, and meanwhile, maybe, I shall think of something. . .' Right!. . . I prayed to God and the Lord put the thought into my mind. . . I clambered up on my chaise and softly,. . . softly so that no one should hear, began pulling out the straw in the thatch, made a hole and crept out, crept out. . . Then I jumped off the roof and ran along the road as fast as I could. I ran and ran till I was nearly dead. . . I ran maybe four miles without taking breath, if not more. Thank God I saw a village. I ran up to a hut and began tapping at a window. 'Good Christian people,' I said, and told them all about it, 'do not let a Christian soul perish. . .' I waked them all up. . . The peasants gathered together and went with me,. . one with a cord, one with an oakstick, others with pitchforks. . . We broke in the gates of the inn-yard and went straight to the cellar. . . And the robbers had just finished sharpening their knives and were going to kill the merchant. The peasants took them, every one of them, bound them and carried them to the police. The merchant gave them three hundred roubles in his joy, and gave me five gold pieces and put my name down. They said that they found human bones in the cellar afterwards, heaps and heaps of them. . . Bones!. . . So they robbed people and then buried them, so that there should be no traces. . . Well, afterwards they were punished at Morshansk."

Panteley had finished his story, and he looked round at his listeners. They were gazing at him in silence. The water was boiling by now and Styopka was skimming off the froth.

"Is the fat ready?" Kiruha asked him in a whisper.

"Wait a little. . . Directly."

Styopka, his eyes fixed on Panteley as though he were afraid that the latter might begin some story before he was back, ran to the waggons; soon he came back with a little wooden bowl and began pounding some lard in it.

"I went another journey with a merchant, too,. . ." Panteley went on again, speaking as before in a low voice and with fixed unblinking eyes. "His name, as I remember now, was Pyotr Grigoritch. He was a nice man,. . . the merchant was. We stopped in the same way at an inn. . . He indoors and me with the horses. . . The people of the house, the innkeeper and his wife, seemed friendly good sort of people; the labourers, too, seemed all right; but yet, lads, I couldn't sleep. I had a queer feeling in my heart,. . . a queer feeling, that was just it. The gates were open and there were plenty of people about, and yet I felt afraid and not myself. Everyone had been asleep long ago. It was the middle of the night; it would soon be time to get up, and I was lying alone in my chaise and could not close my eyes, as though I were some owl. And then, lads, I heard this sound, 'Toop! toop! toop!' Someone was creeping up to the chaise. I poke my head out, and there was a peasant woman in nothing but her shift and with her feet bare. . . 'What do you want, good woman?' I asked. And she was all of a tremble; her face was terror-stricken. . . 'Get up, good man,' said she; 'the people are plotting evil. . . They mean to kill your merchant. With my own ears I heard the master whispering with his wife. . .' So it was not for nothing, the foreboding of my heart! 'And who are you?' I asked. 'I am their cook,' she said. . . Right!. . . So I got out of the chaise and went to the merchant. I waked him up and said: 'Things aren't quite right, Pyotr Grigoritch. . . Make haste and rouse yourself from sleep, your worship, and dress now while there is still time,' I said; 'and to save our skins, let us get away from

ANTON CHEKHOV

trouble.' He had no sooner begun dressing when the door opened and, mercy on us! I saw, Holy Mother! the innkeeper and his wife come into the room with three labourers. . . So they had persuaded the labourers to join them. 'The merchant has a lot of money, and we'll go shares,' they told them. Every one of the five had a long knife in their hand each a knife. The innkeeper locked the door and said: 'Say your prayers, travellers,. . . and if you begin screaming,' they said, 'we won't let you say your prayers before you die. . .' As though we could scream! I had such a lump in my throat I could not cry out. . . The merchant wept and said: 'Good Christian people! you have resolved to kill me because my money tempts you. Well, so be it; I shall not be the first nor shall I be the last. Many of us merchants have been murdered at inns. But why, good Christian brothers,' says he, 'murder my driver? Why should he have to suffer for my money?' And he said that so pitifully! And the innkeeper answered him: 'If we leave him alive,' said he, 'he will be the first to bear witness against us. One may just as well kill two as one. You can but answer once for seven misdeeds. . . Say your prayers, that's all you can do, and it is no good talking!' The merchant and I knelt down side by side and wept and said our prayers. He thought of his children. I was young in those days; I wanted to live. . . We looked at the images and prayed, and so pitifully that it brings a tear even now. . . And the innkeeper's wife looks at us and says: 'Good people,' said she, 'don't bear a grudge against us in the other world and pray to God for our punishment, for it is want that drives us to it.' We prayed and wept and prayed and wept, and God heard us. He had pity on us, I suppose. . . At the very minute when the innkeeper had taken the merchant by the beard to rip open his throat with his knife suddenly someone seemed to tap at the window from the yard! We all started, and the innkeeper's hands dropped. . . Someone was tapping at the window and shouting: 'Pyotr Grigoritch,' he shouted, 'are you here? Get ready and let's go!' The people saw that someone had come for the merchant; they were terrified and took to their heels. . . And we made haste into the yard, harnessed the horses, and were out of sight in a minute. . ."

"Who was it knocked at the window?" asked Dymov.

"At the window? It must have been a holy saint or angel, for there was no one else. . . When we drove out of the yard there wasn't a soul in the street. . . It was the Lord's doing."

Panteley told other stories, and in all of them "long knives" figured and all alike sounded made up. Had he heard these stories from someone else, or had he made them up himself in the remote past, and afterwards, as his memory grew weaker, mixed up his experiences with his imaginations and become unable to distinguish one from the other? Anything is possible, but it is strange that on this occasion and for the rest of the journey, whenever he happened to tell a story, he gave unmistakable preference to fiction, and never told of what he really had experienced. At the time Yegorushka took it all for the genuine thing, and believed every word; later on it seemed to him strange that a man who in his day had travelled all over Russia and seen and known so much, whose wife and children had been burnt to death, so failed to appreciate the wealth of his life that whenever he was sitting by the camp fire he was either silent or talked of what had never been.

Over their porridge they were all silent, thinking of what they had just heard. Life is terrible and marvellous, and so, however terrible a story you tell in Russia, however you embroider it with nests of robbers, long knives and such marvels, it always finds an echo of reality in the soul of the listener, and only a man who has been a good deal affected by education looks askance distrustfully, and even he will be silent. The cross by the roadside, the dark bales of wool, the wide expanse of the plain, and the lot of the men gathered together by the camp fire—all this was of itself so marvellous and terrible that the fantastic colours of legend and fairy-tale were pale and blended with life.

All the others ate out of the cauldron, but Panteley sat apart and ate his porridge out of a wooden bowl. His spoon was not like those the others had, but was made of cypress wood, with a little cross on it. Yegorushka, looking at him, thought of the little ikon glass and asked Styopka softly:

"Why does Grandfather sit apart?"

"He is an Old Believer," Styopka and Vassya answered in a whisper. And as they said it they looked as though they were speaking of some secret vice or weakness.

All sat silent, thinking. After the terrible stories there was no inclination to speak of ordinary things. All at once in the midst of the silence Vassya drew himself up and, fixing his lustreless eyes on one point, pricked up his ears.

"What is it?" Dymov asked him.

"Someone is coming," answered Vassya.

"Where do you see him?"

"Yo-on-der! There's something white. . ."

There was nothing to be seen but darkness in the direction in which Vassya was looking; everyone listened, but they could hear no sound of steps.

"Is he coming by the highroad?" asked Dymov.

"No, over the open country. . . He is coming this way."

A minute passed in silence.

"And maybe it's the merchant who was buried here walking over the steppe," said Dymov.

All looked askance at the cross, exchanged glances and suddenly broke into a laugh. They felt ashamed of their terror.

"Why should he walk?" asked Panteley. "It's only those walk at night whom the earth will not take to herself. And the merchants were all right. . . The merchants have received the crown of martyrs."

But all at once they heard the sound of steps; someone was coming in haste.

"He's carrying something," said Vassya.

They could hear the grass rustling and the dry twigs crackling under the feet of the approaching wayfarer. But from the glare of the camp fire nothing could be seen. At last the steps sounded close by, and someone coughed. The flickering light seemed to part; a veil dropped from the waggoners' eyes, and they saw a man facing them.

Whether it was due to the flickering light or because everyone wanted to make out the man's face first of all, it happened, strangely enough, that at the first glance at him they all saw, first of all, not his face nor his clothes, but his smile. It was an extraordinarily good-natured, broad, soft smile, like that of a baby on waking, one of those infectious smiles to which it is difficult not to respond by smiling too. The stranger, when they did get a good look at him, turned out to be a man of thirty, ugly and in no way remarkable. He was a tall Little Russian, with a long nose, long arms and long legs; everything about him seemed long except his neck, which was so short that it made him seem stooping. He was wearing a clean white shirt with an embroidered collar, white trousers, and new high boots, and in comparison with the waggoners he looked quite a dandy. In his arms he was carrying something big, white, and at the first glance strange-looking, and the stock of a gun also peeped out from behind his shoulder.

Coming from the darkness into the circle of light, he stopped short as though petrified, and for half a minute looked at the waggoners as though he would have said: "Just look what a smile I have!"

Then he took a step towards the fire, smiled still more radiantly and said:

"Bread and salt, friends!"

"You are very welcome!" Panteley answered for them all.

The stranger put down by the fire what he was carrying in his arms—it was a dead bustard—and greeted them once more.

They all went up to the bustard and began examining it.

"A fine big bird; what did you kill it with?" asked Dymov.

"Grape-shot. You can't get him with small shot, he won't let you get near enough. Buy it, friends! I will let you have it for twenty kopecks."

"What use would it be to us? It's good roast, but I bet it would be tough boiled; you could not get your teeth into it. . ."

"Oh, what a pity! I would take it to the gentry at the farm; they would give me half a rouble for it. But it's a long way to go—twelve miles!"

The stranger sat down, took off his gun and laid it beside him.

He seemed sleepy and languid; he sat smiling, and, screwing up his eyes at the firelight, apparently thinking of something very agreeable. They gave him a spoon; he began eating.

"Who are you?" Dymov asked him.

The stranger did not hear the question; he made no answer, and did not even glance at Dymov. Most likely this smiling man did not taste the flavour of the porridge either, for he seemed to eat it mechanically, lifting the spoon to his lips sometimes very full and sometimes quite empty. He was not drunk, but he seemed to have something nonsensical in his head.

"I ask you who you are?" repeated Dymov.

"I?" said the unknown, starting. "Konstantin Zvonik from Rovno. It's three miles from here."

And anxious to show straight off that he was not quite an ordinary peasant, but something better, Konstantin hastened to add:

"We keep bees and fatten pigs."

"Do you live with your father or in a house of your own?"

"No; now I am living in a house of my own. I have parted. This month, just after St. Peter's Day, I got married. I am a married man now!. . . It's eighteen days since the wedding."

"That's a good thing," said Panteley. "Marriage is a good thing. . . God's blessing is on it."

"His young wife sits at home while he rambles about the steppe," laughed Kiruha. "Queer chap!"

As though he had been pinched on the tenderest spot, Konstantin started, laughed and flushed crimson.

"But, Lord, she is not at home!" he said quickly, taking the spoon out of his mouth and looking round at everyone with an expression of delight and wonder. "She is not; she has gone to her mother's for three days! Yes, indeed, she has gone away, and I feel as though I were not married. . ."

Konstantin waved his hand and turned his head; he wanted to go on thinking, but the joy which beamed in his face prevented him. As though he were not comfortable, he changed his attitude, laughed, and again waved his hand. He was ashamed to share his happy thoughts with strangers, but at the same time he had an irresistible longing to communicate his joy.

"She has gone to Demidovo to see her mother," he said, blushing and moving his gun. "She'll be back to-morrow. . . She said she would be back to dinner."

"And do you miss her?" said Dymov.

"Oh, Lord, yes; I should think so. We have only been married such a little while, and she has gone away. . . Eh! Oh, but she is a tricky one, God strike me dead! She is such a fine, splendid girl, such a one for laughing and singing, full of life and fire! When she is there your brain is in a whirl, and now she is away I wander about the steppe like a fool, as though I had lost something. I have been walking since dinner."

Konstantin rubbed his eyes, looked at the fire and laughed.

"You love her, then,. . ." said Panteley.

"She is so fine and splendid," Konstantin repeated, not hearing him; "such a housewife, clever and sensible. You wouldn't find another like her among simple folk in the whole province. She has gone away. . . But she is missing me, I kno-ow! I know the little magpie. She said she would be back to-morrow by dinner-time. . . And just think how queer!" Konstantin almost shouted, speaking a note higher and shifting his position. "Now she loves me and is sad without me, and yet she would not marry me."

"But eat," said Kiruha.

"She would not marry me," Konstantin went on, not heeding him. "I have been struggling with her for three years! I saw her at the Kalatchik fair; I fell madly in love with her, was ready to hang myself. . . I live at Rovno, she at Demidovo, more than twenty miles apart, and there was nothing I could do. I sent match-makers to her, and all she said was: 'I won't!' Ah, the magpie! I sent her one thing and another, earrings and cakes, and twenty pounds of honey—but still she said: 'I won't!' And there it was. If you come to think of it, I was not a match for her! She was young and lovely, full of fire, while I am old: I shall soon be thirty, and a regular beauty, too; a fine beard like a goat's, a clear complexion all covered with pimples—how could I be compared with her! The only thing to be said is that we are well off, but then the Vahramenkys are well off, too. They've six oxen, and they keep a couple of labourers. I was in love, friends, as though I were plague-stricken. I couldn't sleep or eat; my brain was full of thoughts, and in such a maze, Lord preserve us! I longed to see her, and she was in Demidovo. What do you think? God be my witness, I am not lying, three times a week I walked over there on foot just to have a look at her. I gave up my work! I was so frantic that I even wanted to get taken on as a labourer in Demidovo, so as to be near her. I was in misery! My mother called in a witch a dozen times; my father tried thrashing me. For three years I was in this torment, and then I made up my mind. 'Damn my soul!' I said. 'I will go to the town and be a cabman. . . It seems it is fated not to be.' At Easter I went to Demidovo to have a last look at her. . ."

Konstantin threw back his head and went off into a mirthful tinkling laugh, as though he had just taken someone in very cleverly.

"I saw her by the river with the lads," he went on. "I was overcome with anger. . . I called her aside and maybe for a full hour I said all manner of things to her. She fell in love with me! For three years she did not like me! she fell in love with me for what I said to her. . ."

"What did you say to her?" asked Dymov.

"What did I say? I don't remember. . . How could one remember? My words flowed at the time like water from a tap, without stopping to take breath. Ta-ta-ta! And now I can't utter a word. . . Well, so she married me. . . She's gone now to her mother's, the magpie, and while she is away here I wander over the steppe. I can't stay at home. It's more than I can do!"

Konstantin awkwardly released his feet, on which he was sitting, stretched himself on the earth, and propped his head in his fists, then got up and sat down again. Everyone by now thoroughly understood that he was in love and happy, poignantly happy; his smile, his eyes, and every movement, expressed fervent happiness. He could not find a place for himself, and did not know what attitude to take to keep himself from being overwhelmed by the multitude of his delightful

ANTON CHEKHOV

thoughts. Having poured out his soul before these strangers, he settled down quietly at last, and, looking at the fire, sank into thought.

At the sight of this happy man everyone felt depressed and longed to be happy, too. Everyone was dreamy. Dymov got up, walked about softly by the fire, and from his walk, from the movement of his shoulder-blades, it could be seen that he was weighed down by depression and yearning. He stood still for a moment, looked at Konstantin and sat down.

The camp fire had died down by now; there was no flicker, and the patch of red had grown small and dim. . . And as the fire went out the moonlight grew clearer and clearer. Now they could see the full width of the road, the bales of wool, the shafts of the waggons, the munching horses; on the further side of the road there was the dim outline of the second cross. . .

Dymov leaned his cheek on his hand and softly hummed some plaintive song. Konstantin smiled drowsily and chimed in with a thin voice. They sang for half a minute, then sank into silence. Emelyan started, jerked his elbows and wriggled his fingers.

"Lads," he said in an imploring voice, "let's sing something sacred!" Tears came into his eyes. "Lads," he repeated, pressing his hands on his heart, "let's sing something sacred!"

"I don't know anything," said Konstantin.

Everyone refused, then Emelyan sang alone. He waved both arms, nodded his head, opened his mouth, but nothing came from his throat but a discordant gasp. He sang with his arms, with his head, with his eyes, even with the swelling on his face; he sang passionately with anguish, and the more he strained his chest to extract at least one note from it, the more discordant were his gasps.

Yegorushka, like the rest, was overcome with depression. He went to his waggon, clambered up on the bales and lay down. He looked at the sky, and thought of happy Konstantin and his wife. Why did people get married? What were women in the world for? Yegorushka put the vague questions to himself, and thought that a man would certainly be happy if he had an affectionate, merry and beautiful woman continually living at his side. For some reason he remembered the Countess Dranitsky, and thought it would probably be very pleasant to live with a woman like that; he would perhaps have married her with pleasure if that idea had not been so shameful. He recalled her eyebrows, the pupils of her eyes, her carriage, the clock with the horseman. . . The soft warm night moved softly down upon him and whispered something in his ear, and it seemed to him that it was that lovely woman bending over him, looking at him with a smile and meaning to kiss him. . .

Nothing was left of the fire but two little red eyes, which kept on growing smaller and smaller. Konstantin and the waggoners were sitting by it, dark motionless figures, and it seemed as though there were many more of them than before. The twin crosses were equally visible, and far, far away, somewhere by the highroad there gleamed a red light—other people cooking their porridge, most likely.

"Our Mother Russia is the he-ad of all the world!" Kiruha sang out suddenly in a harsh voice, choked and subsided. The steppe echo caught up his voice, carried it on, and it seemed as though stupidity itself were rolling on heavy wheels over the steppe.

"It's time to go," said Panteley. "Get up, lads."

While they were putting the horses in, Konstantin walked by the waggons and talked rapturously of his wife.

"Good-bye, mates!" he cried when the waggons started. "Thank you for your hospitality. I shall go on again towards that light. It's more than I can stand."

And he quickly vanished in the mist, and for a long time they could hear him striding in the direction of the light to tell those other strangers of his happiness.

When Yegorushka woke up next day it was early morning; the sun had not yet risen. The waggons were at a standstill. A man in a white cap and a suit of cheap grey material, mounted on a little Cossack stallion, was talking to Dymov and Kiruha beside the foremost waggon. A mile and a half ahead there were long low white barns and little houses with tiled roofs; there were neither yards nor trees to be seen beside the little houses.

"What village is that, Grandfather?" asked Yegorushka.

"That's the Armenian Settlement, youngster," answered Panteley. "The Armenians live there. They are a good sort of people,. . . the Arnienians are."

The man in grey had finished talking to Dymov and Kiruha; he pulled up his little stallion and looked across towards the settlement.

"What a business, only think!" sighed Panteley, looking towards the settlement, too, and shuddering at the morning freshness. "He has sent a man to the settlement for some papers, and he doesn't come. . . He should have sent Styopka."

"Who is that, Grandfather?" asked Yegorushka.

"Varlamov."

My goodness! Yegorushka jumped up quickly, getting upon his knees, and looked at the white cap. It was hard to recognize the mysterious elusive Varlamov, who was sought by everyone, who was always "on his rounds," and who had far more money than Countess Dranitsky, in the short, grey little man in big boots, who was sitting on an ugly little nag and talking to peasants at an hour when all decent people were asleep.

"He is all right, a good man," said Panteley, looking towards the settlement. "God give him health—a splendid gentleman, Semyon Alexandritch. . . It's people like that the earth rests upon. That's true. . . The cocks are not crowing yet, and he is already up and about. . . Another man would be asleep, or gallivanting with visitors at home, but he is on the steppe all day,. . . on his rounds. . . He does not let things slip. . . No-o! He's a fine fellow. . ."

Varlamov was talking about something, while he kept his eyes fixed. The little stallion shifted from one leg to another impatiently.

"Semyon Alexandritch!" cried Panteley, taking off his hat. "Allow us to send Styopka! Emelyan, call out that Styopka should be sent."

But now at last a man on horseback could be seen coming from the settlement. Bending very much to one side and brandishing his whip above his head like a gallant young Caucasian, and wanting to astonish everyone by his horsemanship, he flew towards the waggons with the swiftness of a bird.

"That must be one of his circuit men," said Panteley. "He must have a hundred such horsemen or maybe more."

Reaching the first waggon, he pulled up his horse, and taking off his hat, handed Varlamov a little book. Varlamov took several papers out of the book, read them and cried:

"And where is Ivantchuk's letter?"

The horseman took the book back, looked at the papers and shrugged his shoulders. He began saying something, probably justifying himself and asking to be allowed to ride back to the settlement again. The little stallion suddenly stirred as though Varlamov had grown heavier. Varlamov stirred too.

"Go along!" he cried angrily, and he waved his whip at the man.

Then he turned his horse round and, looking through the papers in the book, moved at a walking pace alongside the waggons. When he reached the hindmost, Yegorushka strained his eyes to get a better look at him. Varlamov was an elderly man. His face, a simple Russian sunburnt face with a small grey beard, was red, wet with dew and covered with little blue veins; it had the same expression of businesslike coldness as Ivan Ivanitch's face, the same look of fanatical zeal for business. But yet what a difference could be felt between him and Kuzmitchov! Uncle Ivan Ivanitch always had on his face, together with his business-like reserve, a look of anxiety and apprehension that he would not find Varlamov, that he would be late, that he would miss a good price; nothing of that sort, so characteristic of small and dependent persons, could be seen in the face or figure of Varlamov. This man made the price himself, was not looking for anyone, and did not depend on anyone; however ordinary his exterior, yet in everything, even in the manner of holding his whip, there was a sense of power and habitual authority over the steppe.

As he rode by Yegorushka he did not glance at him. Only the little stallion deigned to notice Yegorushka; he looked at him with his large foolish eyes, and even he showed no interest. Panteley bowed to Varlamov; the latter noticed it, and without taking his eyes off the sheets of paper, said lisping:

"How are you, old man?"

Varlamov's conversation with the horseman and the way he had brandished his whip had evidently made an overwhelming impression on the whole party. Everyone looked grave. The man on horseback, cast down at the anger of the great man, remained stationary, with his hat off, and the rein loose by the foremost waggon; he was silent, and seemed unable to grasp that the day had begun so badly for him.

"He is a harsh old man,. ." muttered Panteley. "It's a pity he is so harsh! But he is all right, a good man. . . He doesn't abuse men for nothing. . . It's no matter. . ."

After examining the papers, Varlamov thrust the book into his pocket; the little stallion, as though he knew what was in his mind, without waiting for orders, started and dashed along the highroad.

VII

ON THE FOLLOWING NIGHT THE waggoners had halted and were cooking their porridge. On this occasion there was a sense of overwhelming oppression over everyone. It was sultry; they all drank a great deal, but could not quench their thirst. The moon was intensely crimson and sullen, as though it were sick. The stars, too, were sullen,

　　　　　　　　　　　　　　　ANTON CHEKHOV

the mist was thicker, the distance more clouded. Nature seemed as though languid and weighed down by some foreboding.

There was not the same liveliness and talk round the camp fire as there had been the day before. All were dreary and spoke listlessly and without interest. Panteley did nothing but sigh and complain of his feet, and continually alluded to impenitent deathbeds.

Dymov was lying on his stomach, chewing a straw in silence; there was an expression of disgust on his face as though the straw smelt unpleasant, a spiteful and exhausted look. . . Vassya complained that his jaw ached, and prophesied bad weather; Emelyan was not waving his arms, but sitting still and looking gloomily at the fire. Yegorushka, too, was weary. This slow travelling exhausted him, and the sultriness of the day had given him a headache.

While they were cooking the porridge, Dymov, to relieve his boredom, began quarrelling with his companions.

"Here he lolls, the lumpy face, and is the first to put his spoon in," he said, looking spitefully at Emelyan. "Greedy! always contrives to sit next the cauldron. He's been a church-singer, so he thinks he is a gentleman! There are a lot of singers like you begging along the highroad!"

"What are you pestering me for?" asked Emelyan, looking at him angrily.

"To teach you not to be the first to dip into the cauldron. Don't think too much of yourself!"

"You are a fool, and that is all about it!" wheezed out Emelyan.

Knowing by experience how such conversations usually ended, Panteley and Vassya intervened and tried to persuade Dymov not to quarrel about nothing.

"A church-singer!" The bully would not desist, but laughed contemptuously. "Anyone can sing like that—sit in the church porch and sing 'Give me alms, for Christ's sake!' Ugh! you are a nice fellow!"

Emelyan did not speak. His silence had an irritating effect on Dymov. He looked with still greater hatred at the ex-singer and said:

"I don't care to have anything to do with you, or I would show you what to think of yourself."

"But why are you pushing me, you Mazeppa?" Emelyan cried, flaring up. "Am I interfering with you?"

"What did you call me?" asked Dymov, drawing himself up, and his eyes were suffused with blood. "Eh! I am a Mazeppa? Yes? Take that, then; go and look for it."

Dymov snatched the spoon out of Emelyan's hand and flung it far away. Kiruha, Vassya, and Styopka ran to look for it, while Emelyan fixed an imploring and questioning look on Panteley. His face suddenly became small and wrinkled; it began twitching, and the ex-singer began to cry like a child.

Yegorushka, who had long hated Dymov, felt as though the air all at once were unbearably stifling, as though the fire were scorching his face; he longed to run quickly to the waggons in the darkness, but the bully's angry bored eyes drew the boy to him. With a passionate desire to say something extremely offensive, he took a step towards Dymov and brought out, gasping for breath:

"You are the worst of the lot; I can't bear you!"

After this he ought to have run to the waggons, but he could not stir from the spot and went on:

"In the next world you will burn in hell! I'll complain to Ivan Ivanitch. Don't you dare insult Emelyan!"

"Say this too, please," laughed Dyrnov: "'every little sucking-pig wants to lay down the law.' Shall I pull your ear?"

Yegorushka felt that he could not breathe; and something which had never happened to him before—he suddenly began shaking all over, stamping his feet and crying shrilly:

"Beat him, beat him!"

Tears gushed from his eyes; he felt ashamed, and ran staggering back to the waggon. The effect produced by his outburst he did not see. Lying on the bales and twitching his arms and legs, he whispered:

"Mother, mother!"

And these men and the shadows round the camp fire, and the dark bales and the far-away lightning, which was flashing every minute in the distance—all struck him now as terrible and unfriendly. He was overcome with terror and asked himself in despair why and how he had come into this unknown land in the company of terrible peasants? Where was his uncle now, where was Father Christopher, where was Deniska? Why were they so long in coming? Hadn't they forgotten him? At the thought that he was forgotten and cast out to the mercy of fate, he felt such a cold chill of dread that he had several times an impulse to jump off the bales of wool, and run back full speed along the road; but the thought of the huge dark crosses, which would certainly meet him on the way, and the lightning flashing in the distance, stopped him. . . And only when he whispered, "Mother, mother!" he felt as it were a little better.

The waggoners must have been full of dread, too. After Yegorushka had run away from the camp fire they sat at first for a long time in silence, then they began speaking in hollow undertones about something, saying that it was coming and that they must make haste and get away from it. . . They quickly finished supper, put out the fire and began harnessing the horses in silence. From their fluster and the broken phrases they uttered it was apparent they foresaw some trouble. Before they set off on their way, Dymov went up to Panteley and asked softly:

"What's his name?"

"Yegory," answered Panteley.

Dymov put one foot on the wheel, caught hold of the cord which was tied round the bales and pulled himself up. Yegorushka saw his face and curly head. The face was pale and looked grave and exhausted, but there was no expression of spite in it.

"Yera!" he said softly, "here, hit me!"

Yegorushka looked at him in surprise. At that instant there was a flash of lightning.

"It's all right, hit me," repeated Dymov. And without waiting for Yegorushka to hit him or to speak to him, he jumped down and said: "How dreary I am!"

Then, swaying from one leg to the other and moving his shoulder-blades, he sauntered lazily alongside the string of waggons and repeated in a voice half weeping, half angry:

"How dreary I am! O Lord! Don't you take offence, Emelyan," he said as he passed Emelyan. "Ours is a wretched cruel life!"

There was a flash of lightning on the right, and, like a reflection in the looking-glass, at once a second flash in the distance.

"Yegory, take this," cried Panteley, throwing up something big and dark.

"What is it?" asked Yegorushka.

"A mat. There will be rain, so cover yourself up."

Yegorushka sat up and looked about him. The distance had grown perceptibly blacker, and now oftener than every minute winked with a pale light. The blackness was being bent towards the right as though by its own weight.

"Will there be a storm, Grandfather?" asked Yegorushka.

"Ah, my poor feet, how they ache!" Panteley said in a high-pitched voice, stamping his feet and not hearing the boy.

On the left someone seemed to strike a match in the sky; a pale phosphorescent streak gleamed and went out. There was a sound as though someone very far away were walking over an iron roof, probably barefoot, for the iron gave a hollow rumble.

"It's set in!" cried Kiruha.

Between the distance and the horizon on the right there was a flash of lightning so vivid that it lighted up part of the steppe and the spot where the clear sky met the blackness. A terrible cloud was swooping down, without haste, a compact mass; big black shreds hung from its edge; similar shreds pressing one upon another were piling up on the right and left horizon. The tattered, ragged look of the storm-cloud gave it a drunken disorderly air. There was a distinct, not smothered, growl of thunder. Yegorushka crossed himself and began quickly putting on his great-coat.

"I am dreary!" Dymov's shout floated from the foremost waggon, and it could be told from his voice that he was beginning to be ill-humoured again. "I am so dreary!"

All at once there was a squall of wind, so violent that it almost snatched away Yegorushka's bundle and mat; the mat fluttered in all directions and flapped on the bale and on Yegorushka's face. The wind dashed whistling over the steppe, whirled round in disorder and raised such an uproar from the grass that neither the thunder nor the creaking of the wheels could be heard; it blew from the black storm-cloud, carrying with it clouds of dust and the scent of rain and wet earth. The moonlight grew mistier, as it were dirtier; the stars were even more overcast; and clouds of dust could be seen hurrying along the edge of the road, followed by their shadows. By now, most likely, the whirlwind eddying round and lifting from the earth dust, dry grass and feathers, was mounting to the very sky; uprooted plants must have been flying by that very black storm-cloud, and how frightened they must have been! But through the dust that clogged the eyes nothing could be seen but the flash of lightning.

Yegorushka, thinking it would pour with rain in a minute, knelt up and covered himself with the mat.

"Panteley-ey!" someone shouted in the front. "A. . . a. . . va!"

"I can't!" Panteley answered in a loud high voice. "A. . . a. . . va! Arya. . . a!"

There was an angry clap of thunder, which rolled across the sky from right to left, then back again, and died away near the foremost waggon.

"Holy, holy, holy, Lord of Sabaoth," whispered Yegorushka, crossing himself. "Fill heaven and earth with Thy glory."

The blackness in the sky yawned wide and breathed white fire. At once there was another clap of thunder. It had scarcely ceased when there was a flash of lightning so broad that Yegorushka suddenly saw through a slit in the mat the whole highroad to the very horizon, all the waggoners and even Kiruha's waistcoat. The black shreds had by now moved upwards from the left, and one of them, a coarse, clumsy monster like a claw with fingers, stretched to the moon. Yegorushka made up his mind to shut his eyes tight, to pay no attention to it, and to wait till it was all over.

The rain was for some reason long in coming. Yegorushka peeped out from the mat in the hope that perhaps the storm-cloud was passing over. It was fearfully dark. Yegorushka could see neither Panteley, nor the bale of wool, nor himself; he looked sideways towards the place where the moon had lately been, but there was the same black darkness there as over the waggons. And in the darkness the flashes of lightning seemed more violent and blinding, so that they hurt his eyes.

"Panteley!" called Yegorushka.

No answer followed. But now a gust of wind for the last time flung up the mat and hurried away. A quiet regular sound was heard. A big cold drop fell on Yegorushka's knee, another trickled over his hand. He noticed that his knees were not covered, and tried to rearrange the mat, but at that moment something began pattering on the road, then on the shafts and the bales. It was the rain. As though they understood one another, the rain and the mat began prattling of something rapidly, gaily and most annoyingly like two magpies.

Yegorushka knelt up or rather squatted on his boots. While the rain was pattering on the mat, he leaned forward to screen his knees, which were suddenly wet. He succeeded in covering his knees, but in less than a minute was aware of a penetrating, unpleasant dampness behind on his back and the calves of his legs. He returned to his former position, exposing his knees to the rain, and wondered what to do to rearrange the mat which he could not see in the darkness. But his arms were already wet, the water was trickling up his sleeves and down his collar, and his shoulder-blades felt chilly. And he made up his mind to do nothing but sit motionless and wait till it was all over.

"Holy, holy, holy!" he whispered.

Suddenly, exactly over his head, the sky cracked with a fearful deafening din; he huddled up and held his breath, waiting for the fragments to fall upon his head and back. He inadvertently opened his eyes and saw a blinding intense light flare out and flash five times on his fingers, his wet sleeves, and on the trickles of water running from the mat upon the bales and down to the ground. There was a fresh peal of thunder as violent and awful; the sky was not growling and rumbling now, but uttering short crashing sounds like the crackling of dry wood.

"Trrah! tah! tah! tah!" the thunder rang out distinctly, rolled over the sky, seemed to stumble, and somewhere by the foremost waggons or far behind to fall with an abrupt angry "Trrra!"

The flashes of lightning had at first been only terrible, but with such thunder they seemed sinister and menacing. Their magic light pierced through closed eyelids and sent a chill all over the body. What could he do not to see them? Yegorushka made up his mind to turn over on his face. Cautiously, as though afraid of being watched, he got on all fours, and his hands slipping on the wet bale, he turned back again.

"Trrah! tah! tah!" floated over his head, rolled under the waggons and exploded "Kraa!"

Again he inadvertently opened his eyes and saw a new danger: three huge giants with long pikes were following the waggon! A flash of lightning gleamed on the points of their pikes and lighted up their figures very distinctly. They were men of huge proportions, with covered faces, bowed heads, and heavy footsteps. They seemed gloomy and dispirited and lost in thought. Perhaps they were not following the waggons with any harmful intent, and yet there was something awful in their proximity.

Yegorushka turned quickly forward, and trembling all over cried: "Panteley! Grandfather!"

"Trrah! tah! tah!" the sky answered him.

He opened his eyes to see if the waggoners were there. There were flashes of lightning in two places, which lighted up the road to the far distance, the whole string of waggons and all the waggoners. Streams of water were flowing along the road and bubbles were dancing. Panteley was walking beside the waggon; his tall hat and his shoulder were covered with a small mat; his figure expressed neither terror nor uneasiness, as though he were deafened by the thunder and blinded by the lightning.

"Grandfather, the giants!" Yegorushka shouted to him in tears.

ANTON CHEKHOV

But the old man did not hear. Further away walked Emelyan. He was covered from head to foot with a big mat and was triangular in shape. Vassya, without anything over him, was walking with the same wooden step as usual, lifting his feet high and not bending his knees. In the flash of lightning it seemed as though the waggons were not moving and the men were motionless, that Vassya's lifted foot was rigid in the same position. . .

Yegorushka called the old man once more. Getting no answer, he sat motionless, and no longer waited for it all to end. He was convinced that the thunder would kill him in another minute, that he would accidentally open his eyes and see the terrible giants, and he left off crossing himself, calling the old man and thinking of his mother, and was simply numb with cold and the conviction that the storm would never end.

But at last there was the sound of voices.

"Yegory, are you asleep?" Panteley cried below. "Get down! Is he deaf, the silly little thing?. . ."

"Something like a storm!" said an unfamiliar bass voice, and the stranger cleared his throat as though he had just tossed off a good glass of vodka.

Yegorushka opened his eyes. Close to the waggon stood Panteley, Emelyan, looking like a triangle, and the giants. The latter were by now much shorter, and when Yegorushka looked more closely at them they turned out to be ordinary peasants, carrying on their shoulders not pikes but pitchforks. In the space between Panteley and the triangular figure, gleamed the window of a low-pitched hut. So the waggons were halting in the village. Yegorushka flung off the mat, took his bundle and made haste to get off the waggon. Now when close to him there were people talking and a lighted window he no longer felt afraid, though the thunder was crashing as before and the whole sky was streaked with lightning.

"It was a good storm, all right,. . ." Panteley was muttering. "Thank God,. . . my feet are a little softened by the rain. It was all right. . . Have you got down, Yegory? Well, go into the hut; it is all right. . ."

"Holy, holy, holy!" wheezed Emelyan, "it must have struck something. . . Are you of these parts?" he asked the giants.

"No, from Glinovo. We belong to Glinovo. We are working at the Platers'."

"Threshing?"

"All sorts. Just now we are getting in the wheat. The lightning, the lightning! It is long since we have had such a storm. . ."

Yegorushka went into the hut. He was met by a lean hunchbacked old woman with a sharp chin. She stood holding a tallow candle in her hands, screwing up her eyes and heaving prolonged sighs.

"What a storm God has sent us!" she said. "And our lads are out for the night on the steppe; they'll have a bad time, poor dears! Take off your things, little sir, take off your things."

Shivering with cold and shrugging squeamishly, Yegorushka pulled off his drenched overcoat, then stretched out his arms and straddled his legs, and stood a long time without moving. The slightest movement caused an unpleasant sensation of cold and wetness. His sleeves and the back of his shirt were sopped, his trousers stuck to his legs, his head was dripping.

"What's the use of standing there, with your legs apart, little lad?" said the old woman. "Come, sit down."

Holding his legs wide apart, Yegorushka went up to the table and sat down on a bench near somebody's head. The head moved, puffed a stream of air through its nose, made a chewing sound and subsided. A mound covered with a sheepskin stretched from the head along the bench; it was a peasant woman asleep.

The old woman went out sighing, and came back with a big water melon and a little sweet melon.

"Have something to eat, my dear! I have nothing else to offer you,. . ." she said, yawning. She rummaged in the table and took out a long sharp knife, very much like the one with which the brigands killed the merchants in the inn. "Have some, my dear!"

Yegorushka, shivering as though he were in a fever, ate a slice of sweet melon with black bread and then a slice of water melon, and that made him feel colder still.

"Our lads are out on the steppe for the night,. . ." sighed the old woman while he was eating. "The terror of the Lord! I'd light the candle under the ikon, but I don't know where Stepanida has put it. Have some more, little sir, have some more. . ."

The old woman gave a yawn and, putting her right hand behind her, scratched her left shoulder.

"It must be two o'clock now," she said; "it will soon be time to get up. Our lads are out on the steppe for the night; they are all wet through for sure. . ."

"Granny," said Yegorushka. "I am sleepy."

"Lie down, my dear, lie down," the old woman sighed, yawning. "Lord Jesus Christ! I was asleep, when I heard a noise as though someone were knocking. I woke up and looked, and it was the storm God had sent us. . . I'd have lighted the candle, but I couldn't find it."

Talking to herself, she pulled some rags, probably her own bed, off the bench, took two sheepskins off a nail by the stove, and began laying them out for a bed for Yegorushka. "The storm doesn't grow less," she muttered. "If only nothing's struck in an unlucky hour. Our lads are out on the steppe for the night. Lie down and sleep, my dear. . . Christ be with you, my child. . . I won't take away the melon; maybe you'll have a bit when you get up."

The sighs and yawns of the old woman, the even breathing of the sleeping woman, the half-darkness of the hut, and the sound of the rain outside, made one sleepy. Yegorushka was shy of undressing before the old woman. He only took off his boots, lay down and covered himself with the sheepskin.

"Is the little lad lying down?" he heard Panteley whisper a little later.

"Yes," answered the old woman in a whisper. "The terror of the Lord! It thunders and thunders, and there is no end to it."

"It will soon be over," wheezed Panteley, sitting down; "it's getting quieter. . . The lads have gone into the huts, and two have stayed with the horses. The lads have. . . They can't;. . . the horses would be taken away. . . I'll sit here a bit and then go and take my turn. . . We can't leave them; they would be taken. . ."

Panteley and the old woman sat side by side at Yegorushka's feet, talking in hissing whispers and interspersing their speech with sighs and yawns. And Yegorushka could not get warm. The warm heavy sheepskin lay on him, but he was trembling all over; his arms and legs were twitching, and his whole inside was shivering. . . He undressed under the sheepskin, but that was no good. His shivering grew more and more acute.

Panteley went out to take his turn with the horses, and afterwards came back again, and still Yegorushka was shivering all over and could not get to sleep. Something weighed upon his head and chest and oppressed him, and he did not know what it was, whether it was the old people whispering, or the heavy smell of the sheepskin. The melon he had eaten had left an unpleasant metallic taste in his mouth. Moreover he was being bitten by fleas.

"Grandfather, I am cold," he said, and did not know his own voice.

"Go to sleep, my child, go to sleep," sighed the old woman.

Tit came up to the bedside on his thin little legs and waved his arms, then grew up to the ceiling and turned into a windmill. . . Father Christopher, not as he was in the chaise, but in his full vestments with the sprinkler in his hand, walked round the mill, sprinkling it with holy water, and it left off waving. Yegorushka, knowing this was delirium, opened his eyes.

"Grandfather," he called, "give me some water."

No one answered. Yegorushka felt it insufferably stifling and uncomfortable lying down. He got up, dressed, and went out of the hut. Morning was beginning. The sky was overcast, but it was no longer raining. Shivering and wrapping himself in his wet overcoat, Yegorushka walked about the muddy yard and listened to the silence; he caught sight of a little shed with a half-open door made of reeds. He looked into this shed, went into it, and sat down in a dark corner on a heap of dry dung.

There was a tangle of thoughts in his heavy head; his mouth was dry and unpleasant from the metallic taste. He looked at his hat, straightened the peacock's feather on it, and thought how he had gone with his mother to buy the hat. He put his hand into his pocket and took out a lump of brownish sticky paste. How had that paste come into his pocket? He thought a minute, smelt it; it smelt of honey. Aha! it was the Jewish cake! How sopped it was, poor thing!

Yegorushka examined his coat. It was a little grey overcoat with big bone buttons, cut in the shape of a frock-coat. At home, being a new and expensive article, it had not been hung in the hall, but with his mother's dresses in her bedroom; he was only allowed to wear it on holidays. Looking at it, Yegorushka felt sorry for it. He thought that he and the great-coat were both abandoned to the mercy of destiny; he thought that he would never get back home, and began sobbing so violently that he almost fell off the heap of dung.

A big white dog with woolly tufts like curl-papers about its face, sopping from the rain, came into the shed and stared with curiosity at Yegorushka. It seemed to be hesitating whether to bark or not. Deciding that there was no need to bark, it went cautiously up to Yegorushka, ate the sticky plaster and went out again.

"There are Varlamov's men!" someone shouted in the street.

After having his cry out, Yegorushka went out of the shed and, walking round a big puddle, made his way towards the street. The waggons were standing exactly opposite the gateway. The drenched waggoners, with their muddy feet, were sauntering beside them or sitting on the shafts, as listless and drowsy as flies in autumn. Yegorushka looked at them and thought: "How dreary and comfortless to be a peasant!" He went up to Panteley and sat down beside him on the shaft.

"Grandfather, I'm cold," he said, shivering and thrusting his hands up his sleeves.

"Never mind, we shall soon be there," yawned Panteley. "Never mind, you will get warm."

It must have been early when the waggons set off, for it was not hot. Yegorushka lay on the bales of wool and shivered with cold, though the sun soon came out and dried his clothes, the bales, and the earth. As soon as he closed his eyes he saw Tit and the windmill again. Feeling a sickness and heaviness all over, he did his utmost to drive away these images, but as soon as they vanished the dare-devil Dymov, with red eyes and lifted fists, rushed at Yegorushka with a roar, or there was the sound of his complaint: "I am so dreary!" Varlamov rode by on his little Cossack stallion; happy Konstantin passed, with a smile and the bustard in his arms. And how tedious these people were, how sickening and unbearable!

Once—it was towards evening—he raised his head to ask for water. The waggons were standing on a big bridge across a broad river. There was black smoke below over the river, and through it could be seen a steamer with a barge in tow. Ahead of them, beyond the river, was a huge mountain dotted with houses and churches; at the foot of the mountain an engine was being shunted along beside some goods trucks.

Yegorushka had never before seen steamers, nor engines, nor broad rivers. Glancing at them now, he was not alarmed or surprised; there was not even a look of anything like curiosity in his face. He merely felt sick, and made haste to turn over to the edge of the bale. He was sick. Panteley, seeing this, cleared his throat and shook his head.

"Our little lad's taken ill," he said. "He must have got a chill to the stomach. The little lad must. . . away from home; it's a bad lookout!"

VIII

THE WAGGONS STOPPED AT A big inn for merchants, not far from the quay. As Yegorushka climbed down from the waggon he heard a very familiar voice. Someone was helping him to get down, and saying:

"We arrived yesterday evening. . . We have been expecting you all day. We meant to overtake you yesterday, but it was out of our way; we came by the other road. I say, how you have crumpled your coat! You'll catch it from your uncle!"

Yegorushka looked into the speaker's mottled face and remembered that this was Deniska.

"Your uncle and Father Christopher are in the inn now, drinking tea; come along!"

And he led Yegorushka to a big two-storied building, dark and gloomy like the almshouse at N. After going across the entry, up a dark staircase and through a narrow corridor, Yegorushka and Deniska reached a little room in which Ivan Ivanitch and Father Christopher were sitting at the tea-table. Seeing the boy, both the old men showed surprise and pleasure.

"Aha! Yegor Ni-ko-la-aitch!" chanted Father Christopher. "Mr. Lomonosov!"

"Ah, our gentleman that is to be," said Kuzmitchov, "pleased to see you!"

Yegorushka took off his great-coat, kissed his uncle's hand and Father Christopher's, and sat down to the table.

"Well, how did you like the journey, puer bone?" Father Christopher pelted him with questions as he poured him out some tea, with his radiant smile. "Sick of it, I've no doubt? God save us all from having to travel by waggon or with oxen. You go on and on, God forgive us; you look ahead and the steppe is always lying stretched out the same as it was—you can't see the end of it! It's not travelling but regular torture. Why don't you drink your tea? Drink it up; and in your absence, while you have been trailing along with the waggons, we have settled all our business capitally. Thank God we have sold our wool to Tcherepahin, and no one could wish to have done better. . . We have made a good bargain."

At the first sight of his own people Yegorushka felt an overwhelming desire to complain. He did not listen to Father Christopher, but thought how to begin and what exactly to complain of. But Father Christopher's voice, which seemed to him harsh and unpleasant, prevented him from concentrating his attention and confused his thoughts. He had not sat at the table five minutes before he got up, went to the sofa and lay down.

"Well, well," said Father Christopher in surprise. "What about your tea?"

Still thinking what to complain of, Yegorushka leaned his head against the wall and broke into sobs.

"Well, well!" repeated Father Christopher, getting up and going to the sofa. "Yegory, what is the matter with you? Why are you crying?"

"I'm. . . I'm ill," Yegorushka brought out.

"Ill?" said Father Christopher in amazement. "That's not the right thing, my boy. . . One mustn't be ill on a journey. Aie, aie, what are you thinking about, boy. . . eh?"

He put his hand to Yegorushka's head, touched his cheek and said:

"Yes, your head's feverish. . . You must have caught cold or else have eaten something. . . Pray to God."

"Should we give him quinine?. . ." said Ivan Ivanitch, troubled.

"No; he ought to have something hot. . . Yegory, have a little drop of soup? Eh?"

"I. . . don't want any," said Yegorushka.

"Are you feeling chilly?"

"I was chilly before, but now. . . now I am hot. And I ache all over. . ."

Ivan Ivanitch went up to the sofa, touched Yegorushka on the head, cleared his throat with a perplexed air, and went back to the table.

"I tell you what, you undress and go to bed," said Father Christopher. "What you want is sleep now."

He helped Yegorushka to undress, gave him a pillow and covered him with a quilt, and over that Ivan Ivanitch's great-coat. Then he walked away on tiptoe and sat down to the table. Yegorushka shut his eyes, and at once it seemed to him that he was not in the hotel room, but on the highroad beside the camp fire. Emelyan waved his hands, and Dymov with red eyes lay on his stomach and looked mockingly at Yegorushka.

"Beat him, beat him!" shouted Yegorushka.

"He is delirious," said Father Christopher in an undertone.

"It's a nuisance!" sighed Ivan Ivanitch.

"He must be rubbed with oil and vinegar. Please God, he will be better to-morrow."

To be rid of bad dreams, Yegorushka opened his eyes and began looking towards the fire. Father Christopher and Ivan Ivanitch had now finished their tea and were talking in a whisper. The first was smiling with delight, and evidently could not forget that he had made a good bargain over his wool; what delighted him was not so much the actual profit he had made as the thought that on getting home he would gather round him his big family, wink slyly and go off into a chuckle; at first he would deceive them all, and say that he had sold the wool at a price below its value, then he would give his son-in-law, Mihail, a fat pocket-book and say: "Well, take it! that's the way to do business!" Kuzmitchov did not seem pleased; his face expressed, as before, a business-like reserve and anxiety.

"If I could have known that Tcherepahin would give such a price," he said in a low voice, "I wouldn't have sold Makarov those five tons at home. It is vexatious! But who could have told that the price had gone up here?"

A man in a white shirt cleared away the samovar and lighted the little lamp before the ikon in the corner. Father Christopher whispered something in his ear; the man looked, made a serious face like a conspirator, as though to say, "I understand," went out, and returned a little while afterwards and put something under the sofa. Ivan Ivanitch made himself a bed on the floor, yawned several times, said his prayers lazily, and lay down.

"I think of going to the cathedral to-morrow," said Father Christopher. "I know the sacristan there. I ought to go and see the bishop after mass, but they say he is ill."

He yawned and put out the lamp. Now there was no light in the room but the little lamp before the ikon.

"They say he can't receive visitors," Father Christopher went on, undressing. "So I shall go away without seeing him."

He took off his full coat, and Yegorushka saw Robinson Crusoe reappear. Robinson stirred something in a saucer, went up to Yegorushka and whispered:

"Lomonosov, are you asleep? Sit up; I'm going to rub you with oil and vinegar. It's a good thing, only you must say a prayer."

Yegorushka roused himself quickly and sat up. Father Christopher pulled down the boy's shirt, and shrinking and breathing jerkily, as though he were being tickled himself, began rubbing Yegorushka's chest.

"In the name of the Father, the Son, and the Holy Ghost," he whispered, "lie with your back upwards—that's it. . . You'll be all right to-morrow, but don't do it again. . . You are as hot as fire. I suppose you were on the road in the storm."

"Yes."

"You might well fall ill! In the name of the Father, the Son, and the Holy Ghost,. . . you might well fall ill!"

ANTON CHEKHOV

After rubbing Yegorushka, Father Christopher put on his shirt again, covered him, made the sign of the cross over him, and walked away. Then Yegorushka saw him saying his prayers. Probably the old man knew a great many prayers by heart, for he stood a long time before the ikon murmuring. After saying his prayers he made the sign of the cross over the window, the door, Yegorushka, and Ivan Ivanitch, lay down on the little sofa without a pillow, and covered himself with his full coat. A clock in the corridor struck ten. Yegorushka thought how long a time it would be before morning; feeling miserable, he pressed his forehead against the back of the sofa and left off trying to get rid of the oppressive misty dreams. But morning came much sooner than he expected.

It seemed to him that he had not been lying long with his head pressed to the back of the sofa, but when he opened his eyes slanting rays of sunlight were already shining on the floor through the two windows of the little hotel room. Father Christopher and Ivan Ivanitch were not in the room. The room had been tidied; it was bright, snug, and smelt of Father Christopher, who always smelt of cypress and dried cornflowers (at home he used to make the holy-water sprinklers and decorations for the ikonstands out of cornflowers, and so he was saturated with the smell of them). Yegorushka looked at the pillow, at the slanting sunbeams, at his boots, which had been cleaned and were standing side by side near the sofa, and laughed. It seemed strange to him that he was not on the bales of wool, that everything was dry around him, and that there was no thunder and lightning on the ceiling.

He jumped off the sofa and began dressing. He felt splendid; nothing was left of his yesterday's illness but a slight weakness in his legs and neck. So the vinegar and oil had done good. He remembered the steamer, the railway engine, and the broad river, which he had dimly seen the day before, and now he made haste to dress, to run to the quay and have a look at them. When he had washed and was putting on his red shirt, the latch of the door clicked, and Father Christopher appeared in the doorway, wearing his top-hat and a brown silk cassock over his canvas coat and carrying his staff in his hand. Smiling and radiant (old men are always radiant when they come back from church), he put a roll of holy bread and a parcel of some sort on the table, prayed before the ikon, and said:

"God has sent us blessings—well, how are you?"

"Quite well now," answered Yegorushka, kissing his hand.

"Thank God. . . I have come from mass. I've been to see a sacristan I know. He invited me to breakfast with him, but I didn't go. I don't like visiting people too early, God bless them!"

He took off his cassock, stroked himself on the chest, and without haste undid the parcel. Yegorushka saw a little tin of caviare, a piece of dry sturgeon, and a French loaf.

"See; I passed a fish-shop and brought this," said Father Christopher. "There is no need to indulge in luxuries on an ordinary weekday; but I thought, I've an invalid at home, so it is excusable. And the caviare is good, real sturgeon. . ."

The man in the white shirt brought in the samovar and a tray with tea-things.

"Eat some," said Father Christopher, spreading the caviare on a slice of bread and handing it to Yegorushka. "Eat now and enjoy yourself, but the time will soon come for you to be studying. Mind you study with attention and application, so that good may come of it. What you have to learn by heart, learn by heart, but when you have to tell the inner sense in your own words, without regard to the outer form, then say it in your own words. And try to master all subjects. One man knows mathematics excellently, but has never heard of Pyotr Mogila; another knows about Pyotr Mogila, but cannot explain about the moon. But you study so as to understand everything. Study Latin, French, German,. . . geography, of course, history, theology, philosophy, mathematics,. . . and when you have mastered everything, not with haste but with prayer and with zeal, then go into the service. When you know everything it will be easy for you in any line of life. . . You study and strive for the divine blessing, and God will show you what to be. Whether a doctor, a judge or an engineer. . ."

Father Christopher spread a little caviare on a piece of bread, put it in his mouth and said:

"The Apostle Paul says: 'Do not apply yourself to strange and diverse studies.' Of course, if it is black magic, unlawful arts, or calling up spirits from the other world, like Saul, or studying subjects that can be of no use to yourself or others, better not learn them. You must undertake only what God has blessed. Take example. . . the Holy Apostles spoke in all languages, so you study languages. Basil the Great studied mathematics and philosophy—so you study them; St. Nestor wrote history—so you study and write history. Take example from the saints."

Father Christopher sipped the tea from his saucer, wiped his moustaches, and shook his head.

"Good!" he said. "I was educated in the old-fashioned way; I have forgotten a great deal by now, but still I live differently from other people. Indeed, there is no comparison. For instance, in company at a dinner, or at an assembly, one says something in Latin, or makes some allusion from history or philosophy, and it pleases people, and it pleases me myself. . . Or when the circuit court comes and one has to take the oath, all the other priests are shy, but I am quite at home with the judges, the prosecutors, and the lawyers. I talk intellectually, drink a cup of tea with them, laugh, ask them what I don't know,. . . and they like it. So that's how it is, my boy. Learning is light and ignorance is darkness. Study! It's hard, of course; nowadays study is expensive. . . Your mother is a widow; she lives on her pension, but there, of course. . ."

Father Christopher glanced apprehensively towards the door, and went on in a whisper:

"Ivan Ivanitch will assist. He won't desert you. He has no children of his own, and he will help you. Don't be uneasy."

He looked grave, and whispered still more softly:

"Only mind, Yegory, don't forget your mother and Ivan Ivanitch, God preserve you from it. The commandment bids you honour your mother, and Ivan Ivanitch is your benefactor and takes the place of a father to you. If you become learned, God forbid you should be impatient and scornful with people because they are not so clever as you, then woe, woe to you!"

Father Christopher raised his hand and repeated in a thin voice:

"Woe to you! Woe to you!"

Father Christopher's tongue was loosened, and he was, as they say, warming to his subject; he would not have finished till dinnertime but the door opened and Ivan Ivanitch walked in. He said good-morning hurriedly, sat down to the table, and began rapidly swallowing his tea.

"Well, I have settled all our business," he said. "We might have gone home to-day, but we have still to think about Yegor. We must arrange for him. My sister told me that Nastasya Petrovna, a friend of hers, lives somewhere here, so perhaps she will take him in as a boarder."

He rummaged in his pocket-book, found a crumpled note and read:

"'Little Lower Street: Nastasya Petrovna Toskunov, living in a house of her own.' We must go at once and try to find her. It's a nuisance!"

Soon after breakfast Ivan Ivanitch and Yegorushka left the inn.

"It's a nuisance," muttered his uncle. "You are sticking to me like a burr. You and your mother want education and gentlemanly breeding and I have nothing but worry with you both. . ."

When they crossed the yard, the waggons and the drivers were not there. They had all gone off to the quay early in the morning. In a far-off dark corner of the yard stood the chaise.

"Good-bye, chaise!" thought Yegorushka.

At first they had to go a long way uphill by a broad street, then they had to cross a big marketplace; here Ivan Ivanitch asked a policeman for Little Lower Street.

"I say," said the policeman, with a grin, "it's a long way off, out that way towards the town grazing ground."

They met several cabs but Ivan Ivanitch only permitted himself such a weakness as taking a cab in exceptional cases and on great holidays. Yegorushka and he walked for a long while through paved streets, then along streets where there were only wooden planks at the sides and no pavements, and in the end got to streets where there were neither planks nor pavements. When their legs and their tongues had brought them to Little Lower Street they were both red in the face, and taking off their hats, wiped away the perspiration.

"Tell me, please," said Ivan Ivanitch, addressing an old man sitting on a little bench by a gate, "where is Nastasya Petrovna Toskunov's house?"

"There is no one called Toskunov here," said the old man, after pondering a moment. "Perhaps it's Timoshenko you want."

"No, Toskunov. . ."

"Excuse me, there's no one called Toskunov. . ."

Ivan Ivanitch shrugged his shoulders and trudged on farther.

"You needn't look," the old man called after them. "I tell you there isn't, and there isn't."

"Listen, auntie," said Ivan Ivanitch, addressing an old woman who was sitting at a corner with a tray of pears and sunflower seeds, "where is Nastasya Petrovna Toskunov's house?"

The old woman looked at him with surprise and laughed.

"Why, Nastasya Petrovna live in her own house now!" she cried. "Lord! it is eight years since she married her daughter and gave up the house to her son-in-law! It's her son-in-law lives there now."

And her eyes expressed: "How is it you didn't know a simple thing like that, you fools?"

"And where does she live now?" Ivan Ivanitch asked.

"Oh, Lord!" cried the old woman, flinging up her hands in surprise. "She moved ever so long ago! It's eight years since she gave up her house to her son-in-law! Upon my word!"

ANTON CHEKHOV

She probably expected Ivan Ivanitch to be surprised, too, and to exclaim: "You don't say so," but Ivan Ivanitch asked very calmly:

"Where does she live now?"

The old woman tucked up her sleeves and, stretching out her bare arm to point, shouted in a shrill piercing voice:

"Go straight on, straight on, straight on. You will pass a little red house, then you will see a little alley on your left. Turn down that little alley, and it will be the third gate on the right. . ."

Ivan Ivanitch and Yegorushka reached the little red house, turned to the left down the little alley, and made for the third gate on the right. On both sides of this very old grey gate there was a grey fence with big gaps in it. The first part of the fence was tilting forwards and threatened to fall, while on the left of the gate it sloped backwards towards the yard. The gate itself stood upright and seemed to be still undecided which would suit it best—to fall forwards or backwards. Ivan Ivanitch opened the little gate at the side, and he and Yegorushka saw a big yard overgrown with weeds and burdocks. A hundred paces from the gate stood a little house with a red roof and green shutters. A stout woman with her sleeves tucked up and her apron held out was standing in the middle of the yard, scattering something on the ground and shouting in a voice as shrill as that of the woman selling fruit:

"Chick!. . . Chick!. . . Chick!"

Behind her sat a red dog with pointed ears. Seeing the strangers, he ran to the little gate and broke into a tenor bark (all red dogs have a tenor bark).

"Whom do you want?" asked the woman, putting up her hand to shade her eyes from the sun.

"Good-morning!" Ivan Ivanitch shouted, too, waving off the red dog with his stick. "Tell me, please, does Nastasya Petrovna Toskunov live here?"

"Yes! But what do you want with her?"

"Perhaps you are Nastasya Petrovna?"

"Well, yes, I am!"

"Very pleased to see you. . . You see, your old friend Olga Ivanovna Knyasev sends her love to you. This is her little son. And I, perhaps you remember, am her brother Ivan Ivanitch. . . You are one of us from N. . . You were born among us and married there. . ."

A silence followed. The stout woman stared blankly at Ivan Ivanitch, as though not believing or not understanding him, then she flushed all over, and flung up her hands; the oats were scattered out of her apron and tears spurted from her eyes.

"Olga Ivanovna!" she screamed, breathless with excitement. "My own darling! Ah, holy saints, why am I standing here like a fool? My pretty little angel. . ."

She embraced Yegorushka, wetted his face with her tears, and broke down completely.

"Heavens!" she said, wringing her hands, "Olga's little boy! How delightful! He is his mother all over! The image of his mother! But why are you standing in the yard? Come indoors."

Crying, gasping for breath and talking as she went, she hurried towards the house. Her visitors trudged after her.

"The room has not been done yet," she said, ushering the visitors into a stuffy little drawing-room adorned with many ikons and pots of flowers. "Oh, Mother of God! Vassilisa, go and open the shutters anyway! My little angel! My little beauty! I did not know that Olitchka had a boy like that!"

When she had calmed down and got over her first surprise Ivan Ivanitch asked to speak to her alone. Yegorushka went into another room; there was a sewing-machine; in the window was a cage with a starling in it, and there were as many ikons and flowers as in the drawing-room. Near the machine stood a little girl with a sunburnt face and chubby cheeks like Tit's, and a clean cotton dress. She stared at Yegorushka without blinking, and apparently felt very awkward. Yegorushka looked at her and after a pause asked:

"What's your name?"

The little girl moved her lips, looked as if she were going to cry, and answered softly:

"Atka. . ."

This meant Katka.

"He will live with you," Ivan Ivanitch was whispering in the drawing-room, "if you will be so kind, and we will pay ten roubles a month for his keep. He is not a spoilt boy; he is quiet. . ."

"I really don't know what to say, Ivan Ivanitch!" Nastasya Petrovna sighed tearfully. "Ten roubles a month is very good, but it is a dreadful thing to take another person's child! He may fall ill or something. . ."

When Yegorushka was summoned back to the drawing-room Ivan Ivanitch was standing with his hat in his hands, saying good-bye.

"Well, let him stay with you now, then," he said. "Good-bye! You stay, Yegor!" he said, addressing his nephew. "Don't be troublesome; mind you obey Nastasya Petrovna. . . Good-bye; I am coming again to-morrow."

And he went away. Nastasya once more embraced Yegorushka, called him a little angel, and with a tear-stained face began preparing for dinner. Three minutes later Yegorushka was sitting beside her, answering her endless questions and eating hot savoury cabbage soup.

In the evening he sat again at the same table and, resting his head on his hand, listened to Nastasya Petrovna. Alternately laughing and crying, she talked of his mother's young days, her own marriage, her children. . . A cricket chirruped in the stove, and there was a faint humming from the burner of the lamp. Nastasya Petrovna talked in a low voice, and was continually dropping her thimble in her excitement; and Katka her granddaughter, crawled under the table after it and each time sat a long while under the table, probably examining Yegorushka's feet; and Yegorushka listened, half dozing and looking at the old woman's face, her wart with hairs on it, and the stains of tears, and he felt sad, very sad. He was put to sleep on a chest and told that if he were hungry in the night he must go out into the little passage and take some chicken, put there under a plate in the window.

Next morning Ivan Ivanitch and Father Christopher came to say good-bye. Nastasya Petrovna was delighted to see them, and was about to set the samovar; but Ivan Ivanitch, who was in a great hurry, waved his hands and said:

"We have no time for tea! We are just setting off."

Before parting they all sat down and were silent for a minute. Nastasya Petrovna heaved a deep sigh and looked towards the ikon with tear-stained eyes.

"Well," began Ivan Ivanitch, getting up, "so you will stay. . ."

All at once the look of business-like reserve vanished from his face; he flushed a little and said with a mournful smile:

"Mind you work hard. . . Don't forget your mother, and obey Nastasya Petrovna. . . If you are diligent at school, Yegor, I'll stand by you."

He took his purse out of his pocket, turned his back to Yegorushka, fumbled for a long time among the smaller coins, and, finding a ten-kopeck piece, gave it to Yegorushka.

Father Christopher, without haste, blessed Yegorushka.

"In the name of the Father, the Son, and the Holy Ghost. . . Study," he said. "Work hard, my lad. If I die, remember me in your prayers. Here is a ten-kopeck piece from me, too. . ."

Yegorushka kissed his hand, and shed tears; something whispered in his heart that he would never see the old man again.

"I have applied at the high school already," said Ivan Ivanitch in a voice as though there were a corpse in the room. "You will take him for the entrance examination on the seventh of August. . . Well, good-bye; God bless you, good-bye, Yegor!"

"You might at least have had a cup of tea," wailed Nastasya Petrovna.

Through the tears that filled his eyes Yegorushka could not see his uncle and Father Christopher go out. He rushed to the window, but they were not in the yard, and the red dog, who had just been barking, was running back from the gate with the air of having done his duty. When Yegorushka ran out of the gate Ivan Ivanitch and Father Christopher, the former waving his stick with the crook, the latter his staff, were just turning the corner. Yegorushka felt that with these people all that he had known till then had vanished from him for ever. He sank helplessly on to the little bench, and with bitter tears greeted the new unknown life that was beginning for him now. . .

What would that life be like?

A Note About the Author

Anton Chekhov (1860–1904) was a Russian doctor, short-story writer, and playwright. Born in the port city of Taganrog, Chekhov was the third child of Pavel, a grocer and devout Christian, and Yevgeniya, a natural storyteller. His father, a violent and arrogant man, abused his wife and children and would serve as the inspiration for many of the writer's most tyrannical and hypocritical characters. Chekhov studied at the Greek School in Taganrog, where he learned Ancient Greek. In 1876, his father's debts forced the family to relocate to Moscow, where they lived in poverty while Anton remained in Taganrog to settle their finances and finish his studies. During this time, he worked odd jobs while reading extensively and composing his first written works. He joined his family in Moscow in 1879, pursuing a medical degree while writing short stories for entertainment and to support his parents and siblings. In 1876, after finishing his degree and contracting tuberculosis, he began writing for St. Petersburg's *Novoye Vremya*, a popular paper which helped him to launch his literary career and gain financial independence. A friend and colleague of Leo Tolstoy, Maxim Gorky, and Ivan Bunin, Chekhov is remembered today for his skillful observations of everyday Russian life, his deeply psychological character studies, and his mastery of language and the rhythms of conversation.

A Note from the Publisher

Spanning many genres, from non-fiction essays to literature classics to children's books and lyric poetry, Mint Edition books showcase the master works of our time in a modern new package. The text is freshly typeset, is clean and easy to read, and features a new note about the author in each volume. Many books also include exclusive new introductory material. Every book boasts a striking new cover, which makes it as appropriate for collecting as it is for gift giving. Mint Edition books are only printed when a reader orders them, so natural resources are not wasted. We're proud that our books are never manufactured in excess and exist only in the exact quantity they need to be read and enjoyed.

bookfinity™

Discover more of your favorite classics with Bookfinity™.

- Track your reading with custom book lists.
- Get great book recommendations for your personalized Reader Type.
- Add reviews for your favorite books.
- AND MUCH MORE!

Visit **bookfinity.com** and take the fun Reader Type quiz to get started.

Enjoy our classic and modern companion pairings!

Classic & Modern

Bookfinity is a registered trademark of Ingram Book Group LLC. © 2023 Bookfinity. All rights reserved.

Printed in the USA
CPSIA information can be obtained
at www.ICGtesting.com
JSHW022342140824
68134JS00019B/1642